FAST TRACK TO GLORY

FAST TRACK TO GLORY

A NOVEL BY
TOMASZ CHRUSCIEL

AGATO HOUSE

Fast Track to Glory is a work of fiction. Names, characters, businesses, places, events, and incidents are either the products of the author's imagination or used in a fictitious manner. Any resemblance to actual persons, living or dead, or actual events is purely coincidental.

Fast Track to Glory is a registered trademark of Tomasz Chrusciel

Copyright © 2016 by Tomasz Chrusciel

Published by Agato House

ISBN: 978-0-9929574-3-8

Cover design by Damonza
www.damonza.com

Printed by CreateSpace

FOR MY PARENTS

CHAPTER 1

NINA JUMPED OFF the Intercity the moment it pulled into Heidelberg Central Train Station. A growing crowd of passengers absorbed her and carried down the open roof platform. Seeing a gap in the flow of bodies, she squeezed through and stepped aside between two metal benches.

A digital clock hanging over the platform showed 21:50. She grimaced and put her business suitcase down.

On her tiptoes, she craned her neck, scanning the surroundings over groups of excited travellers who were moving to the exit.

Did she arrive too late? No one was holding a sheet of paper with her name on it.

She reached down to a side pocket of her suitcase and pulled out the pearl-black envelope with an Italian Ministry of Culture seal. A bicycle courier had handed it over three hours ago, just when she was calling a taxi to take her to the airport so she could catch the last flight home from Frankfurt to Venice.

Inside was an invitation to a confidential meeting in the Heidelberg Castle tonight at ten. Massimo Campana had scribbled his signature at the bottom. Above it she read: "Again, please excuse the short notice. I will be sending a chauffeur to collect you, Signora Monte. Please wait at the platform."

Nina had never met Campana. She suspected he was relegated from another department lately, as she knew employees in the Ministry well. They had called her to consultations before. Most recently on interpretation of religious rituals depicted on walls of the ancient Roman harbour, dated second century A.D., that were unearthed close to Rome's Fiumicino airport.

But the Ministry had always informed her in advance what they expected from her.

Tonight was odd in this respect. One hour and seventeen minutes' journey from Frankfurt left her without any valid conclusion as to why her professional advice was required, why they organized such a gathering that late and outside of Italy.

Shivers crawled over her body despite the cashmere jacket wrapped around her torso. Early September in Germany was cooler than she was prepared for.

She bounced on her feet to warm herself up. She was supposed to be at home now, relaxing in a long, hot, scented bath with a glass of red wine in her hand.

The crowd on the platform thinned out. Then it was only Nina.

Feeling abandoned, without a sign of a promised driver, in the city she didn't know, she grabbed the handle of her briefcase and rolled it behind her to the station's hall.

When she entered the building, the rich smell of coffee, toasted sandwiches, and pastries reminded her of a half-eaten almond croissant she carried in her handbag. She hadn't had time to finish it when rushing to catch the train over here, and then she had forgotten about it.

She navigated her way to the exit.

In a lane adjacent to the station, taxi after taxi drove off, but the queue of customers was long. Those more impatient continued on foot.

'Signora Monte!'

Nina turned to her left. Four metres away, a man wearing a navy suit and a hat in the same colour came up to a skinny girl in her early twenties dressed in a chiffon blouse, tight blue jeans and shiny metallic sneakers. The chauffeur towered over her one-metre-sixty, give or take, frame.

Had he really confused her with Nina? What had Massimo Campana told him she looked like?

Although Nina had to admit that the girl was the same height. Her straight black hair cut at the shoulders was similar too. When she turned her head, Nina also caught a glance of her face, the olive skin tone and subtle jaw line mimicking her own.

But despite the resemblance, Nina didn't look as if she were going to a Justin Bieber concert, and the time when she starved herself to fit into a size six glorified by *Vogue* had long been left behind. After all, she turned thirty-six last month.

She felt growing irritation at the chauffeur for his mistake, and at Massimo Campana for robbing her of the pleasure of the hot, soothing bath she deserved. This morning, she had gotten up at five o'clock to prepare for a hectic conference day in Frankfurt on ancient scientific thought, where she had given two long lectures on social and religious movements in the Mediterranean.

The girl smiled at the chauffeur, who was close to her age, and shook her head. He winced and excused himself, took off the hat and ran his fingers through his short auburn hair.

The passengers dispersed, and now only two of them were left standing by the main entrance to the train station.

He noticed Nina, and rushed towards her. 'Signora Monte. I'm sorry for the delay. My name is Felix,' he said in Italian with a noticeable German accent. 'With that crowd coming to see the fireworks, I couldn't find a parking space closer to the station. Whew, I thought you were already gone.'

'Buonasera, Felix,' she said. 'Good evening.'

He picked up her briefcase. 'I'll take you to the castle. Follow me, please.'

He started to walk off.

Nina shadowed him two steps behind. 'How long have you been doing this job, Felix?'

'Ahem … this is the first time, Signora,' he said, glancing at her over his shoulder. 'I do all sorts of things to pay for my college.'

At least that explained his lack of professionalism and coming late. Her students were the same.

Nina meant to ask what he was studying, but at times she had to jog to keep up with his swift pace. She preferred to concentrate on the road so as not to sprain her ankle on some sidewalk pothole where the sporadic street light wasn't reaching.

He led her away from the stream of people. After two hundred metres, Nina sighed when he finally stopped at a parking square neighbouring a shopping mall.

'I'm sorry, Signora Monte,' he said, opening the rear door of an Audi A6. 'Was it too fast? My girlfriend is teasing me that I should walk like normal people.'

'She might have a point,' Nina said and clambered into the car. 'Unless you're training for a marathon.'

'No, Signora. I just don't like wasting my time moving from one place to another.' He closed the door and put her suitcase into the boot.

Then he took a seat behind the steering wheel. 'If I could, I would run everywhere.'

He turned around to her. 'Do you like running, Signora?'

Nina never pictured herself to be one of those people who got up at five or six to go jogging in the park. With spending too many hours behind her desk at university, though, perhaps she needed to think about it.

'I presume you don't know anything about the meeting you're taking me to,' she said, fastening the seatbelt.

'Oh no.' He pressed a button and the engine hummed to life. 'I wouldn't know anything about that. My job is just to bring you to the castle.'

The car pulled out from the shopping mall, and soon Felix drove into congested human traffic. He used the horn now and then to shove off pedestrians who were marching in the middle of the road. Nina saw groups of teenagers, families with small children, a man carrying on his shoulders a boy who was waving an inflated crocodile balloon attached to his forearm, and an ambling older couple, holding hands.

It took twenty minutes to reach the point beyond which the car traffic was not permitted. Two men clad in fluorescent yellow vests moved a heavy barrier aside. Felix touched the rim of his hat and gave them a quick nod.

The Audi swung sharply left and then right, narrowly avoiding a scattered group of schoolboys who stepped on the asphalt. From there, the ride up the road, leading to a hill overlooking the city and the Neckar River, was swifter.

A few minutes later the car pulled over in front of the gateway to Heidelberg Castle.

'Here we are, Signora,' Felix said. 'This is the entrance.'

Nina pressed the button on the door and the car window slid down silently.

The castle looked as if it were becoming deserted, and the several men she saw through the gate walking in the dim yard were staying to make sure no elders, children or sick people were left behind.

'Signora, this is it. Please follow through the gate tower, then straight through the yard. Someone will meet you there.'

Nina took another glance at the gloomy yard. No one awaited her. 'Are you sure?'

'This is what I have been instructed to tell you,' Felix said.

'Of course you have.'

'Please leave your luggage in the car. I will pick you up after the meeting.'

She opened the door and stepped onto the cobblestone pavement. The moment she shut the door, the car drove off.

The tower was built from red brick and was as high as a four-storey building. Above the entrance, two statues of medieval knights, armed with swords and lances, guarded the gate. Next to them, two lions stood on their rear legs. There was a clock on top of it, but it was too dark to read the time.

Nina rubbed her shoulders with her hands. Then she went through the entrance and walked into the vast courtyard, which was surrounded on all four sides by the castle buildings. She relaxed, seeing that it was better lit than what she had seen from the car. More people bustled about the square, carrying boxes, some tools, briskly crossing the yard.

Across the square, there was a brighter lit entrance; probably the main building of the whole complex.

When a man came out of there, and made merely ten steps, Nina knew he was there to bring her in, and not only because he walked straight in her direction and seemed to smile at her. He wore an elegant grey or cream suit while everyone else around was in their working clothes.

He held out his arms when he was the last four metres away from her. 'Signora Monte, welcome! My name is Massimo Campana.'

He stopped to let through two workers who were carrying long pipes.

Campana was a good-looking, fifty-something, stylish man, and Nina thought that it must be stressful work at the Ministry that covered his forehead and eyes with too many furrows. His short hair had grey streaks at the sides and was thinning.

When the workers went about their job, Campana stepped forward, took Nina's hand and squeezed it firmly. 'Welcome. Welcome, Signora!'

'Good evening, Signor Campana.'

He pulled her towards the castle entrance. 'Everyone is waiting.'

He was taller than Nina, but not by much as he hunched forward.

'I was hoping for a briefing before the meeting. Your invitation was quite vague,' Nina said.

'I know, and I truly apologise for that,' he replied. 'You will find out everything soon enough. I can only tell you that the name of our host is Christoph Gerst from the German Ministry of Education, Science and Culture. Our French partners sent a representative of their Ministry of Culture and Communication in the person of Julien Traverse. Although, from his bearings, I'd say he works for Defence.'

Campana had a low, self-assured voice, the kind that was in the habit of giving instructions, not taking questions.

When they were in the middle of the courtyard, the lights changed to a red colour, engulfing the castle in a crimson glow.

'Aha, the show is about to begin,' he said and pouted his lips. 'Pity we will miss it.'

For one short moment Nina lost her sense of direction, and let him guide her. She felt as if she were being dragged from behind the scene to the main stage of a school theatre, to be thrown into penetrating spotlights to perform a play without knowing its script.

He released his soft grip on her arm when they entered the castle.

Inside was murky, and Nina smelled a slight whiff of fresh paint in the air. They walked out of the shadows into a well-lit corridor. To her left, she saw man-sized figures of former nobles of the castle, or so she guessed. To the right, horned animal trophies lined the wall. Nina shuddered. She would have never put up anything like that in her home—it felt like an alley in an animals' graveyard.

Her high heels clanked hurriedly on the corridor's marble floor, giving the sound she considered inappropriate in any graveyard.

Massimo Campana, who was two steps ahead of her, stopped abruptly at a door guarded by a bulky man dressed in a black suit. His head and face were clean shaven; he looked like a celebrity bodyguard. Without a word, the man opened the door.

Campana gestured to Nina.

'After you, Signora.'

CHAPTER 2

NINA SAW TWO men sitting at a wooden few-hundred-year-old table set in the middle of a ten-by-ten metre room. They were engaged in a conversation, oblivious to her and Massimo Campana's arrival.

Above the men, a single chandelier hung from a stucco ceiling decorated with colourful paintings. A stove stood in the left corner. Court scenes were depicted on its green tiled walls. Beside it was a second door. Was it also guarded?

'Gentlemen! I'm back with our charming expert. Let me introduce Signora Nina Monte,' Campana said in impeccable English. 'We can continue in untroubled fashion now.'

Nina exchanged brief pleasantries with both men, and took a seat at the table across from them in the carved, upholstered arm chair that harmonized well with fuchsia walls and a polished marble floor.

Campana sat next to her. He put his burgundy briefcase on the table, pulled out a stack of documents, and browsed through them.

Four bottles of water, glasses, coffee cups, a jug, and appetizing pastries lay on the table, untouched.

Christoph Gerst pretended to be interested in Campana's documents, but he kept glancing at Nina with a nonchalant smile. He was dressed in a burgundy turtleneck sweater and a dark-yellow sports jacket with elbow patches. His short blond hair was trimmed in a stylish manner and combed to the side. If that bodyguard was indeed hired by celebrities, Gerst could be one of them.

Julien Traverse, who was the oldest person in the room, maybe in his late sixties, wore an exquisite Italian suit and a purple mosaic tie. Nina thought that behind the old-fashioned, thick lenses, his eyes looked oddly large.

'As you all have been already informed...' Campana started, and then paused, looking at everyone.

Nina asked herself who, in his mind, *all* was.

'...the progress in the search for the item of our interest is at its peak.'

'Signor Campana, do you mind presenting the credentials of your associate?' Traverse said and folded his hands on the table.

Nina looked at the brownish patches on the back of his hands. Then her eyes shot up. *What did he say?*

'I've only been informed that Ms Monte is a professor at the University of Padua,' he added.

She raised her eyebrows.

'We shouldn't have any doubt in the competences of our Italian friends, Monsieur Traverse,' Gerst said flatly.

For a person who represented as powerful a country as Germany, Christoph Gerst looked surprisingly young.

Traverse disconnected his magnetic glasses at the bridge. 'Dear Christoph, the matters we discuss here are too grave. I will leave nothing to chance.'

Campana frowned at the Frenchman. 'Monsieur Traverse, Signora Monte has been studying and teaching history of religions at the Department of Historical and

Geographic Sciences and the Ancient World at the University of Padua, which she is also head of. I can assure you that her credentials are flawless.'

The firework show set off above the castle. Gerst pushed his chair back, crossed to the windows and shut them. The explosions stifled to a level allowing a conversation.

When he sat down, Nina felt his gaze boring into her with increased interest.

'I doubt there's another individual in Italy able to overshadow the credentials of Signora Monte,' the Italian went on. 'In addition, Signora and the Italian Ministry of Culture are well acquainted. Nevertheless, details of our previous dealings will not be the subject of this meeting.'

'So what is it?' Nina's words came out in an uncontrolled manner. 'I'm sorry, Signor Campana, but you're making me guess what is expected of me, and I feel quite confused at being kept in the dark.' She paused when three muffled explosions made the water in the bottles vibrate. 'And *why* are you organizing this meeting during the fireworks?'

'I agree.' Gerst sent her an emphatic smile. 'Signora Monte must be thoroughly briefed.'

'This was exactly what I was getting to,' Massimo said.

Traverse spread his palms on the table and opened his mouth, but the blasts of fireworks grew to a deafening level for a moment.

Nina touched her forehead. She started feeling uneasy in a small medieval castle room with three strangers who couldn't tell her why she was there. She opened the bottle of water and drank straight from it. Glancing back at the door she had walked through, she saw that it was now secured by another man.

She flinched, feeling a hand on her arm.

'Are you all right, Signora?' Campana said.

'Yes,' she said in a low voice. 'Although, I might have lost track of this conversation. But please—continue.'

Campana hesitated for a second and then dug out another document.

'Before tonight, only four persons have been allowed to see it. Now, you've joined our group.' He offered her a large picture. 'Do you know what this is?'

Nina looked at the underwater photograph of a shipwreck. Her anxiety at being in the wrong place at the wrong time receded.

'It's a warship galley, I presume,' she said.

'You *presume*,' Julien Traverse said.

Nina shot him a glance over the frame of the photo. 'I'm not an expert at underwater treasure hunts, if this is why I'm here.'

The Frenchman averted his gaze. It felt like a tiny triumph; so he wasn't as threatening as she imagined.

Campana cleared his throat.

A discreet smirk crossed over Gerst's face. 'It *is* about a treasure hunt,' he said. 'Sort of.

'This picture was taken three days ago on the bottom of Lake Garda,' Massimo Campana said. 'It was quite a coincidence that the whereabouts of the ship has been discovered only now. As it so happens with many great things, they often come unexpected, Signora.'

Her head started to throb. 'Signor Campana, I may be an expert at history of religions, but I am certainly not an expert at underwater excavation. I still don't understand.'

'True; however, we are hopeful that you *are* an authority on what we intend to find inside this galley,' Campana said.

Nina scanned the photograph.

'What you see,' he went on, 'is a galley that sank during the battle of Maderno in 1439. It was a period of wars between Venice and the Visconti family.'

'Wars in Lombardy. The history of Italy before unification,' Nina said. 'Venice, being at war with Milan, went to great lengths to help Brescia, their protectorate, which was under siege. As Milan controlled the south of Lake Garda, Venetians sailed their ships up the Adige River. From there they used five hundred oxen and three hundred men to drag six galleys over the mountains to the north of the lake. Each galley weighed one hundred tons. A third of the people perished in that gruelling expedition.'

The Italian glanced at Traverse with an expression of: "I told you."

'The Venice fleet was eventually defeated, and this,' Campana said, pointing at the picture in her hands, 'is *Santa Lucia*, one of their ships that went down.'

'And … you have found something valuable on board and you want my expertise to confirm its authenticity. Am I right?'

'We don't have it in our hands yet,' Traverse said. 'We are confident it will be found any time now.'

Nina put the picture on the table. 'Do you mind me asking what the French government has to do with all of that? And,' she said, looking at Gerst, 'German, for that matter?'

Traverse winced. 'Ms Monte, I think I can also speak in the name of our German partner.' He pointed at Gerst with his open palm, as if she needed a clue who the German partner was. 'The artefact in question might be lying on the bed of an Italian lake, but it never belonged to Venice, or to Milan, or to the later Kingdom of Italy.'

'Monsieur Traverse,' Campana cut in, 'the item might not belong to Italy, but Lake Garda certainly *is* part of my country. The ship in which the item lies is our heritage. And you gentlemen are here due to ... let's call it, friendly surveillance.'

Traverse raised his chin and pouted his lips as if finding an insult in that statement.

Nina understood where the tension among them came from. The three countries spied on each other. Germany, France and Italy had sent their men to something that, on the surface, was a joint undertaking.

Christoph Gerst propped his elbows on the table and leaned towards her. Nina could smell his citrus aftershave. 'Signora Monte, let me tell you about your part in all of this. As soon as the item is located and secured, you will be kindly asked to confirm its authenticity.'

Nina frowned. She had already said that, hadn't she?

'We count on you,' Campana said. 'There are great hopes in regard to what we will unveil, but we need an interpreter. It may change many things.'

'What kinds of things?' she asked.

'What kinds of things?' Traverse said with a half-smirk. '*All* kinds of things. The world without terminal disease, poverty, without limitations that plague our population.'

She couldn't imagine such a place. But she could easily imagine the world without Julien Traverse.

'It has potential to become an enormous step in our evolution! I only wish the French nation had its men among

15

the crew who are right now exploring the wreck,' Traverse added coarsely.

'If I understand correctly,' Nina said, 'you're fighting over something that you haven't even seen yet.'

Both Gerst and Traverse started to speak at once. Nina raised her outstretched palm over the table, causing the gibberish to die away.

Massimo Campana spoke first. 'Monsieur Traverse, you will be pleased to know that Mister Lammert van der Venn and his crew of experts in underwater exploration are the best possible choice for this enterprise. And,' he said, glancing at Nina, 'if Signora Monte will join them, we couldn't have assembled a better team.'

Traverse stared into Campana's eyes, as if they were continuing their argument on a non-verbal level.

The Italian gathered his documents. 'Unfortunately, we have to wrap up for now. We will reconvene in the same place in three days. Thank you, all.'

Nina lifted her eyebrow and bent her neck forward. Was that all?

Traverse and Gerst stood up and shook hands with each other. Nina noticed that the Frenchman wasn't looking at Campana when he held out his hand to him. The handshake she received from Traverse was a brief limp grip of the tips of her fingers.

'Let me walk you to your car,' Gerst said to Nina.

'Herr Gerst,' Massimo said, 'you've been an excellent host. Signora Monte and I have further arrangements. Have a good night.'

Gerst set his lips into a disillusioned grin. 'Absolutely. Good night. Have a safe journey, Signora. I hope to see you again.'

When he and Traverse left the room, Nina turned to Campana. 'What is going on here?'

He finished shovelling the documents into his briefcase, and said, 'Our German colleague has a great impression of you, Signora. I don't think there would be anyone to blame him for that affection.'

Nina felt a flush on her cheeks. 'What did he mean by saying "have a safe journey", and what did you mean by "Signora Monte will join them"? Do you really expect me to get involved after that farce?'

'Let's walk,' he said.

When they stepped onto the courtyard, the firework show was over. The stink of burned charcoal and sulphur drifted through the air, stinging at the inside of Nina's nose.

'The meeting took place in Germany for your convenience, Signora, as you were already in this country,' Campana said. 'The gathering of the ministerial employees in the castle wouldn't draw too much unwanted attention, but if it did, it would be explainable why we met: cultural exchange, et cetera. But...' He sighed and said, 'This is an official version. The truth is I had no other choice but to involve France and Germany. They already knew what we were up to. And as we gave them no choice when we asked for your and van der Venn's cooperation, they insisted on meeting you immediately. That, we couldn't refuse. Although I knew that by organizing our gathering at such a short notice they had aimed at discouraging you from coming here at all. I'm sorry for that, I'm glad you came. Then, as you've witnessed, the meeting wasn't going well. If we carried on, we wouldn't have come to any valid conclusions.'

He stopped before the gate tower. 'You see, Signora, I wish I knew better what's exactly happening on Lake Garda, and if our German and French partners made an impression on you that they do know, don't let them fool you.'

Campana handed her a leather binder. 'Inside is everything that you need to know about Lammert van der Venn, and your next steps—if you accept, of course.'

'Signor Campana, I have my du—'

'We've informed the university that you'll be off for a couple of days.'

'What?'

'The Ministry thinks it won't take longer. After this is over, we will award your department a generous grant. Think how much your studies would benefit. Naturally, we will add a special bonus for your involvement and for any inconvenience we might have caused.'

Nina furrowed her eyebrows. Never before had the Ministry been so determined to recruit her.

'Let's *assume* I agree to your proposal,' she said slowly. 'What exactly would you expect me to do?'

Massimo pointed through the gate. 'The same driver will take you to Milan. Journey shouldn't take more than six hours. We know that you have an apartment there. Tomorrow morning you will meet Cardinal Vittorio Ermanno Esposito and present him a short briefing from tonight's gathering.'

He must have read her puzzled face. 'Signora Monte, you are the last person I thought I would have to explain to that the Church is always engaged where serious sacral matters are at stake,' he said. 'In the afternoon you will take a train to Peschiera del Garda, and from there a direct bus to Malcesine by the lake, where you will finally catch a breath.

Van der Venn will get in touch with you later on the next day.'

'I can see you've already arranged everything,' Nina said.

'We've booked a hotel for you. Although, without a lake view. We have to think about taxpayers. We went overboard with spending this year,' he said, then winced. 'Media are only waiting for any dodgy move a politician would make.'

'No problem. Although, I do hope you booked me for a full board. Three hefty meals a day.'

'Please keep your receipts. We will reimburse your expenses,' Campana said, ignoring her sarcasm. Then he headed to the car that had brought her to the castle.

Resigned, Nina shook her head and followed him.

'Please have a thorough look into those documents. If there's anything unclear, van der Venn promised to explain every aspect.'

Campana came to a stop by the car. He dropped his eyesight for a short moment, then looked up at Nina. 'Actually, it was van der Venn who insisted it was better if you learned everything from him.'

He reached into his inside pocket. 'My private number. You can get in touch with me in case of an emergency.'

Felix opened the door for Nina. She put the folder on the seat and turned back to ask Campana what kind of emergency he had in mind, but he was already halfway back to the castle.

'How was the meeting, Signora?' Felix said when they both settled in the car. 'Have you got your answers?'

Nina switched on the light above her head and opened

van der Venn's portfolio. 'I will have to wait for that a bit longer.'

CHAPTER 3

FELIX DROVE THE car down the hill, dancing between pedestrians, but the Audi's speed was much slower than before. It took forty minutes before the car shot onto the A5 highway and sped south.

Nina put down the folder she had gotten from Campana and tried to relax. She reached into her bag and rummaged around for the leftovers of her croissant. She took a bite. It was a bit stale and the vanilla almond custard had dried out slightly, but she was grateful for it nonetheless.

Lammert van der Venn's dossier both saddened and impressed her.

She had read that he was fifty-two years old, birthplace unknown, parents unknown. He had been raised in an orphanage in Amsterdam. At fourteen he escaped and joined the crew of a cargo ship. Then it looked like he had hardly ever put his foot on dry land. At sixteen, South America became his home, where he worked on a Colombian beach in tourism.

When he turned twenty-two, he bought his own boat. He searched for underwater treasures off the coast of the Dominican Republic, Jamaica, St. Martin, the Cayman Islands, and the Bahamas. He had a flair for this business; at thirty-five he owned a small fleet of boats.

He became a millionaire art collector in his early forties, but hadn't ceased in his quest for rare artefacts.

Further, Lammert van der Venn was acquainted with a number of prominent figures from the Caribbean and Africa. Nina read their names. Some of them were hard-bitten dictators from countries that considered human rights a redundant privilege.

Van der Venn's latest project, commissioned by the Haitian government, was a vast excavation off their coast. Nina's eyes opened wider when she read that he discovered two tons of artefacts, jewellery, and gold of a total value of 192 million US dollars.

But it was the last sentence of his portfolio that enhanced Nina's curiosity: "Now he is on an ultimate quest for a spiritual treasure."

She leaned her head back and closed her eyes. Nothing in the folder gave her a clue what they were after, what lay deep in the waters of Lake Garda.

And the Ministry kept her on a tight schedule. She was to meet the cardinal tomorrow at 8:30 a.m.

She peered forward at the glowing clock embedded into the Audi's dashboard. She rubbed her eyes. Ten minutes past two. No wonder she couldn't gather her thoughts.

The speedometer showed 190 kilometres per hour. She looked out the window and up. It felt like sitting on a soft armchair in an astrological observatory and staring at Milky Way after Milky Way. It was celestial. She could watch it all night, if only her eyelids weren't so heavy…

'Signora Monte.' Someone shook her arm. 'Signora, we have reached the destination. Do you want me to walk you to the door?'

She shuddered, feeling the cool wind blowing in through the open door. Felix was leaning over her, as if he wanted to kiss her. She recoiled. 'What?'

'My job is done, but I could walk you to the door, Signora?'

She covered her mouth and yawned, glancing around.

The car was parked by the entrance to an apartment building in Milan, her second home in Italy. Her suitcase stood outside, behind Felix.

'No. You must also be exhausted,' she said, giving him a sympathetic smile. 'I'm glad only one of us closed their eyes.'

'I'm very well, Signora. I could walk back to Heidelberg,' he said. 'They pay me lots of money for this job.'

Nina scrambled out of the car. 'Then I'm glad even more.'

He squeezed her hand. 'Thanks, Signora. Good luck!'

Nina headed straight to the gate, thinking about Lake Garda, Lammert van der Venn, and a world without Julien Traverse. And Felix's sincere "good luck."

When she closed the door to her apartment behind her, she went to her bedroom and fell onto the bed. Once her head touched the pillow, marvellous visions of medieval castles, fireworks, and sunken galleys whirled in her head, and pulled her in to taste their abundance.

And something else awaited her there; something, she sensed, that had been there a long, long time. Something of value that was far beyond measurable.

CHAPTER 4

LAMMERT VAN DER Venn swam slowly below the surface of Lake Garda. A depth gauge on his wrist showed one hundred metres. The temperature close to the surface was a pleasant twenty-two degrees Celsius; here it was hardly ten degrees. Clad in a seven-millimetre-thick drysuit, he didn't feel the cold.

In his hand, he held a powerful but fragile HID dive light. High intensity discharge increased the output of the bulb to five thousand lumens. The other two torches mounted to his lightweight helmet weren't as strong. The lights gave him a field of vision of eleven metres ahead in otherwise zero-visibility surroundings.

He made thirty-five meters along the rugged lakebed, but there was nothing to be seen yet.

He swam slowly for another reason. At this depth, his ninety-five-kilo body consumed a combination of oxygen, helium and nitrogen, supplied in twin cylinders on his back, five times faster than on the surface. Another three decompression cylinders to safeguard his ascent were strapped to his side.

Through the thick glass of his helmet, in the penetrating glow of HID light, he saw a one-metre-high pillar protruding from the lakebed, five metres ahead.

When he had dived in the same spot yesterday, he had almost disregarded it, but his hunch hadn't let him pass. Rightly, because that pillar turned out to be the tip of a mast.

He shifted his torch off the mast and down.

Emptiness—as if the lakebed were gone.

He broke three Cyalume glow sticks and let them descend. Then another two.

A reddish glow engulfed the majestic shape of *Santa Lucia*.

Van der Venn stared, amazed, at her thirty-metre-long body that was sitting in a straight position jammed in a cavity, as if made to hide the galley from the very first day when she sank, more than half a millennium ago.

Hundreds of shattered oars on both sides let the ship fit into the hollow. Her second mast was smashed—its broken half jabbed into the deck in the middle of the galley.

Van der Venn broke two more sticks and left them on the edge. Then he regulated a pressure valve of his diving wing—a horseshoe-shaped inflatable buoyancy bladder fitted in between the twin tanks and an ultralight aluminium back plate that was held by a harness tightened to his body.

He descended ten metres and hovered over the once glorious ship, then swam along her length, manoeuvring between the ropes that floated loosely, still attached to the broken mast. With great care, he touched the decayed planks of the main deck.

He moved down into a black hollow where the deck was smashed open.

The visibility plunged in the belly of the ship. Jagged, decaying walls were swallowing the light. As though to compensate that, he heard his steady breath and heartbeat much louder, as if the sound could be trapped in here and bounce off. But not the light.

Van der Venn swam through the opening in the wall, three metres ahead. He saw an entrance to another room, turned his body and swayed his legs, letting the momentum propel him forward. He grabbed the doorframe and pulled.

A chunk of wood stayed in his hand. He squashed it between his fingers like a jellyfish, and then looked around.

Several barrels, chests loaded with cannon balls, swords, spears and muskets were scattered across the room. In the corner was a cage. It looked like a jail for one person. Behind metal bars there was a wide open coffer with untouched soldiers' pay.

His gaze slid off the gold and travelled to the far end of the armoury.

Van der Vann knew he wasn't alone.

Two fleshless skeletons floated by the wall. In the glow of his torches, he recognized on them the remains of Venetian infantry uniforms, which somehow prevented the skeletons from complete disintegration. They weren't part of the regular galley's crew. Two loaded crossbows with bolts still hung on their necks.

He pushed the water with his fins.

One foot of each soldier was chained to the massive, one-metre-tall-and-wide chest that stood between them. It was made from solid wood and reinforced with iron bars all over. Van der Venn believed that it would take four strong men to lift it off the ground when not submerged. In spite of that, it was still nailed to the deck.

Four huge padlocks protected its load. They were the reason he had failed to open it yesterday.

He smiled. Tonight he came better prepared.

He reached for a nickel-plated hydraulic cutter from a pocket on his thigh, and clutched the first padlock between its blades. The six-hundred-year-old iron gave up with ease. So did the second, the third and the fourth.

Van der Venn lifted the lid and held it upright. Even in the water it felt heavy. Lights on his helmet illuminated another chest the size of plane-cabin luggage. A discoloured Christian cross was painted on its top.

He slowly opened a smaller lid.

A nearly overwhelming sensation of relief swept over him. Every muscle in his body responded and relaxed.

Finally. Finally, he had found it.

A stone tablet, which measured twenty-five centimetres in length and width and three centimetres wide, lay on something that once must have been an expensive purple satin. Strange writing was engraved into the stone. Van der Venn could not read it. Only a handful of people could. Maybe even less than that, but he didn't worry about that now.

He took it into his hand with care, as if it might fall apart with the slightest touch. If it was really much older than the galley, it could crumble.

Tingles ran through his fingers and farther up and down his body, as if the tablet were charged with electrical energy that penetrated the synthetic rubber of his gloves.

He felt happy and mellow, like after a glass of whiskey. He felt like dancing, although he had never danced. Now he could, if not for the tight drysuit clinging to his body. What if he took it off? He would be free to succumb to that growing sensation of tranquillity and glee.

Not that fast. Listen. Listen to it, Lammert! And he heard it. He heard that thought rattling at the back of his head that he had tried to chase away for the last five minutes, but it kept coming. Two words kept coming louder. And louder.

Nitrogen narcosis.

The mixture of gas he was breathing wanted to deceive him. To make him careless. It was impairing his ability to make the correct decisions and to focus. He had experienced this before when he was exposed to the elevated pressure of deep waters for too long.

If he stayed longer down here, the gas would keep interfering with his judgment. It would provoke him to be bolder than he should.

Van der Venn calmed his mind and his breath. He unclipped a desert-sand-coloured carbon-fibre briefcase from his harness, opened it, and slid the tablet in. The water was pushed away when he sealed it back. Then he closed the heavy chest.

He turned away to make his way back.

Wait. Not so fast.

Another thought popped up in his head. Nitrogen narcosis was something to worry about, but he had it under control. He was an experienced diver. He had more time.

What if there was something else in that big chest—something he didn't notice before because his eyes went straight to the tablet?

He lifted the lid. It was super light this time, and he let it fall back, peering inside. Nothing else was there. Van der Venn shrugged his shoulders.

Then he heard a muffled crack. It was funny because he thought it was his shoulders that cracked when he raised them. Only he knew that wasn't true.

He glanced up. The wall behind the chest had been smashed by the lid. The torches on his helmet penetrated nothing but darkness.

Another sound. It was louder. Coming from somewhere above.

He wasn't sure if he was hallucinating or if something was really happening on the upper deck. Hallucinations were the next stage of nitrogen intoxication—loss of consciousness would follow.

He looked up just in time to see the tip of the broken mast sliding towards him. Two seconds later it crashed into his back, slipped to his side between the decompression cylinders, and pinned him to the deck.

Van der Venn cursed in a loud voice. He choked on the air and coughed. His heart rate accelerated, his lungs burned. He let go of the briefcase. With his vision blurred he watched the water current caused by the crash take it away deeper into the guts of the galley.

He felt dizzy. If he could only sit down on solid ground, take one deep breath of fresh air, feel a strong breeze on his face.

He let the torch fall, pulled out a titanium knife from a pocket on his forearm and cut off the cylinders. He freed himself, but the cylinders stayed under the mast. The light floated on a cord attached to his arm, and for a moment it blinded him. Disorientated, he squeezed his eyes shut.

When he opened them, he saw a distorted shape of Venetian infantry illuminated by the lights in his helmet. The infantry seemed to be upside down.

He grabbed the soldier by his legs, turned his own body and climbed up. With each grip, van der Venn's fists crushed the skeleton's bones until there was nothing left.

Then he pushed himself lightly up off the open chest, watching the Venetian crossbow falling down from the fragmented soldier.

The instant the weapon touched the deck, a lead bolt blasted off and hit van der Venn under his armpit. It punctured the skin of the buoyancy wing. Bubbles of air rushed from it, shooting up. He gritted his teeth. His safeguard to ascending without a risk of decompression sickness became useless.

Careful not to touch anything, he swam out of the galley and sat on the cavity, clutching his fingers to its edge. The glow of the sticks he had left there before was fading.

Along with the air left in his twin tanks and a pony bottle strapped to his arm, he calculated that it should be just enough to make it to the decompression back-up cylinders that he had left secured to the diving shot-rope attached to a buoy floating on the surface of Lake Garda. The other end of the rope was held by a thirty kilo lead weight dropped to the lakebed.

He closed his eyes; around him was almost darkness anyway. The pounding in his skull made it hard to remember in which direction the rope was.

CHAPTER 5

AFTER TWO HOURS of a controlled ascent, during which van der Venn kept his eyes glued to the depth gauge, his crew hoisted him on board an ultra-modern yacht, *Snovia*. When his feet touched the deck, he winced and leaned, propping his hands on his knees to relieve the strain on his lower back.

He removed his helmet and took a few shallow breaths. His lungs still burned. The air was crisp. The night was warm and quiet. The waters of the lake kept its serenity.

'Are you all right, boss?' Waaberi asked, helping him take off the diving suit.

Van der Venn replied with a short nod.

Waaberi remained still, fiddling with the suit. His chest muscles were nervously flexing and relaxing under his T-shirt that featured two leopards supporting a shield with the white star—Somalia's national emblem.

'Boss … to me it looks like you should use a decompression chamber.'

'Start the engines, Waaberi!'

'Yes, boss!' He put the wet suit down and sprinted to the captain's bridge.

'Stop staring,' van der Venn said to Sander Klaff. 'There's nothing to celebrate yet. Be patient.'

The three diesel engines roared to life.

'Why don't you let me go down there with you, as we usually do? You're taking avoidable risks,' Klaff said and pointed at the cylinder with the mark left by the mast, and the punctured wing. 'And where's the rest of your tanks?'

'It was more complicated this time. *Different* and complicated.'

'It's the same as on the day you hired me seven years ago,' he said and stretched out his slender arms. 'There's water, something deep underneath, and we take it out. Simple.'

'This must be done my way,' van der Venn answered. 'Besides, if I needed help, I would take Waaberi.'

'What?' Klaff craned his veined neck forward, stretching the rigged boat tattooed under his left ear. 'That little African shit? He's too young for a dive like that!'

Van der Venn took a step towards him and rested his heavy arm on Klaff's shoulder. Klaff's head was at the level with van der Venn's chest. 'Seven years, or seven seconds. As long as you work for me, you will do as I say.'

Klaff's weather-beaten face was blank. He said in a low voice, 'Waaberi might be right about that decompression chamber.'

'I don't need decompression. I'm just tired. It shows, apparently,' he said and turned away from Klaff. 'Go and help to navigate. I want to be out of here immediately.'

That was the end of discussion. Klaff wouldn't dare to test his patience any more. Besides, van der Venn didn't pay his men to fear him. That was self-destructive. That was wishing for a day when his crew would fail him. No. He needed them to be efficient. And they were efficient, because he paid them not only in cash.

He kept them in a constant state of excitement. He made them explorers. He made them adventurers. He made them gamblers, always eager to see what came from the depths of oceans, seas or lakes.

Van der Venn always handpicked his men to his liking. He needed to know they were properly suited to the hard work at sea. But often he preferred doing things alone. He was used to it because it had started a long time ago.

The place where he grew up, St. Augustine's orphanage in Amsterdam, had left him no other choice. He'd had to fight with other kids. It was never pretty. At twelve, he broke an arm of one boy, and a wrist of another. A third one escaped with a bleeding nose.

He had a reason. A good one.

Respect.

They laughed at his plump and short body. They called him names from strip cartoon books. Van der Venn had erased those nicknames from his memory. If he wanted, he could bring them back, but that wouldn't do him any favours. Forty years later, the abuse would taste the same.

After that, the people who ran the orphanage isolated him from the other kids. They said he had antisocial personality disorder.

Idiots. How can a twelve-year-old be antisocial?

They gave him pills. He refused to take any. They forced them down his throat. He tried to bite off two of his minder's fingers. They left him alone.

When they let him out of isolation, no one annoyed him anymore—he annoyed no one.

One good thing that came out of those years in Amsterdam was that they had taught him how to read and write. How to fight, he learned on his own. It came naturally.

Those years hardened him in a way no family would ever be able to do.

And those years made him promise something. The promise he kept fulfilling every day of his life: he would never allow anybody to push him around. He would be the strongest. He would be independent. He would have everything he needed. And he would despise weak and pathetic human beings.

All of that became reality.

But despite having enough money to never work again and being able to live whatever life he wished, how could he do it? How could he do it if the world held secrets that only people like him had enough courage to reach for? Things compared to which his wealth meant no more than a lousy overcoat to a beggar who'd won the lottery.

Tonight he had in his hands one of those secrets.

Tonight he held the tablet in his hands. It was special. Not exactly like he had imagined it, but at least now he knew that it existed.

Could it really give him immortality?

Nina Monte would know the answer.

Van der Venn looked into the distance, at the towns built around the shoreline of the lake. They shone with thousands of flickering dots. Tens of thousands lived there, unaware what their lake had preserved on its bed for half of a millennium.

And what a glory it was to bring to the one who took it.

CHAPTER 6

THE SUN WAS picking through the purple curtains of Nina's bedroom. She opened her eyes and squinted at her wristwatch. Nearly 7:30 a.m. She rolled to the side, yawned and stretched her arms and legs. Incredibly, after three hours of sleep, she felt rested.

She took a shower, had breakfast, and before she put on her clothes, it was ten minutes past eight. But she wasn't going to be late for the meeting. Her apartment was three metro stops from Piazza del Duomo.

Nina reached the Duomo metro station at 8:27 a.m. She climbed up the stairs and into the open.

The seventeen-thousand-square-metre piazza was already besieged by tourists. In the middle of the square, to her right, she passed the monument of King Victor Emanuel II, who watched over the Gothic cathedral and other surrounding buildings like the Royal Palace, Carminati Palace, and Galleria, an old prestigious shopping mall named after the king.

Duomo di Milano, the Milan Cathedral, took the central point of the piazza. Every time Nina visited this place, she stood speechless for a moment, staring at the white-and-pink carved marbles of an elaborate façade covered with more than one thousand statues and gargoyles. Over one hundred cathedral spires reached into the sky, the tallest of them as far as one hundred eight metres.

It had to take an architectural genius to put it all together. But not one genius only. Many prominent figures had been involved in the construction that lasted four hundred years.

Nina came to a stop in front of a visitors' entrance; groups were not allowed in until 9:30. The queue was short and when her turn came, a tall guard pointed at her bare shoulders. She pulled out a floral-print silk scarf from her purse and threw it around herself to comply with the cathedral's rules. The guard gave her an approving nod.

She walked into Duomo di Milano. It was quiet and pleasantly warm inside. Among the smell of flowers and candles, she inhaled a faint scent of incense used by priests during a mass.

Daylight slipped through vibrant religious scenes depicted on the stained glass of huge Gothic windows. Forty twenty-five-metre-high columns supported the ornamented ceiling of a stunning structure able to accommodate forty thousand worshippers. Every square metre of the church was decorated with something.

Nina ambled down the central nave and then turned into a parallel aisle, admiring the sculptures of saints, the sarcophagi of bishops, and the woven tapestries that hung on the both sides.

Other visitors mirrored her behaviour. Some were taking pictures, but only those with yellow bands on their wrists. Those who didn't pay for the right to use their cameras were now and then still sneaking a photo with their mobile phones.

Nina scanned the surroundings in search of the cardinal. She had no idea what he looked like. She deduced that he must have been better informed than she had.

She paused at the end of the aisle in front of the statue of a saint. When Nina had seen it for the first time in her early teens, she hadn't given a second thought about the long cloth thrown around the man's arm and across his waist. Later she had found out that he held his own skin.

'The statue of Saint Bartholomew by Marco d'Agrate,' she heard a voice say behind her, and turned around.

An elderly man with an oval face and brown eyes behind rimless rectangle glasses stood two metres in front of her. He was clad in a black cassock with scarlet piping and buttons. A little above his waist he wore a scarlet fascia, which hung down on his left side. On his chest, a pectoral cross hung on a cord. A scarlet zucchetto covered his head.

'One of the twelve apostles of Christ, flayed and crucified in Armenia in the first century,' Nina said, glancing back at the statue. 'For bringing Christianity.'

'I was told you are an outstanding historian, Signora Monte,' the man said and smiled. Lines on his face shaped a heart around his lips and down to his chin. He extended his hand. 'My name is Cardinal Vittorio Ermanno Esposito.'

'Pleased to meet you, Cardinal,' Nina said and shook his hand.

'You must be tired, having travelled all the way from Heidelberg last night,' he said. 'Would you prefer to reschedule our meeting?'

'Cardinal, as far as I know, I should only inform you about the progress of yesterday's gathering,' Nina said. 'The problem is that I'm not sure if there *was* any progress. For me to be of any help, you would have to tell me first what it is that everyone, with all due respect, including you, wants so badly.'

'Do you know, Signora Monte, for what reason the Ministry called you?'

'They know me and they know I'm reliable,' Nina said with confidence. 'Besides, apparently the man who leads the search had something to do with it.'

'Do you really think that a *man* can be in charge of such a divine operation?'

'I don't believe in God, Cardinal Esposito.'

'So I've been told,' he said, amused.

Nina raised her eyebrows. 'I'd really like to know what my role is and what you are looking for.'

He put his hands together, like for a prayer, and raised them to his chest. 'Signora, do you know what the biggest wish of a human being is?'

'My first guess is money, power, and sex.' She bit her lower lip. Had she gone too far with her honesty?

Esposito let out a discreet chuckle. 'Yes, all of those. Unfortunately. But they are desires of sinful men. I'm asking you what the desire of a pure heart is. Although, a desire that should not be.'

He spoke slowly, articulating every word to the point that she thought he was reciting from a script. She felt no authority in his voice, which she expected she should in the presence of such a high priest in a Catholic church. But she wasn't a member of his church.

'How many men of a pure heart have you met, Cardinal?'

His grin disappeared. He turned away from Nina and looked at the altar. 'I will tell you, Signora, what that desire

I'm talking about is.' He paused as if making sure she was listening. 'We would like to find God in ourselves.'

It made no sense. Wasn't it the pillar of the Christian faith? Maybe he had said "to find God *for* ourselves."

She brushed those thoughts aside and said, 'I don't understand how it is relevant to what is happening at the lake, Cardinal.'

Esposito glanced at her. 'Come. Tell me about the meeting.'

He took a seat on the closest pew, smoothed his cassock, and motioned to Nina to join him.

While she was reporting what happened in the castle eleven hours ago, the cardinal listened to her with his hands clasped together on his lap, and with his eyes closed.

When she finished, he did not move. Nina thought that he had fallen asleep. Then he knelt and started talking in a low voice. She joined him on her knees to hear his words. Was this what a person felt during confession?

'My child, you must be vigilant with what politicians have to say. Their promises always have a double meaning,' he whispered.

'Promises? No one promised me…' She trailed off, thinking about funds for her department. 'How do you know I've been promised something?'

'What they're looking for,' he continued, 'doesn't belong to any of them. It belongs to the faithful men of our holy congregation. It was under Church protection a long time ago, but was lost. For those reasons, it cannot fall into the hands of infidels.'

The cardinal turned to her. His eyes were watery.

He wagged his finger at her. 'You will be *personally* responsible for bringing it to me, no matter what.' His tone of voice changed into a conspicuous threat.

'But, Father, I can't—'

He put his hand on her head. Nina spontaneously bowed.

'My child, everything we do is, in the end, God's will. A thin line separates conscience and our obligation to the Almighty. I trust you will understand when the time comes.'

Then, as suddenly as he tensed, he relaxed, and that heart-shaped humble smile he had welcomed her with returned. 'You must not be afraid of anything, for God will be at your side at all times. You will have my prayers with you.'

With awe, and on her knees, feeling awkward, she watched him briskly walk away. The soft soles of his shoes let out no sound on the stone floor of the cathedral. Soon he disappeared behind the altar.

Nina pushed herself to her feet and hastened to the exit, wondering if she did well accepting Massimo's Campana job offer. So far the riddle from Lake Garda had only brought her more frustration.

She felt as if all the statues of saints and martyrs were picking at her, especially Saint Bartholomew, the man who was flayed for praising the word of God.

Her shoulders became heavier and heavier. She trudged the last few metres like a drowning person to the surface of the water.

Outside, the sunrays engulfed the Piazza Duomo. Long queues of organized pilgrims waited for their turn to visit the holy cathedral. Nina put on her sunglasses and headed through the square, mingling with tourists, their cameras recording every image around them.

She pulled the scarf from her shoulders, letting her bare skin absorb the warmth of the early September sun.

In daylight, what Esposito told her was not only abstract, but also made her uneasy. If there were a God, the Almighty, the one who began everything on Earth, for whom people erected majestic structures like Duomo di Milan, she would never find him in herself. Regardless of if that was a sin or not.

CHAPTER 7

NINA SAT DOWN at a table outside a small restaurant in Via dei Mercanti, close to Piazza Duomo, and ordered an espresso.

Half of the tables around her were taken. At a few, she saw shopping bags from designer outlets like Armani, Versace, and Roberto Cavalli, proving that the fashion week in Milan was in full swing.

She tore two small bags of brown sugar, poured them into the cup, stirred it with a silver-looking spoon, and took a slow sip. Sweet and strong flavour of freshly brewed coffee had always sharpened her senses. That and Sudoku. Now, though, she wasn't in the mood for a puzzle. Since last night, she'd had enough mystery.

Nina lifted her gaze to the chaos and noise of the morning in the city. Cars, trams, buses carried people to work. Normally, she would have been aboard one of them in Padua.

Somehow, now more than before, she enjoyed the presence and flow of average people. People like her, whose daily worries evolved around less spiritual matters.

That unpleasant sensation she experienced when leaving the cathedral had been dissolved, although it left behind a dilemma.

How would the first person on the street respond to the question asking if they had found God in themselves, and, if not, at what stage was their quest? Probably they would give her a confused look and walk away. Or maybe not. What if not? What if some might actually have an answer?

She shook her head. If there were a God, someone would have already found concrete proof.

She pulled out a tablet computer from her handbag and logged into her academic mailbox.

Odd. She had fifteen new emails since she had checked her account yesterday, so why were all of them marked as read? Then, astounded, she looked around herself, and back to the screen. Nina blinked a few times—the e-mails showed as unread now.

She really needed to run the updates on her computer more often. Either that or not to use the public Wi-Fi that much.

The last e-mail she received was a thank-you note from Massimo Campana. It was short. He had again apologized for the inconvenience and wished her a safe journey.

Indeed the Ministry had been handling the discovery in the lake with extreme seriousness, and wanted to keep it quiet. Nina understood why she had never met Campana. She was convinced they had hired him exclusively for this case. Even his email address had a slightly different domain extension.

The rest of the communication required no immediate attention, so she logged off.

Nina took a deep breath, glanced around again, and signed on to her dating account for professionals.

If someone asked, she had always stressed that it wasn't her idea to find a partner online. As her tight schedule at the university rarely gave her a chance to hook up with an interesting man, she capitulated to an idea by three of her work friends. They called the project: modern technology in service of Nina's Monte romantic life. Although she didn't think there was anything romantic in that.

She read the profile she had agreed to after two glasses of wine.

Nina Monte is thirty-six years old, one metre sixty, curvy build but everything shaped gorgeously. Besides beautiful (what you have already noticed) she's honest, cares for the elderly, is independent, and has a successful career.

She studies archaeology: history of medieval art, roman history; philosophy: aesthetics, history of ancient scientific thought, history of Christianity, history of religions.

So you shouldn't be surprised or intimidated that she's a professor of History of Religions at the Department of Historical and Geographic Sciences and the Ancient World.

She would like to meet a responsible and mature man who has similar views of the world, meaning he hates liars, unreliable people, those who neglect their families, and those who hurt others.

Looks are less important than a clear view as to where a potential relationship is going.

Nina read the last line again, the only paragraph she had written herself. Was desperation screaming between those words?

She received messages from three handsome men who had the courage to reply. She leaned closer to the screen. One of them wore makeup. She flinched and deleted all of them.

Once, she had been opposed to the cliché that average guys were apprehensive about educated, strong-minded women. Today she was inclined to agree.

Strongly agree.

CHAPTER 8

Es ITALIA 9741, destined for Peschiera del Garda, glided on the rails through Milan. Nina listened to the train's characteristic *click, click* trying to compose her thoughts after she trapped herself in fruitless speculation about what lay at the end of her trip. What lay at the bottom of Lake Garda.

She looked out the window. The sun was low. For many, it was time to go home after hours of a hectic day.

She tried to catch her image in the glass. What she saw was mostly a reflection of the carriage inside. Beside her, there were seven or eight people travelling in the car that could easily squeeze in thirty passengers.

After Nina had returned to her apartment earlier, she had tried to catch up on her sleep. But despite her tiredness she hadn't been able to close her eyes for longer than ten minutes. Now, she felt physically and mentally weary.

Something else was stealing her sleep, though. She was angry with herself, because unconsciously she knew that her decision to accept Massimo Campana's offer was greatly due to Massimo Campana's promise of extra funds for her department. However many times she explained to herself that she did well, and that she didn't care if there was something additional for her in it, she still felt guilty.

Maybe her guilt wouldn't have resurfaced with such strength if not for Cardinal Esposito. Were the people she met in Heidelberg like those politicians he mentioned? Did she take the job because they had bought her?

Nonsense. It was the Ministry. She trusted them, and they respected her.

The train picked up speed and soon pulled out of the city.

Nina opened her briefcase and drew out the documents she had received from Campana.

She gazed at the picture of the man she was to meet tomorrow.

Lammert van der Venn looked as if he were forged from one solid block by a sculptor who hated to waste too much of his precious material. His skin was darkish. She couldn't say if it was a tan or if he was born with it.

He stood straight with his legs planted onto the deck of a yacht—Nina presumed, his own. His arms, crossed on his chest, and his forearms were almost of the same width, packed with muscles. He had a rectangular silhouette with shoulders only a little wider than his waist. She saw an oval outline of his belly under his T-shirt, but he was not overweight.

Nina took in her hands a second picture of him, a portrait.

His rounded, flat nose and his squinty, sharp eyes that were brown or green revealed no nationality.

The top half of his head was round, with short, curly hair and a furrowed forehead. The bottom half was square with a distinct jaw and a short, cropped beard.

Nina recalled Campana's assurance that he was the ideal man for the job. Although she knew little about that man, to her, Lammert van der Venn didn't look like a person who was for hire.

She checked the time on her phone. The journey to Peschiera del Garda was going to last one hour and seven minutes. Thirty-five more minutes left on the train. Thirty-five more minutes of being ogled by a man with a juvenile smile.

Nina had noticed him in Milan straight after he had taken a seat cornerwise, three rows in front of her.

He was no older than twenty-eight, wore a yellow polo T-shirt, blue striped suit, and red sneakers. Handsome and immature. He could have been one of her students. But he resembled a footballer.

That game had a corrupt charm to put every woman on a secondary position. Always. She never understood what was fascinating about twenty-two men, some of them grown, chasing after a ball. When one of them tried to snatch it from under the legs of another player, and succeeded, the first guy tumbled down in his despair as if he were practising a shooting scene for a new mafia movie.

The boy in the polo T-shirt combed his hair with his hand over and over. He was preparing himself. That was supposed to draw Nina's attention, and give him guts to come over and talk to her. Simple and obvious.

One glimpse in his direction would suffice. For the whole half an hour, she was careful not to encourage him. Until she had just glanced at him absent-mindedly.

He got up and headed towards her. A bottle cap lay on the floor. He kicked it aside like a penalty at a stadium full of screaming fanatics.

Nina lowered herself in the seat, pretending to be engrossed in the document she had already read three times.

'My name is Cesare,' he said, sitting down next to her. 'Where are you going?'

Nina closed the folder. 'Is this the best line you could come up with, Cesare?'

He raised his hands in a gesture of surrender. A boyish smile crossed his mouth. 'Why so hostile? I just wanted to get to know you.'

'Okay, go on,' she said, business-like.

He raised one eyebrow and said in flirtatious manner, 'Just like that?'

Nina slid her folder into her briefcase. 'Yes. Shoot. Impress me.'

'Impress you?' He ran his fingers through his hair again. His hand paused on his neck. He stared out the window as if someone held a blackboard with script lines for the first-time seducers.

'What would you like to talk to me about, Cesare?'

He was still smiling at her, but only just. 'What would *you* like to talk about?'

Nina pressed her lips together and closed one eye. 'Hmm, something meaningful. Football?'

'Phew,' he said and extended his hands in front of him. 'I knew you were cool. Did you watch—?'

'How old are you, Cesare?'

'Twenty-nine,' he replied. 'How old are *you*?'

'There's enough of an age difference between us, I can safely say, that you're wasting your time with me.'

She saw no more confusion on his face. He looked embarrassed.

'I just wanted to talk,' he stammered.

Then he rose slowly. Nina watched him shuffling his feet away. She felt a sting in her stomach. Discrediting him as her possible partner was justified. But why did she have to be so bitchy about it, repelling him when he was just being friendly?

She grabbed her belongings and crossed to his seat.

'My name is Nina,' she said to him. 'I'm a bit grumpy today, but it's not your fault. I wouldn't mind a chat if you're not angry with me.'

He wasn't.

For the next half an hour, Nina let herself engage in a trivial but calming conversation, forgetting Massimo Campana, Cardinal Esposito and Lammert van der Venn— and that enigmatic item all of them wanted.

CHAPTER 9

AT CLOSE TO midnight, Lammert van der Venn walked into an Irish pub in Malcesine. They had in stock his favourite whiskey—the only apt alcohol to mark his fifty-second birthday.

The inside smelled of beer and a mixture of stronger liquors. Glasses clinked against glasses. A group of people chatted loudly over music that had little to do with indigenous Irish tunes. Now and then someone burst into a jarring laugh.

It was the closest thing to a sailor's tavern he would get in this town. He hated neat restaurants where everything was sterilized and new. Besides, after having a heaped plate of saltfish fritters on *Snovia*, he wasn't hungry.

Behind the bar a man in a white shirt and a green apron served a small crowd of customers. Van der Venn pushed his way to the counter. The barman poured a pint of Guinness. Then he put the three-quarters-filled glass on the bar top and looked at him.

'What can I get you today, sir?'

Before he answered, someone pushed on his back, wedged himself between him and another customer, and put his beer down. Some of it splashed on the sleeve of van der Venn's shirt.

'Sorry about that, mate!' he said and put his hand on van der Venn's forearm. 'This is a nice frock you wear. Going somewhere fancy?'

Van der Venn clenched his fist, looking at his three-hundred-forty-dollar woven black shirt. Then he glanced up at the man who was easily twenty years younger than he, thinking which of the drunkard's bones to break first.

The barman leaned over and pushed the man aside so that his arm was no longer touching van der Venn. 'What do you want, Gerry?'

'Switch on the telly, Sean. Myself and the lads want to see rugby highlights,' he said in a scratchy voice. 'What's the point of having that bloody *giant* screen, if nobody's watching it?'

'Okay, just behave yourself.'

'Always, mate, always,' he replied and walked off.

The barman reached for the remote and flicked to life the sixty-inch screen that covered half of the wall, opposite the bar.

'I'm sorry, sir,' he said. 'What will it be tonight?'

'Eighteen-year-old whiskey. One bottle, one glass.'

'Right away!'

He turned around and scooped a bottle of Jameson from the shelf, opened it, and along with a glass, he set it on the counter.

Van der Venn grabbed the whiskey and pushed himself from the bar. He headed to the farthest room of the pub, to the same table he had taken yesterday. On his way, he passed an overexcited group who screamed and gesticulated at the players fighting over an oval ball.

He looked at the one who had almost spoiled his evening.

The barman had done van der Venn a favour when he intervened.

Tonight was about being alone and in peace, and he didn't even think about diving. What had to be discovered, had been discovered. Tonight he preferred to keep his feet on dry land, and his throat content.

The two-seat table in a secluded cubicle far from TV noises and sweat of rugby fans, flanked by three walls painted in deep red, was free. Pictures of rural Ireland hung on them. Two halogen lights built into the ceiling cast down a low light.

Van der Venn placed the bottle on a wooden top and sat down in an upholstered chair. He felt an intense strain in his lower back. That should ease off; he had already taken two pills. Over the last six months, he had felt this way more often. Especially after a dive. His back would start to hurt in protest that the restful weightlessness had been broken.

It was an irony that the underwater world was the only place where he could breathe deeply. Whatever he had ever done, good or bad, merciful or brutal, was meaningless. There, no one judged him, no one envied him, no one hated him. Under the water, he could forget about the pain in his back from being squashed by that damned cannon on a wreck off the Jamaican coast, three years ago.

Klaff had wanted him to see someone about it, but that idea was ludicrous for van der Venn. He never went to a doctor, never got sick. Except for that one time when he got chikungunya two years ago. Those bloodsucking mosquitoes had put him to bed with a high fever for three days. Even then he didn't let his men call a doctor. The worst was that, afterwards, his back pains had become more frequent.

He poured whiskey into the glass, raised it and admired its dense texture and golden colour. He inhaled the scent of sherry notes, spice and toffee.

Then he lowered it back on the table. Patience was what he trained into himself; it hardened him. In life, nothing came easy. Few people knew that better than him.

He smiled, thinking that the real change in his life began exactly with the lack of patience when, at fourteen, he had decided he'd had enough of the orphanage. There was nothing left to learn there. He had escaped and gotten on a cargo ship transporting building materials to the Port of Cartagena in Colombia. He'd told them he was seventeen. Luckily he looked much older than his age.

He worked as a deck boy in a pantry, on a deck and a kitchen. He cleaned lavatories, scrubbed the deck, set the tables, served, cleared leftovers. For twelve hours a day, seven days a week.

After twenty-one days he had gone ashore in Colombia, without a word of goodbye.

He deserved a better life. He learned to speak Spanish from fishermen, and English from Americans. He got a job behind a bar on a beach.

At seventeen he started working for a French treasure hunter, Basile Lemaire. Basile taught him navigation and everything a sailor should know about boats and the sea. Learning new things from him turned out to be the best time of his life.

Five years later, van der Venn managed to save enough to buy a boat. Nothing special, nothing like *Snovia* was now, but it had been enough then.

At thirty-five he got bored of the Caribbean, and expanded his territory. He bought houses on three continents: in Port Elizabeth, South Africa; in Sardinia, Italy; and in the Caribbean, Dominica. The only purpose of these places was to accommodate the wealth he had picked up from the sea floor. He became a professional art collector.

Van der Venn let a smirk cross his face.

He usually never brooded on his past. The time around his birthday was the only exception. It was his revision time. He could see things as they truly were and where he came from. Tomorrow he would forget about that again. For another twelve months.

He raised the glass and took a small sip.

Flavours he already knew so well and their warmness enveloped him as if someone had thrown a soft blanket around his shoulders. Moments like this helped him remember to wait for his treasures patiently, even if they were at his fingertips but not yet ready to be exposed.

Like now, when he had to wait for her.

Nina Monte would know if he was right, if the stone tablet was genuine. He would see the truth in her face. He had made sure she was not to be fully briefed. Her reaction would be sincere.

He had suppressed his excitement for the last forty-eight hours. His people had noticed a change in his behaviour. He had become less strict with them. Otherwise, Klaff would never have dared to question his instructions.

He took another sip. Whiskey travelled down his throat, disconnecting him from his surroundings, relaxing him in a way he only felt under the water.

'Buonasera,' someone said, too happily for his taste. 'Good evening.'

His fictional blanket had been robbed. He gritted his teeth and glanced up.

A slightly overweight, grey-haired man with a tanned, clean-shaven face—except for a grey soul patch just below his lower lip—was grinning at him. He wasn't much older than van der Venn.

In one hand, he held an empty pint; just a tiny amount of dark liquid still covered its bottom. In the other, he had a whiskey glass full to the brim with ice cubes.

He plumped down on a chair. '*Scusi.*'

'I'd rather be alone,' van der Venn replied in English.

'Excuse me. Do you mind company?' the man said with an Italian accent. 'I can see you are not a rugby enthusiast. Me neither. Personally, I prefer football. But they serve here *superb* stuff.' He waved with his glass and burped. '*Scusi.* Sorry.'

'Go. Away,' van der Venn said, keeping his bearing calm.

The man put out his hand. 'My name is Gianluigi.'

He remained impassive. 'Go away, Gianluigi.'

'I could, but I can't. I can see that something bothers you.' The Italian raised his chin as if to encourage van der Venn to speak.

'When someone needs to get something off his chest, I'm there for him,' Gianluigi said, and pointed his finger ahead. 'Tonight, I'm here for you, my friend! And … if on that occasion, I can have a nice drink, then I make one heck of a listener.'

It was hard to distance himself from the babbling man; his hands were constantly moving as if each word had its own gesture. And the Italian called him a friend. If someone called you a friend, he wanted something from you.

Van der Venn emptied his glass lazily. He had no friends. Only associates. Gianluigi didn't strike him as either of those two kinds.

The man threw most of the ice into his pint and reached over for van der Venn's glass, but he covered it with his palm.

'I understand. Nothing should spoil a high-quality whiskey.'

Van der Venn stared into his eyes. The Italian didn't flinch, so he poured Jameson for both of them.

'God bless you, my friend,' he said and tasted the liquor, smacking his lips. 'Superb, *superb* stuff.'

Van der Venn emptied his glass, and looked expectantly at Gianluigi who, after a second of hesitation, did the same. He poured more.

'Where do you come from, my friend?' Gianluigi said.

'I have no home.'

'But where have you been born? Everyone knows that.' Gianluigi's words became prolonged and clunky, his hands not as nimble as before.

'I don't know,' he replied and filled the glasses to the half.

'You are not an easy person to talk to you, you know.' Gianluigi leaned back in his chair, then over the table, clasping his glass, and said zestfully, 'Tell me something about yourself.'

Van der Venn sipped from his glass, emotionless. 'Do you want to know who I was before I killed my first man?'

Gianluigi sat back. Dismay took over his exhilaration. 'I beg your pardon?'

'Drink. Isn't it what you came for?'

Gianluigi tried to get up, but van der Venn grabbed an armrest of his chair and pulled him back to the table. Although he couldn't have been heavier than seventy kilos, van der Venn scowled in pain from the effort. He fished out a small box from his pocket, opened it, popped another painkiller and washed it down.

'I said drink.'

Gianluigi looked back towards the empty corridor that led to the main room. Screams of rugby fans came out of there. Then he glanced at van der Venn and, with his trembling hand, guided the glass to his mouth. He gulped the whiskey.

Van der Venn refilled the glasses. 'Why are you scared of me?'

'I'm … I'm not,' Gianluigi said and raised his chin. His Adam's apple rose and fell jerkily.

'Then there's nothing you should worry about. I only despise cowards. They're like a plague.' He closed his eyes. 'I wish I were a cure. I wish I could clean this planet of every worthless, whining wimp.'

Van der Venn heard the scrape of the chair against the floor. 'I thought we were friends.'

The chair didn't move again.

He leaned forward and outstretched his massive arms, grasping the edge of the table on Gianluigi's end. 'I've been lucky to be surrounded by courageous men. After what they went through, little can scare them.'

Gianluigi lowered his head and rested his palms on his thighs.

'You wanted a story. Here it is. I'll tell you a story of a courageous man,' van der Venn said, sitting up in his chair. 'His name is Waaberi. Before his parents die during the

Somalian famine in 1992, they beg his uncle to take him. He agrees, but soon the foster family kicks the boy out. He has no home, no education, nowhere to go. He goes into piracy.'

Van der Venn paused to take a sip.

'Eleven years ago, with three other idiots, he attempts to hijack my yacht after dusk. I shoot dead his fellows on the spot. Someone from my crew fires at fourteen-year-old Waaberi. When I approach him, blood is oozing between his fingers from a wound in his stomach. But the boy bucks like a trapped panther. I see hatred and fury in his eyes. In his other hand he is squeezing a thirty-centimetre blade. If I'm not careful, he will cut my throat.'

Drops of sweat loomed on Gianluigi's forehead.

'I leave him bleeding on that small boat, without water, and haul it behind my yacht. I shout to him that if he gets through the night, I will look after him. I see how he hates me. I see he accepts.'

'My *God*,' Gianluigi whispered. 'Poor boy.'

Van der Venn squinted at him. 'It's funny that you mention him.'

'Who did I mention?' Gianluigi said in a broken voice.

Van der Venn stood up. 'Are you a religious man?'

'Yes … yes, I am.'

He circled the table and stopped behind Gianluigi. 'Tell me something. How come a religious man can be a coward?'

'I don't … What do you want from me?'

'You lied to me. I hate liars. Liars and beggars, who think they can came to me without respect and have what's mine, what I earned through tough slog.'

Gianluigi tried to get up, but van der Venn's arms pushed him down.

'You like stories? There's another one. When I'm under the water, I like to push myself over the edge. Sometimes I run out of air. It's like a game. Highly addictive game.' He enclosed his hands on Gianluigi's neck. 'When my tanks and lungs are almost empty, I have to stay calm. Would you like me to show you?'

Gianluigi raised his head and looked up. 'You're insane. I—'

Van der Venn's big palm cupped his chin and nose, cutting off the air. With the other hand, he pushed hard on the Italian's shoulder.

'How long can you keep your breath, Gianluigi, my *friend*?'

Van der Venn held his breath and closed his eyes. He imagined himself underwater, without air, without light, his body drifting slowly upwards. It would be some time before his lungs would start to burn.

He felt Gianluigi wriggling in the chair. He looked down. The Italian tried to catch him, but only waved his hands helplessly. His face turned scarlet. He kicked the table. The bottle and glasses hit the floor, but the sound of shattered glass blended into the thunderous booing of rugby fans.

Van der Venn let him go and restarted his own breathing.

Gianluigi gasped for air, the palms of his hands clutched to his chest.

'My heart,' he mumbled. '*Help*.'

Van der Venn watched him blankly.

Gianluigi pulled out his mobile. It slipped and landed on the table. He attempted to reach for it, but his hands were cramped to his body.

'I should get going,' van der Venn said casually, with one finger moving the phone closer to Gianluigi. 'If you happen to meet your God, tell him that Lammert is coming to say hello.'

CHAPTER 10

ALESSANDRO DROVE HIS Piaggio scooter through the narrow streets of Malcesine to the hotel his family had owned since 1980. It was nearly 9:00 a.m. on his Maserati wristwatch, and the sun had yet to warm up the shadowed alleys he rushed along.

He pressed on the horn to ward off pedestrians, ignoring their right of way. Then he heard them screaming at him, but he was already too far away to recognize the words. He raised his hand in apology and accelerated.

September mornings were his favourite part of the year. Especially the first week of the month. The air was crisp and fresh after the night, just on the brink of changing into the much higher temperatures of midday.

He turned the steering bar to the left and sped up the twenty-metre-long driveway leading to the hotel's main entrance. When he reached the car park, the engine of his old scooter let out a last hiss and died away.

He needed a new bike. He would have gotten one two weeks ago, a brand new Piaggio Typhoon with a 125 cc 4-stroke engine. He would have, if not for his mother who insisted he should wait until the end of this season, after they close the books to account for the hotel's earnings.

Alessandro took off his helmet and looked around. Five out of the seven cars parked by the two-storey, sandy front of the hotel had German registration plates. The other two belonged to families from Sicily who'd had enough of the Mediterranean swelter and had come to Lake Garda to cool down.

'Buongiorno,' he said happily, waving to the guests who were having breakfast on a room's sunlit terrace. 'Good morning.'

'Guten Morgen,' they replied in German and waved back to him.

He walked into the dining room that was on the ground floor. Its wide windows overlooked the lake. The room could accommodate thirty-eight guests for breakfast, which was the full capacity of the hotel. Outside, five more tables were set for people who liked to smoke with their meal, or otherwise enjoyed eating out in the open.

In the middle of the restaurant, Alessandro saw his new waitress, Mirabella, dressed in a white shirt and a burgundy apron tied at her back into a cockade. As he'd done for the last few mornings, he watched her slim figure as she negotiated her way with grace between the tables. Her black, curly hair was made into a ponytail, but he knew that, when freed, it reached almost to her waist.

'Mirabella, buongiorno,' he said.

'Buongiorno, Alessandro,' she replied, and passed him by, carrying a jug of fresh coffee.

He inhaled the aroma of coffee, and a whiff of vanilla perfume.

'Mirabella, can I talk to you?' he said and headed to the reception.

From the corner of his eye he noticed that she put the jug down and followed him.

Standing behind the counter, Alessandro propped his hands on its top. 'You are so frosty to me this morning.'

'Alessandro, I'm busy.'

'They can wait.'

He tried to reach for her hand but she made one step back. 'Alessandro, I told you that you are not the type I'd like to settle down with.'

He laughed. 'I know. I'm too young for that, too.'

Mirabella cocked her head and crossed her arms on her chest. 'You're thirty-one. I'm twenty-four. You're too *old* for me.'

He put his palms on his heart and winced. 'Ouch! So beautiful, and yet so cruel!'

'Besides, Mrs Pini warned me about you.'

Alessandro raised his eyebrows. 'Mama? What did she say?'

'Mirabella, please get back to work,' Francesca Pini said, walking into the reception.

Mirabella nodded politely and left.

'Alessandro Pini! Stop flirting with our staff,' she said and put out her hands with her palms up. 'Treat them with the respect they *deserve*!'

Alessandro grimaced. 'But I always treat everyone with respect.'

His mother frowned and stood her ground. 'How many waitresses has this hotel had since the beginning of the season?'

'Ahem … two.'

She glanced at him with annoyance and stuck out four fingers in front of his face.

'Four? Are you sure, Mama?'

'I *hired* them!'

'Okay,' he said and shrugged his shoulders. 'But I don't flirt with everybody. They just know that I'm lonely and busy and … well, lonely…'

He trailed off under his mother's hard look. 'You are my only *son*. And I *love* you. If you want to run this hotel, you have to act like a *real* manager.'

'But I *am* the manager!'

'You must learn how to be responsible, Alessandro,' she said in a soft voice. 'I'm almost sixty-two. Only God knows how much time I have left.'

'Mama! Please. Don't say things like that. You are still young. God knows that I love you so much. He wouldn't want to break my heart, would he?'

'I suppose.' She smiled and touched his cheek. 'And shave yourself. You look like a criminal.'

She headed to the kitchen.

Alessandro glanced at his reflection in the mirror that hung on the wall in the reception. Three days' stubble covered his tanned face. He liked that. Women liked that.

He ran his hand over his sandpaper-like chin. It was well suited to his bushy eyebrows and black, curly hair that covered his forehead and ears.

He smiled and smoothed the collar of his purple cotton slim-fit shirt. Then he pushed his chest forward and took another look in the mirror at his slender one-metre-eight body. He was in great shape, he thought.

'And I *am* a real manager,' he said to himself.

Piles of documents waiting for him in his office at the back of the reception desk didn't mean he wasn't capable of being in charge of the business.

He pressed the function button on his laptop, typed the password, and logged into his Facebook account. He had a message from a friend. Luca had gotten two tickets for the next match at San Siro in two days. AC Milan would host Fiorentina. Alessandro rubbed his hands. He, Luca, and eighty thousand people cheering, singing, and yelling at both teams.

'Excellent!'

Then he checked the hotel mailbox. A broad smile crossed his face when he saw six new reservations. One from Poland, two from Norway, and three more had come from Germany. The peak of the season had ended a week ago in Italy, but he hoped to gain more newcomers from northern Europe. The problem of lower occupancy had resolved itself.

'Mama,' he screamed in the empty reception room, 'look at this, I'm a *great* manager!'

A mobile phone in his front jeans pocket vibrated. He took it out and listened to the lyrics of "Siamo Chi Siamo" by Luciano Ligabue.

He sang the first few lines, and then touched the icon of the green receiver.

'Good morning,' he said.

'Alessandro, this is Raffaele Lombardi from the municipal police.'

'*Raffaele*, how are you? Why are you so official? Was yesterday's dish in my restaurant not fresh?'

'No, it's—'

'What was it? Spaghetti Frutti di Mare by Gianluigi?'

'Alessandro, I'm—'

'Then I will have to cut Gianluigi's salary in half,' Alessandro said and laughed.

'He is dead, Alessandro.'

'Exactly, but please don't arrest him yet. Where would I find a better chef?'

There was silence on the other side.

'Hello? Are you there, Raffaele?'

'Gianluigi was found dead last night,' he replied in a low voice.

Alessandro's smile faded away. Heat waves built in his stomach and rushed up to his head. His body froze. Only his hand holding the phone started to shake. He had to sit down.

'I'm terribly sorry, Alessandro. I know he was like a father to you.'

Alessandro opened his mouth, but his throat had dried out.

'In ten minutes, I'll be in the restaurant by the castle. Come see me. I will tell you more,' Raffaele said and hung up.

Alessandro's smartphone slipped through his fingers. He watched it fall in slow, perfect motion, bouncing two times before it landed between his feet on the sanded wooden floor.

CHAPTER 11

ALESSANDRO'S THIRD ATTEMPT to start the engine of his scooter failed. It was as if he suddenly forgot how to operate it, as if he had never ridden it before. He let it fall to the side and kicked the saddle. Then he dropped down on a patch of grass by the car park.

He slid to hide himself behind a Mercedes. He breathed deeply, pushing back the tears. He put his hands around his head, covered his ears. No matter how hard he pressed on them, Raffaele's words forced their way into his mind over and over again: "Gianluigi was found dead. Gianluigi was found dead!"

Alessandro sprang to his feet and sprinted towards the centre of Malcesine.

He ran, oblivious to horns of cars and motorbikes, to people whom he elbowed or pushed out of his way. He ignored greetings of his friends.

He came to a halt by the restaurant. His shirt clung to his back, and he felt sweat trickling down his spine. He glanced over a low fence. A dozen tables were set behind it. Tourists and locals alike chattered over their drinks, sandwiches or pastries.

Raffaele waved to Alessandro from the far corner. His short and stocky physique was easy to notice in a police uniform, but that was strange as Alessandro had never seen him dressed so officially. It had to be out of respect for Gianluigi.

Alessandro moved his way to the table and plopped onto a seat next to Raffaele. His heart wouldn't slow down the thumping, although he steadied his breath.

Raffaele raised his hand towards a waiter. 'Two espressos, please.'

Alessandro didn't want to meet Raffaele's gaze. He stared at something that twenty minutes ago was a stunning view of Lake Garda. Now it was just a vast pool of water where boats, ferries, and yachts crossed each other's paths.

'It was an accident, wasn't it?' Alessandro said.

The waiter put two small coffee cups in front of them and then moved to another table.

Alessandro glanced at Raffaele. He stroked his pedantically kept, greyish beard.

'What makes you think that?'

'What else could it be?' Alessandro raised his voice.

Raffaele dropped two cubes of sugar into his espresso. 'Gianluigi was found dead in a pub. He drank too much, and I was told that most likely it was a heart attack.'

Alessandro put his palms together at the level of his face. 'If it was a heart attack, it is not Gianluigi we're talking about. You made a mistake, and it must be someone else.'

Raffaele raked his fingers through his bushy hair. 'I'm really sorry, Alessandro. Gianluigi was a sociable person. Everyone in town knew him, not only because he was a talented chef.' He paused and glanced at the lake with an absentminded gaze. 'He had something inside that made people confide in him. When they had problems they went often to him first, rather than to me.'

Alessandro shook his head. 'But it cannot be! Gianluigi is one of the fittest people I know. Maybe in better shape than I am!'

Raffaele sipped on his espresso. 'He was fifty-six years old, Alessandro.'

'So what?'

'He liked to drink.'

'Who doesn't drink? And how old are you?'

Raffaele raised one eyebrow and pulled on his beard. 'Almost the same.'

Alessandro grabbed on his arm. 'Do you know that Gianluigi cycles along the lake for an hour every day? He also told me that he did his thorough medical check-up last month. And everything was fine!'

'I think he didn't want to worry you.'

'Nonsense!'

Raffaele sighed. 'I spoke to his doctor. Gianluigi had a heart condition.'

Alessandro lowered his head. His gaze wandered around. He couldn't focus on anything. 'You're wrong. You must be wrong. He would have told me.'

'Doctor said that he kept that even from his own family.'

Alessandro looked up. 'I don't believe you.'

Their waiter approached them. 'Will there be anything else, signori?'

'No, grazie,' Raffaele said, then turned back to Alessandro. 'Gianluigi lost his wife not that long ago. I think it played a major factor. He drank more; his disorder deteriorated.'

Alessandro grasped at his espresso, but couldn't force himself to raise the cup.

'Your mother was friends with his wife. Wasn't she?' Raffaele said.

Alessandro nodded slowly. 'After her death, Mama cared a lot about Gianluigi. He was fond of her too. Only out of respect for his wife, Mama never let him think there might be something serious between them.' He buried his face in his palms. 'Mama will be devastated.'

After a minute he raised his head. 'Who found him?'

Raffaele took out a black jotter and put on his glasses. 'Sean, the owner of the pub. Around one in the morning. He told me that Gianluigi had two or three beers. Then he probably drank whiskey with someone.'

Alessandro squinted at him. 'How come three pints and one glass of whiskey can give you a heart attack?'

Raffaele looked at him over the rims of his reading glasses. 'I'm not a doctor, Alessandro.' Then he browsed forward a few pages in his jotter. 'I gathered information on the man he was with.'

Alessandro sat straighter.

'I don't have a name, but Sean told me that he came to his pub for the third time in a row. I have here his description.' He cleared his throat. 'He's in his mid-fifties, tall, muscular build, furrowed forehead. A peculiar shape of his head. Apparently it looks like those LEGO mini figures.'

'That's all?'

'We've established that he has a fancy yacht. It was seen off the coast of Malcesine, but only after sunset.'

'After sunset? But where does it come from?'

Raffaele took off his glasses. 'The whole shoreline of Lake Garda is one hundred sixty kilometres long. Having three men at my disposal, whose primary job is to look after three thousand residents of Malcesine plus one thousand tourists, how do you propose I check every pier to know where that yacht is anchored?'

Alessandro clenched his hands into fists.

'I would have to involve police from every town surrounding the lake,' Raffaele said. 'And here comes up something else. But it must stay between us. I'm only telling you this because I know how close you were with Gianluigi.'

Alessandro wondered if he should lean over the table but decided that it would be ridiculous.

'I got a phone call from Roma this morning. I was informed that a group of scientists are carrying out sea-bottom exploration on the lake, and that I should assist them if they request so,' Raffaele said. He paused for a moment. 'The description of their grey yacht matches the one in question.'

'Who phoned you?'

He shook his head to say "It's confidential."

'Did you talk to him? To that man from the yacht?'

Raffaele let out a heavy sigh. 'I was told that people on the yacht cannot be disturbed, as their work'—he lowered his voice to a whisper—'is of a huge importance to the state.'

'To the state?'

'Shush.' Raffaele put his finger to his own mouth.

Alessandro squinted at him. 'What kind of *nonsense* is that?'

Raffaele straightened the flaps of his uniform. 'Alessandro, Gianluigi's death is not being treated as suspicious.'

'If you were Gianluigi's family would you not want to know his last words?' Alessandro said on one breath.

'My hands are tied.'

'Don't worry. Mine are not,' he said and stood up. 'I will talk to him.'

Raffaele's face blushed. 'Didn't you hear what I've just told you?'

Alessandro emptied his cup and smacked it down on the table. 'Thanks for the coffee.'

CHAPTER 12

ALESSANDRO KNOCKED ON the frame of the wide-open red door. 'Anyone there?'

He looked back. Outside the pub, on a small square surrounded by clay flower pots, the chairs were upside down on the tables. He poked his head through the door. The chairs and stools were also upturned. It smelled of a floor scrubber. The lights were off, as was the music.

'Hello! Sean?'

Alessandro waited for a moment, then walked in.

'Don't slip.' A slim-built man in his late forties with a worried face came out of a back room. 'I've just given it a proper cleaning.'

He crossed to Alessandro to shake his hand. 'I knew you would come. How are you?'

Alessandro felt as if someone had tied a knot in his throat.

'Can you show me where you found Gianluigi?' he muttered.

Sean flicked a switch with his finger and the lights brightened the pub. 'Follow me.'

Alessandro shadowed him three steps behind. He felt like his breath had shortened, his steps were sluggish, as if he were carrying stones in his pockets. He leaned on the table.

Sean turned back to him. 'Are you okay?'

Alessandro let out a weak smile and motioned to him to go on.

After twenty steps, the pub owner stopped in front of a cubicle with a table and two chairs. Faint light reflected in a polished black table top. Two paper coasters lay evenly on its ends. Between them stood a candle stuck into an empty beer bottleneck. Alessandro stared at dried streaks of wax that marked the bottle.

He made a sign of the cross and averted his gaze. 'He wasn't alone, was he?'

'Nobody was with him when I found him.'

'It's unfair if he died alone,' Alessandro said in a low voice. 'Gianluigi was always surrounded by people.'

'Customers loved him. Last night he was drinking with that new guy. That's at least what I presume, and what I told the police.'

'Was there anything else?'

Sean scratched the back of his head. 'Let's go to the bar.'

Alessandro took a seat on a stool. Sean went behind the bar top. 'You look like you wouldn't mind a drink.'

Sean raised his hand before Alessandro uttered his protest. 'It's never too early for a good whiskey.'

He turned back and grabbed a green bottle. 'This is what that guy ordered, yesterday. The *whole* bottle.'

Sean poured a small amount of the alcohol into two glasses.

'Looks expensive,' Alessandro said.

'It is. If I were in Gianluigi's shoes, I would surely strike up small talk with the lad who has the old Jameson for a friend.'

Alessandro pulled his glass closer. 'Tell me about that guy.'

'He came to my place for the third time yesterday. Always well-mannered, always paying with big notes.' Sean pulled a cloth from his shoulder and wiped the bar counter. 'Yesterday, I found on that table a two-hundred-euro note.

Alessandro looked at the glass in his hand curiously. It didn't look that expensive.

'I've been in this business for twenty-seven years,' Sean went on. 'I know faces. When I saw that guy three days ago, my first thought was: "Sean, be polite, smile, and don't encourage him to come back." '

'Why?'

Sean drank the whiskey up and glanced at the empty glass. 'This is as good as it gets.'

Alessandro tasted his drink. He twisted his mouth but quickly made a straight face, then said, 'Why did he make such a bad impression on you?'

'Sometimes you don't need a reason, Alessandro. Sometimes you just know when you meet someone that this is a person to keep yourself away from.'

'Do you think he had something to do with what happened to Gianluigi?'

Sean narrowed his eyes, as if attempting to read something on the opposite wall. Alessandro glanced back at the enormous TV screen. It was off.

'No, I don't,' Sean said. 'By the way, how's Gianluigi's family taken the dreadful news? He must have relatives.'

Alessandro cursed under his nose. He hadn't thought about it. He should have asked Raffaele.

'Gianluigi had two daughters,' Alessandro said, fiddling with his glass. 'They live in Naples. They both got married and gave birth to twins. One of his daughters has two baby boys and the other two girls. Gianluigi adored those kids beyond…'

He slipped off the stool. 'I have to go.'

***

Alessandro sat down on a small rocky beach by the lake, staring at the water shimmering in the midday sun. He picked up a stone, weighed it on his palm, and threw it as far as he could. Then another one. He stood up and hurled one after another, until the muscles in his shoulder started to burn.

Then he collapsed onto the ground, watching the ripples he caused fifty metres away.

It was unfair. Life was unfair. He laughed bitterly. Maybe it was as good as it gets.

He looked up at the mountains and their peaks that surrounded the lake.

They had fascinated him when he was six years old. He had dreamt that he climbed each of them, and waved down from their heights to his parents.

When he was eleven he promised his mother that he would climb the one that was the highest to see where his father had disappeared.

His mother had hugged him. Then she took him for ice cream. He got his favourite flavour of cherry, pistachio, and chocolate. She said that the man who taught Alessandro how to play football had found himself another wife. Before he understood what she meant, the ice cream had melted between his fingers.

Alessandro rubbed his eyes with the back of his hand. He had to tell his mother about Gianluigi. The sooner the better. He took a few deep breaths and stood up.

On his way back to the hotel, he passed the quayside in the town centre, where several companies offered cruises on the lake. Tourists could go from there to every other port around Lake Garda. Two large, anchored boats were almost full. Another one had just returned with newcomers from Limone, a town across the lake.

He quickened his steps, manoeuvring between tourists who strolled down the streets of the town centre.

Then he walked briskly along the shoreline and soon reached a less-frequented pier where he noticed an old man basking in the sunrays.

Giovani was eighty-five years old. He always sat on the same bench in boots and a beige fleece jacket. He leaned on his walking stick and observed the lake from the early morning until late in the day.

'Good morning, Signor Giovani,' Alessandro said and took a seat next to him.

The old man took off his beret, revealing for a second wisps of white hair. He bowed his head in a welcoming manner.

His craggy face brightened. 'It's you, Alessandro.'

'How are you today, Signor Giovani?'

'Very well,' he said and nodded, leaning his body forward.

'Signor Giovani, have you seen a big grey yacht recently?'

The old man turned his glassy eyes to Alessandro. 'This is a big lake. Yachts, boats, ferries come and go every day.'

'Yes, but this one appears only after the sunset.'

Giovani lifted his walking stick and pointed it straight ahead. 'There they come. I don't know if it's grey. My eyes are not as good as they used to be, and the boat comes always late. Shortly afterwards it's time for me to go.'

Alessandro considered his next question. 'Have you ever noticed anything suspicious about it?'

'No,' he said, and then laughed. 'But someone should tell them that there are no squids in the lake.'

'How come?'

'I can see a light coming out of the bottom of the yacht each time they anchor in the middle of the lake.' He pointed his stick again. 'This is how you fish for squids. The light lures squids.'

Alessandro squinted. His gaze travelled two hundred metres away. He stared at the empty spot on the lake and didn't register that the old man was speaking again. Then he heard him laughing.

'Excuse me? Did you say something, Signor Giovani?'

'The lady had a better sense of humour than you.'

'The lady?'

'The lady who asked me about the big yacht.'

Alessandro's pulse quickened. 'Do you know her name? What did she look like?'

Giovani turned and hit the top of Alessandro's head with his stick, baffling him with the efficiency with which he handled it.

Then he chuckled and said, 'I used to be like you. I had only one thing on my mind … She is very pretty.'

Giovani raised the stick. Alessandro sheltered his head, but the old man pointed in a different direction. 'You see that red spot?'

'No, but I see a woman,' Alessandro said, massaging his head.

'Go and ask her for her name, if you want to.'

CHAPTER 13

'MI SCUSI, SIGNORA,' Alessandro shouted, running after the woman dressed in a red, sleeveless blouse and an orange skirt, who walked along the lake path. 'Excuse me!'

She didn't react.

'Signora!'

He ran another five metres and was about to reach for her shoulder when she turned around and he almost knocked her down. He snatched her, wrapped his arms around her waist and held her up. The subtle scent of roses engulfed him.

He looked into her green eyes and the anger building in them. He stepped back. 'I'm sorry. I have to talk to you.'

'Aren't you moving too far?' she said, infuriated, smoothing her skirt. 'If I wanted to take a boat trip, I'd come and buy a ticket.'

'It's not about a boat. Well, in a way. Can we sit down and talk?'

Two elderly women who were sitting on a bench three metres to Alessandro's right moved to one side, leaving enough space for two more persons.

The woman in the red blouse looked at them in surprise, then she turned to Alessandro. 'Most certainly we cannot!'

'Why have you asked Signor Giovani about that yacht that comes here after dusk?'

She looked at him, bewildered. 'Who's Signor Giovani? And who are you?'

'My name is Alessandro Pini. Signor Giovani is the old man you have just asked about the yacht.'

'Are you spying on me?' The anger in her voice didn't ease off. She pushed a wisp of her black hair behind an ear.

'No! On *him*!' Alessandro pointed at the lake. 'Do you know the owner of the yacht? He's around fifty years old, big, furrowed forehead, funny head.'

'Even if I knew, this would be none of your business.'

Alessandro stepped up, closing the already small distance between them. 'He likes to drink in a pub close by. One dodgy fellow.'

The woman extended her hand, pushed him back and rummaged in her purse. 'I'm calling the police.'

'They know nothing. I've already talked to them,' he said without hope.

She pulled out her phone.

'Alessandro Pini, behave yourself or else I will have a word with your mother,' said a lady sitting on the nearby bench.

'Signora Lazzari?' Alessandro said. 'I didn't notice you. How are you today?'

The elderly woman sent him a look of rebuke.

Alessandro's shoulders slumped. He looked at the woman in red. 'I'm sorry. Signora Lazzari is right. I shouldn't have shouted at you.'

The woman in red stared at him. Her fingers hovered over the screen of her phone. She said sternly, 'You have exactly one minute to explain to me what this is really about.'

He gritted his teeth and felt his eyes welling up.

'Alessandro is a good boy,' Signora Lazzari said. 'He will do you no harm, Signora.'

When the woman in red slid the phone back to her purse, Alessandro gently took hold of her arm and pushed her aside.

'This morning the police called me and said that my friend, Gianluigi, was found dead in a pub. The man from that yacht is probably the last person who talked to him,' he said. 'I must know if this is true.'

Alessandro saw her face muscles relaxing. 'Oh. I'm very sorry for your loss.'

'Can you help me? Please.'

The corners of her mouth pulled back in a consoling smile. 'I don't know the man you want to talk to. Not yet.'

Alessandro turned around and glanced at the bench one hundred metres away where Giovani continued his daily practice, and then he turned back to her. 'What is your name?'

She extended her hand. 'Nina Monte.'

Alessandro accepted her firm shake. 'Nina, would you like to have an early lunch with me?'

CHAPTER 14

'THIS IS A nice place,' Nina said, breaking a chunk of fresh bread in half. She put it into her mouth and looked around.

When after a short walk along a narrow alley they went through an archway, she hadn't expected to find herself surrounded by walls painted in warm yellow tones, and open skies.

'I come here sometimes,' Alessandro said. 'It has an ideal location. Few places in Malcesine are like this one.'

Nina swept up the crumbs that dotted a coral-pink tablecloth.

'See that balcony with flower pots on the first floor?' He pointed over his shoulder. 'People actually live there. It makes dining here a family gathering.'

Alessandro reminded her of Cesare from the train. Both had the same body type, the same way of speaking, and were close in age. Why did she only seem to attract the immature ones?

'Do you know every restaurant in this town?' she asked.

'Yes, I do,' he said, raising his chin proudly.

'Because you can't cook, I presume,' Nina said, without knowing where her presumption came from.

He stared at her for a short moment and then said, 'Signor Giovani was right. You do have a sense of humour.'

Nina took a sip of water, to avoid commenting on that. She was a scientist and a historian. There was nothing humorous about the world she lived in.

'I'm familiar with the dining business because I own a hotel and a restaurant in Malcesine,' he told her. 'Where are you staying?'

'I think that is—'

'None of my business,' Alessandro finished her sentence. 'It's just a professional curiosity.'

A waitress placed the food they had ordered in front of them.

Nina looked at her smoked salmon dressed in a rocket salad, honey and mustard sauce. She realized how hungry she was. After waking, she had struggled to find her appetite, having only a cup of coffee and a small croissant; all because of the anticipation that built up before meeting with van der Venn.

She took a mouthful of salmon, and watched Alessandro digging into his tagliatelle.

'I'm sorry about earlier,' he said. 'I'm desperate.'

She cut off an even piece of salmon. With grace, her back straight, elbows close to her torso, she led the fork to her mouth. Just like her mother had taught her to do.

Alessandro chewed his pasta slowly and long. He kept his eyes low, playing with the tagliatelle on his plate.

'Is something wrong with your food?' Nina asked.

'It's great, as always.' He looked up at her. 'The pasta is al dente, the bacon crisp. I'm just not hungry.'

She put her fork and knife down, and tapped her mouth with a napkin. 'So why did you invite me for lunch?'

'It seemed like the only way to keep you from running away, and to find out if you can get me to that man who talked to Gianluigi before his…' Alessandro fisted his hands, squeezing the cutlery. He suspended his gaze on ice cubes floating in the glass of water, and whispered, 'I miss him so much.'

Nina glanced to her left. A couple with two young children and their granny were having lunch at the only other occupied table. They were so quiet that she hardly noticed their presence.

'Alessandro, you know,' Nina began, turning to him, 'in some cultures when a family loses someone, they're sad, of course, but they accept their loss like something inevitable, although they show their grief in different ways. Some mourners wail and cry to the point of exhaustion; others express no emotions, accepting the death as liberation.'

He chewed the pasta with his head low.

Nina gesticulated with her hands, as she always did when giving a lecture to her students. 'Around the globe death is considered in diverse ways. It largely depends on traditions, culture or religion of the bereaved. Despite those differences, the common factor is how to find meaning in dying. I think that for those who believe death is a transition to a better place, it's easier to cope with their loss. You might know that the followers of all principal religions believe in an afterlife. Some cultures go even further. For them the dead coexist with the living. As an example, let's take—'

'What are you talking about?' Alessandro said, gaping at her with a string of tagliatelle hanging from his mouth.

Her professional consolation wasn't going too well. She readjusted her hair nervously. 'I'm sorry. I teach history of religions at the University of Padua.'

He raised his glass and swallowed. 'That is where you're from?'

'I was born in Milan, but now my life revolves around Padua, although I live in Venice,' she said. 'I arrived in Malcesine yesterday to join the crew on that yacht.'

'Sea-bottom exploration?'

She looked at him, surprised. 'How do you know that?'

'The police told me.'

'Aha … Well, I will be meeting the crew tonight. If I have a chance, I will ask Mr van…'

'He must be an important person since they asked the police to assist him if requested.'

Nina tilted her head. 'You are better informed than I am, Alessandro.'

She wondered how much he really knew, and how much the police knew about the search.

'The local inspector is my friend,' he explained.

'All I can promise is that I will ask them about your friend.'

'That's all I'm asking for.'

Alessandro patted his pockets frantically. His face turned pale. 'Oh no!'

'What happened?'

'I think I lost my wallet.'

Nina gave a shrug. 'It's a small town. I can see that you all know each other. Someone will find it and return it to you.'

He lifted one corner of his mouth. 'Yeah, if it's found by a local.'

Nina finished her salmon, put the cutlery together on her plate, and took a gulp of water. Then she put twenty-five euros on the table.

'This treat is on me.' She stood up. 'In regards to what we discussed, I will know how to find you, Alessandro Pini. But if you don't hear from me, I wish you good luck with everything,' she said, and left the restaurant.

On her way back to the hotel, Nina pondered if everything that she had heard from him wasn't just a shameless lie to wangle a free lunch.

CHAPTER 15

WITH EVERY STEP, Alessandro's walk to his hotel was becoming more and more laboured. But he had to speak to his mother. It was better if she found out from him. If *he* was shocked, he tried not to think how she would take the news about Gianluigi's death.

He reached the hotel, rehearsing for the fifth time what to tell her, how he should say that the person she without a doubt loved, had died last night.

His mother wasn't at the reception reading the papers as she usually was in the midday. He didn't find her in the empty kitchen, either.

When he finally saw Francesca Pini sitting on a wooden swing in a shadowed corner of a small orchard at the back of the hotel, he realized he had come too late.

Her hair was a mess. Her shoulders sagged. She had swollen eyes that stared into emptiness, in which her motionless figure seemed to be suspended. An empty wine glass dangled between her fingers.

Alessandro came up to her, knelt on one knee and said, 'You already know, Mama, don't you?'

She nodded, first slowly, then vigorously and long. Then she leaned and buried her head into his shoulders.

He stroked her hair. 'How did you find out?'

She sniffled. 'Raffaele phoned half an hour ago. He wanted to talk to you … He said it was police business. I forced him to tell me what the police wanted from my son. I sensed in his voice that something bad had happened. But … not *this*.'

'What did he want from me?'

'To tell you that he contacted Gianluigi's daughters,' she said and raised her puffy eyes to him. 'And that you should stay away from this. He knows that you spoke to Sean. What is going on, Alessandro?'

'Nothing, Mama.'

'Raffaele said it was a heart attack, but that you didn't believe him.'

'It's not like that. I just need to talk to someone.'

She stood up and styled her hair. 'Leave this matter to the police.'

'But, Mama, they're not—'

'Alessandro Pini! A tragedy has happened. This is a time to mourn Gianluigi, not to play detective.' She brushed his cheek. 'Go and rest for a while. I don't think that all of our scheduled arrivals will be coming today. They said on the radio there is a strike on the German rail.'

She took a shallow breath and moved to the hotel's back door. Then she disappeared inside.

'Yes, Mama,' Alessandro said to himself.

She was right. He shouldn't think about that man from the pub. At least not until he could better organize his thoughts.

He headed to the hotel and pushed open the door to his windowless office. Three walls in a rectangular, four-square-metre room were cramped with metal shelves, yielding under the weight of thick folders, and a thin layer of dust.

90

In the middle stood a small table with an old computer screen on top and a picture of him and Gianluigi. The photograph had been taken five years ago to commemorate the thirtieth anniversary of the restaurant's opening. Alessandro was shaking the hand of his first chef.

He took it into his hands and touched Gianluigi's face. He shut his eyes, flexed all his muscles, and wished to go back to that happy moment to give him another five years of life alongside Gianluigi. He would spend it better, differently, knowing that his time was limited.

But nothing happened.

He kissed the photograph. 'Rest in peace, my friend.'

Suddenly, he felt a boiling anger towards Sean, his pub, his whiskey. He hated him for the saying that beset his mind like lyrics of an obnoxious song: "as good as it gets."

What did it mean? Did horrible things have to happen? Were they inevitable?

He would never agree with that. Otherwise, apart from a few exceptional moments of happiness, life would be nothing more than a one-way street towards an end. A dead-end.

CHAPTER 16

THE SUN WAS low when Nina paced the floor of her hotel room, wondering why she hadn't heard from Lammert van der Venn yet. She had tried to reach him two hours ago, then one hour later; twenty minutes ago she left him a voice message and sent a text. He still didn't answer.

She perched on the bed and glanced around. As promised, the Ministry hadn't overpaid for her accommodation.

Furniture made from solid oak consisted of a single bed, a nightstand, a wardrobe with fitted large mirror, and a desk with an old TV set. All was set on twenty-five square metres, including a bathroom.

The windows overlooked a back yard, the employees' parking lot. She didn't have a lake view to distract her from thinking about her new assignment, or about what she had said to that boyish hotelier earlier.

The lecture about death she had given him was appalling. Why had she even dwelled on that? It was one thing to teach her students. It was an entirely different story to brag about it to someone who had just lost a dear person. If she had been in his situation, that sort of speech would only serve to annoy her.

Nevertheless, she had made a promise. She was going to ask van der Venn about last night. It would have to be discreet, though. It was none of her business how he was spending his free time. A false first impression would leave an unpleasant aftertaste.

Nina opened the folder she had brought from Heidelberg and found Campana's business card.

He answered after the second ring. 'Massimo Campana speaking.'

'Good evening, Signor Campana. This is Nina Monte.'

'Ah, Signora Monte. Good evening.'

'Signor Campana, I cannot get in touch with van der Venn,' she said, aware of the chilling tone of her voice.

'What time is it, Signora?'

'Why is it important?'

'It *is* important,' he said. 'If it is before eight p.m., Mr van der Venn is most likely unavailable.'

She put the phone to the other ear. 'Why?'

'Signora, Ministry is paying Mr van der Venn for his working hours, and he starts after eight p.m. and finishes when he considers necessary,' he said matter-of-factly. 'Outside these hours, he doesn't wish to be disturbed.'

Nina looked at her wristwatch. 'It's a quarter to eight.'

'Ah, you see. I'm sure he will contact you soon. Is there anything else I can do for you?'

'Is there anything else I should know but haven't been informed about?'

There was a short silence on the line, then he said, 'I believe there isn't.'

'Thank you.'

'You're welcome, Signora.'

At 8:00 p.m. sharp, Nina's phone let a single short tone. She read a message: "Ms Monte, welcome to Malcesine. My associates will pick you up in fifteen minutes. Lammert van der Venn."

Nina took a glance into the mirror. If she was to change her mind about what to wear tonight, it was her last chance.

She decided that a herringbone-pattern blazer with collar and lapels, and a matching slim-hip pencil skirt gave her the right dose of a business-like appearance without exposing her to the voracious eyes of sailors.

She shook her head, smiling to herself with sympathy and pity; she wasn't going to meet the crew of a fifteenth-century galley.

At exactly quarter past eight, came another text: "Please come down. The car is waiting."

She slid her mobile into a leather handbag, zipped it up, and hooked it over her forearm. *Ready.*

When she stepped out of the hotel, the rear door to a black Audi was wide open. The car looked similar to the one she had ridden in from Heidelberg to Milan. Would she also meet the same chauffeur?

She got inside and pulled the door, which closed silently.

The man in a navy-coloured tank vest, who kept his hands on the wheel, was shorter and slimmer than Felix.

'Good evening, Ms Monte,' he said in English, looking at her through the rear-view mirror. 'My name is Sander Klaff.'

It was the same car. The crumbs of her croissant were still scattered on the back seat.

Nina buckled up. 'Good evening.'

Klaff had a swallow tattooed on his right arm, and a compass rose on his left wrist. His head was bald and he had a straight, Greek nose. He wasn't older than forty-five.

He lit up a cigarette and the car pulled out of the hotel's door. 'You don't mind me smoking, do you?' he said.

His French accent reminded her about the meeting in the castle and Julien Traverse's complaints about an absence of his countrymen among the crew on the lake. Then again, the French language was spoken in a number of countries outside Europe.

'Only if you have to, Mr Klaff.'

The car already stank of cigarettes. She opened the window, parted her mouth and inhaled.

Klaff drew on his fag, dropped down his window and blew the smoke outside. Then he squeezed the cigarette between his fingers and flicked it outside. A glowing butt landed in someone's garden.

'Mr Klaff—'

He punched the horn, and Nina jumped in her seat.

'Out of my way, arseholes!' he shouted at two cyclists who were riding their mountain bikes next to each other.

When they formed a line, Klaff changed gears, accelerated, and Nina felt her back pushing into the Audi's seat.

Klaff slowed down after another fifty metres and then turned right. The car skidded to a halt in front of a private pier.

'Let's go,' he said and jumped out of his seat.

Nina observed him trotting to an anchored two-engine white speedboat. She got out and slammed the door.

Klaff hopped in, started the engine and unhooked a mooring rope. The boat swayed on the calm, deep-blue water. He turned back to look at Nina; he seemed to be surprised at seeing her on the pier walking at a casual pace.

As soon as she stepped into the speedboat, he pushed on the throttle. Nina lost her balance, but her tumble ended on the soft cushions of the rear seats.

Klaff glanced at her. 'You all right?'

Nina smoothed her skirt, with the other hand holding onto handrails. She was glad she wore flat shoes; otherwise she would have sprained her ankle.

'Mr Klaff, something is telling me that you wouldn't give a thing if I fell overboard,' she said in a loud voice to outcry the roar of the engines.

Klaff laughed. 'If you fell overboard, Lammert would break my legs and throw me into the lake!'

'I would gladly assist Mr van der Venn in the process of doing so.'

He laughed louder. The speedboat swung for a moment, but he regained control. They were headed straight to the middle of the lake.

Nina looked ahead. The distance to the big, grey yacht was shrinking. Fifteen metres before the yacht, Klaff cut the engines.

All possible lights on the yacht seemed to be on. She heard raised voices. Three crew members stared into the water. A puzzling blue-and-green glow was emerging from underneath the vessel. It was getting brighter and brighter.

Then it cut the surface of the lake, and Nina saw someone in a scuba diving suit that resembled a cosmonaut outfit. The man was holding something in his hands.

CHAPTER 17

ALESSANDRO AWOKE FROM limbo with a numb sensation in his neck. Lazily, he stood up from the chair and stretched his spine. He didn't remember falling asleep. Maybe he dozed off for ten minutes or so. He looked at his watch.

It was 7:00 p.m. He cursed and ran out of the office.

When he reached the kitchen, he winced in guilt upon seeing his mother's fatigued face.

On eleven square metres of the kitchen floor, she slaved to cope with dinner orders, peeling potatoes, washing lettuce, and controlling the flames on a gas cooker.

Strands of hair stood out from under a scarf she wore on her head. A thin layer of sweat covered her forehead.

'Where have you been, Alessandro?' she said in a weary voice. 'I've sent Mirabella for you but she couldn't find you.'

If even his staff didn't think to look for him in his office, maybe he really should start spending more time in there.

The lid on a boiling pot started to rattle. She lowered the flame under it and pushed an extra button on the hood to absorb vapour. Then she wiped her forehead with the back of her hand.

Alessandro put on an apron. 'I'm sorry, Mama.'

A trout was sizzling in a frying pan. He took a spatula and flipped the fish. Drops of oil splashed on his hand. He grimaced and recoiled, then crossed to a sink and put his fingers under the cold running water.

Mirabella came in. Her face was pale. It looked as if she had applied a whitewash instead of makeup. 'Another two tables are taken,' she said on one breath.

'Why did everyone decide to come at the same time?' Francesca said, flustered.

'We'll be okay, Mama. I'll help you with everything.'

'Mirabella,' Francesca said, 'tell them it takes a bit longer today.'

Mirabella grabbed two bread baskets and made to rush to the guests, but Francesca screamed after her, 'Wait! Tell them that tonight we serve only pizza, pasta and fish, no meat dishes.'

'Yes, Signora,' she said and pushed the door open with her shoulder.

'What do I do?' Alessandro asked.

'I don't remember the last time I cooked for more than three people,' his mother said, wiping more droplets of sweat from her forehead. Then she handed him a peeling knife and pointed at the stack of carrots. 'After you're finished with them, cook more pasta.'

Alessandro peeled vegetables, leaving out patches of skin, then chopped them into uneven pieces. Doing so, he cut three of his fingers, which stung at contact with water.

From there it got worse. He overcooked the pasta. Unfortunately, or not, half of it ended up in the sink when he drained it. How was he supposed to manage all of that with his hurt fingers?

Mirabella returned, holding more orders in her hand. She hesitated, wondering if she should read them when she noticed Alessandro's fingers.

'This is nothing, Mirabella. I've been much worse,' he said, although he didn't remember if that was true.

She kept staring at him. It was only then that Alessandro saw that his white apron looked as if he worked at a butcher's and they had just gotten a fresh meat supply.

Mirabella put the order on the table, and read, 'One parma ham pizza, one napoletana, two mussel linguine.'

The next hour, and eight more orders, later confirmed what Alessandro already knew about himself: he was terrible at having to work under pressure.

His mother had to finally come to the same conclusion, because she called Agostina, an experienced housemaid who worked for the hotel and who used to assist Gianluigi during the peak season.

Alessandro gave a huge sigh of relief. So huge that he almost stabbed Agostina with a bread knife when she came in; cutting bread was the only thing his mother asked him to do. Because there were no more newcomers—at least this was what he had been told—Francesca let him go.

In the open, he expanded his lungs in a long, deep breath. The air was pleasantly cool, although it had no chance to circulate between his body and clothes. Every piece of his garment clung to him, bound by his sweat.

He ran to his office and found a fresh T-shirt. Then he took off the jeans and pulled on combat cargo shorts.

His eyes met Gianluigi's smile radiating from the picture he had left on the office table. Alessandro stared at it for a long moment without blinking until his eyes started to sting.

'I'm sorry, Mama,' he whispered to the empty room while putting on a black cotton hoodie. 'I have to know.'

CHAPTER 18

NINA FOLLOWED KLAFF and, for the first time in her life, she found herself on a luxurious yacht.

On the deck, two well-built men, probably twins in their mid-twenties, helped the diver out of his suit. They spoke to each other in Arabic, coordinating their task. Next to them, on the floor, Nina saw the item the diver had brought up with him: an ancient-looking, wet, wooden chest.

A young man of African origin knelt by it, tugging on its padlock. A man dressed in a dirty apron, who was much older than the rest, leaned over him, and said something in a language Nina didn't recognize. He held a spatula in his hand with which he gesticulated. She noticed an ancient Greek coin dangling on his neck from a golden chain.

No one paid any attention to her.

She glanced around, and her frustration triggered by Klaff's crude behaviour returned tenfold.

Artefacts were scattered all over the deck. An antique silver tray was being used as an ashtray for Klaff's awful addiction. Dried in the sun, pasta leftovers lay on blue-and-white china plates that looked like they were from the Ming Dynasty. All of that must have come from sunken ships.

'Waaberi, step back,' the diver said. 'Raul, get back to the kitchen!'

Nina looked up and recognized the man from the picture she had received from Campana.

Lammert van der Venn stood straight in his swimming trunks. His shoulders, now pumped with blood, looked even bigger. His curly hair was much longer than in the picture, and his skin darker. His face was clean shaven.

Nina stepped forward. 'Mr van der Venn, what is—?'

His outstretched arm cut her off. He pulled a knife from his ankle holster, crouched down, and wrecked the padlock off the chest.

Nina's jaw went down.

Van der Venn lifted the lid.

'Yeah!' the twins shouted.

Waaberi made a sound that resembled something between 'butchered animal' and the last yelp of a drunkard before he would lose consciousness. Nina cringed and covered her ears.

Klaff and the cook made no noise. Only their eyes were narrowed, mouths slightly open.

When the howl lessened, van der Venn said, 'Gentlemen, it was another productive enterprise.'

Then he plunged his hand into a chest full of gold coins, and fished out a fistful of them.

'Catch!' He threw one coin to each of the five men on board. 'This is your prize. Go onshore and get yourself a drink. Stay as long as you want.'

A bigger roar shot through the air. Nina's face must have turned scarlet because even if there was some blood left in her legs, she felt that she needed to sit down instantly.

The crew jumped into the speedboat. Another person, who wasn't on the main deck, joined them in the last moment before the boat's engine whined, and they headed off. Then they made a U-turn and circled the yacht. For a second Nina thought that she caught a glimpse of a familiar face. But it was too dark, and then they were gone, though the yelling seemed to still hang around.

'This is outrageous!' She had found her voice. 'Those coins belong to the Italian Republic and its people. You cannot splash them around like … like popcorn!' She swung her hand around. 'And how can you treat those artefacts in such a disrespectful manner?'

Van der Venn put on a white polo shirt and a pair of flip-flops.

Nina crossed her arms on her chest.

He was ogling her, oblivious to her outburst.

She thumped her foot down. 'Did you hear what I said?'

'You are temperamental, Ms Monte,' he said. 'Quite the opposite of how I imagined you.'

Nina ran her hand through her hair. 'What's that supposed to mean?'

He started to talk, but she waved her hand dismissively. 'Mr van der Venn, if you think that all that I've witnessed here will remain forgotten, then you are…'

She trailed off, seeing that van der Venn wasn't listening to her. He crouched down next to the chest and tucked his hand inside.

Nina placed her hands on her hips. 'Do you think that you can bribe me with a coin, like that herd of yours? You must be out of your mind!'

'What about fifty coins?' he said and looked up at her. 'Think about it. You could fetch for them a nice house by the lake.'

Nina struggled to find an adequate answer. The longer

the silence lasted, the more she was afraid he thought she was considering his offer.

She calmed her breath and said, 'You are insane.'

'Have you ever heard about the concept of diversion, Ms Monte?' he said, unimpressed.

Nina angled her head. 'What?'

'I had to get rid of them, to show you this.'

He pulled out something from the wooden chest. Nina blinked a few times, perplexed, seeing a contemporary sand-yellow, heavy-plastic briefcase.

'How … how did this get there?'

'I put it in here two nights ago to secure the reason of your visit.'

He closed the lid of the chest and moved it aside with his foot. 'Let's get inside.'

Nina noticed that he walked in a funny way, as if he didn't want to bend his knees too much. Under the roof, van der Venn flicked a few switches and the lights on the boat died out.

He stepped into a dim office, followed by Nina, and switched on a table lamp on a writing desk. What she saw next was most intriguing compared to how barbaric he treated the other medieval stuff.

He placed the briefcase on the table tenderly, as if it were an armed explosive device seconds away from going off, and pushed some buttons underneath it. It clicked and hissed open, giving a two-centimetre-wide gap.

He slipped on white gloves and handed a pair to Nina. 'Put them on, please.'

She accepted the gloves, thinking that he wasn't completely irresponsible when handling artefacts.

His hands never parted with the case when he glanced at her. His eyes shone with a deep-green shade. The smirk in the corner of his mouth was devilish.

Goose bumps prickled Nina's skin. An unwelcome mishmash of irritation, anticipation, and ungrounded fear fought for domination inside her.

'Whatever you're experiencing now, Ms Monte, I'm not the cause of it,' he said and opened the lid. 'This is.'

Nina let out her breath. She was staring at a stone tablet on which something was engraved.

The trio of her feelings crescendoed into disarray. Then into disappointment. Maybe she wasn't expecting to see a marvellous piece of craft, but … this?

Letting her academic side take over, she put out her hands. Van der Venn placed the tablet onto them, and they dropped down a little under its weight.

The back side of the tablet felt coarse under her fingers. The front was meticulously polished—except for the engraved text. While the tablet had a coppery colour, the letters were much lighter. Her thumbs ran over it like wiper blades on a cracked car windscreen.

She felt weird energy radiating from the stone and travelling through her hands and, farther, to her heart, evoking a tingling sensation, dispersing her confusion and disappointment.

She concentrated on reading the text.

Her pulse accelerated. The letters weren't just a scribble as she had thought at first sight, and their order wasn't accidental. They were set in words and short sentences. It was calligraphy written in an ancient language.

Was that possible? But how?

That language hadn't been heard for more than four thousand years.

'Ms Monte?' The soft voice of van der Venn brought her back to now.

She glanced up at his blurred figure. Had she tears in her eyes? She shut and opened them several times—the only move she could make, and her vision returned to normal.

The words of Cardinal Esposito echoed in Nina's head: "We would like to find God in ourselves."

Then, in the cathedral, for a split second a thought had occurred to her, but she had dismissed it as too abstract, letting her mind's cold reasoning stifle her intuition.

'Judging from your expression, what we have here is authentic,' van der Venn said. 'As far as I'm concerned, you might be only one, out of a few living persons, who knows about it.'

Nina looked up at him.

'All I need from you, Ms Monte, is to tell me how to make this work.'

CHAPTER 19

ALESSANDRO CROUCHED DOWN on a small pier one kilometre off Malcesine's town centre. The night was warm and windless, the shoreline deserted except for two teenagers who sauntered hand-in-hand along the path scarcely lit by streetlamps. They didn't notice him; they were talking and laughing, looking into each other's eyes.

He waited until they passed him by. Then he turned his gaze to the water, two hundred metres away, and he whistled, impressed.

He hadn't pictured the yacht he had heard about to be quite like this. Its body was at least thirty-five metres long, and it looked like a military vessel. It must have cost the owner a small fortune to transport it here.

Alessandro had once been asked by a guest to calculate the cost of bringing over a twelve-metre boat from Venice. He wrote back that seven thousand euros should suffice.

Five or six persons were bustling around aboard the well illuminated yacht.

All of a sudden, screams like a goal celebration at a match travelled on the water straight to Alessandro. He cocked his head and squinted. Crewmen ran to the back of the yacht. He heard a whirr of an engine. A motorboat was set free from the yacht, circled around it, and sped towards him. Directly towards him.

He stood up but instantly crouched back. Then he stood up again. His eyes wandered between the upcoming men and the yacht.

A person aboard the yacht—judging from the body language, a woman—gesticulated with her hands. Alessandro couldn't see with whom she was speaking.

His pulse quickened and he hunkered down. Was it Nina Monte? Had she found out something about Gianluigi?

Alessandro glanced around and, with little consideration if his idea made any sense, rose up, ran ten metres and jumped over a fence overgrown from the inside with a dense hedge.

He landed on a soft lawn of someone's holiday villa between two sunbeds, three metres from a swimming pool. The front yard was empty, as it was for most of the year; Alessandro knew that the occupants were rarely guests here.

Now the shadowy smoke of an extinguished barbecue and a faint smell of grilled meat drifted towards him.

Behind the fence, the roar of the speedboat reached its peak. Then they cut the engine. Alessandro put his ear to the hedge. Twigs prickled his cheek and forehead.

He heard shouts and heavy steps on the pier. Men spoke in a language he couldn't decipher. Arabic? Or Hebrew? Then someone said, in English, 'Shut up and everyone follow me!' There was more prattling, but it faded away soon.

Alessandro sat back against the hedge and exhaled. He put his face into his hands and rubbed his eyes. Why was he hiding like a thief? He hadn't done anything. His mother was right. He shouldn't play detective. He was sweating again.

His black hoodie was supposed to make him less visible; instead, it made him perspire. He smelled like a wet dog.

He propped his hand on the lawn to lift up his body. And froze.

The big eyes of a German Shepherd stared at him with curiosity. A long tongue hung from the dog's open mouth. Alessandro sat back down and slowly raised his hands.

'Gooood doggy.'

The dog tilted its head and barked. Then it put its paw on Alessandro's shoulder and barked again. It was a deep woof, right in front of his nose, which brought out a stench of digestion. Alessandro shrank his body. The paw slipped down.

Then the dog moved back, wagged its tail in what Alessandro hoped was a friendly manner, leaned down, and picked up a tennis ball. He reached out, pulled the ball from the dog's snout and threw it to the other end of the garden. When the dog sprinted to fetch the toy, he scrambled over the fence to the outer side.

Alessandro uttered a silent thanks to the people who hadn't trained their animal as a watchdog. His hands trembled a little, so he shook them.

The pier was empty, apart from a newly arrived speedboat, and another smaller boat anchored at the other side. It had to belong to the owners of the house and the German Shepherd.

Alessandro stepped into it and pulled out a pair of paddles. He decided that they wouldn't mind since he had, after all, made friends with their pet.

He glanced at the yacht. For a second he thought that it had disappeared; its lights were out except for the safety ones. He saw one on the side, one at the back, and one at the front. Even if there were a full crew standing aboard, Alessandro wouldn't know about it.

The first fifty metres, he rowed vigorously. Then his pace decreased, but he was still closing the distance. And he had a much better view.

Three satellite dishes were mounted above the captain's bridge. One of them was swivelling around like sonar. The back was packed with machinery, which resembled a small crane.

The last sixty metres were slower. He had gotten tired, but he also wanted to approach the yacht unseen.

Twenty metres from the yacht, almost in the middle of Lake Garda, it occurred to him that the man he wanted to talk to might not be aboard at all. He might have been one of those who came ashore. He hesitated.

It was too late to return. He grabbed the oars tighter and continued paddling.

When he was three metres away from the rear of the yacht, he put the paddles inside and cushioned the contact with his outstretched hand.

He tightened the boat to a hook, and put one foot on board, as silently as possible. Then another one. He kept his body half bent. He pricked up his ears and listened, motionless. Steady water lapping against the frame of the vessel was the sole sound.

Alessandro climbed a few rungs of the ladder. One slow step up, five beats of his heart. At the top he raised his head to probe what lay ahead. From the inside, the yacht looked even bigger.

On the deck there was a lot of machinery that must be used for sea-bottom exploration. He saw diving equipment and other tools, but he wasn't sure what they were used for.

He stepped with care between ropes, and other stuff that didn't look new to him at all. Through the wide-open door he peered into the cabin. Although he couldn't see details, the spare lights gave him enough to know that the owner didn't have to worry about money.

Everything smelled exotic and brand new. It reminded him of an extravagant, kept-in-pristine-condition penthouse he had visited once in Milan, after he and his friend Luca had picked up two girls who had wealthy connections. Then and now, the growing sensation of being out of place took over him.

In dimmed lights embedded in three circles in the ceiling, he saw a long, white sofa that stood against the right cabin wall. He caressed the soft and delicate leather with his hand.

Table lamps with modernistic rectangular shapes were placed between the sofa and a window. In the middle there was something like an elliptical conference table fitted with small monitors. The left side was occupied by a mahogany bar with dozens of bottles that Alessandro knew he would never serve in his restaurant, because his guests would never be able to afford them.

A big picture of an old sailing ship hung on the far wall, although it might have been a screensaver.

The cabin was peaceful, but he felt as if something dire was on guard.

He considered his options. Two came up in his mind. He could continue sneaking around, and risk being caught red-handed. Or he could reveal himself, shout out to get someone's attention and explain the intrusion.

The second option was better. Yes. No. It didn't mean

that whoever showed up would be happy, seeing him sneaking around.

He craned his neck and glanced out the window at the shore. Lights of his home town sparkled, as if trying to tell him that he was a loony if he thought he could get away with this trespassing, because people from this boat probably weren't fond of unexpected visitors.

He lowered his head and moved towards the front of the yacht. After a few steps, he paused to listen for anyone's presence. Then he pushed forward. Another pause.

Voices.

He couldn't tell them apart—his heart was thumping in his chest too loudly—but they were coming from below the deck.

On his tiptoes, he stepped down into the innards of the yacht.

One voice belonged to a man. He spoke Italian with a hard foreign accent. Alessandro heard broken sentences: 'And as far as I'm ... you might be only one out of two living ... who knows...'

Then after a while he spoke again.

'All I need from ... is to tell me how to make this...'

The conversation was taking place in a cabin just a few metres away from Alessandro. He saw an entrance and the light coming out of there.

Silence again. Alessandro thought that the man was talking to someone on the phone.

'I don't know.'

His pulse quickened. It was Nina Monte's voice.

He moved closer to them.

'Be honest with me, Ms Monte. I guarantee you that whatever is being said here won't leave this room,' the man said.

The tone of his voice was hard and emotionless, like his accent. Alessandro's new confidence vanished. He glued his back to the wall.

'Although I find your manners a bit unorthodox, in light of this discovery, that has little importance,' Nina said.

Alessandro heard a brief laugh. 'I knew we would find common ground.'

After a short silence, Nina said, 'I wrote an essay about it years ago.'

'"Fast Track to God,"' the man said. 'Don't look so surprised, Ms Monte.'

'I *am*. I had published it online, but a few days afterwards it disappeared from the university website. No one could tell me why. I uploaded it again, but the same thing happened.'

Silence.

'*You* did it?' Nina said.

Alessandro heard anger in her voice.

The man replied calmly, 'Ms Monte, discoveries like that one should not be publicised until a thorough examination has been completed.'

A sudden draught of air enveloped Alessandro's sweaty torso, causing goose bumps to prickle his skin. An irresistible urge to sneeze came over him. He squeezed his nostrils with his thumb and index finger. The pressure bounced back to his head, and for a moment blocked his ears. He leaned his back against the wall and took a breath in and out. It would have been a ridiculous way of being discovered.

He cleared his throat, making enough noise to give up his presence. 'Hello!'

A split second later, a bullet smashed into the wall right next to his left ear.

Chapter 20

ALESSANDRO SPRINTED UP the stairs, keeping his head low. Another bullet exploded somewhere close when he reached the main deck.

'Halt!' he heard the man he had eavesdropped on yell from behind him.

Alessandro obeyed.

'Van der Venn, stop it!' Nina screamed. 'Are you mad?'

'Turn around!' the man said.

He did as he was told. A bulky man was pointing a gun at his head. Alessandro raised his hands.

Nina came up after him. 'Don't shoot—' She saw Alessandro. 'What are you doing here?'

'Ms Monte, do you know this man?'

'Alessandro, are you all right?' she said, then turned to the man she called van der Venn. 'You could have killed him! I can't believe it!'

The man grinned. 'Hardly. Although then we wouldn't have to watch him panting and sweating like that.'

Nina made her way towards Alessandro, but the man shoved her aside.

'Get off me!' she screamed.

Van der Venn ignored her and looked at Alessandro. 'Who do you work for?'

'What? Nobody!'

'Answers like that will get you nowhere,' he said.

Alessandro's legs got wobbly. 'I work for no one. My name is Alessandro Pini. I'm a hotelier here in Malcesine.'

Van der Venn turned to Nina. 'This is how you met him? Do you stay in his hotel?'

'Hardly,' Nina said.

'Why are you here? And for your own good, it'd better be Ms Monte's charm,' he said, squinting at Alessandro.

'No! I came here to talk to you.'

The man lowered his gun.

'Who *sent* you?'

'Nobody.'

He raised his pistol. 'Haven't I told you something before?'

'No! Wait! I can explain!' Alessandro took a few intermittent breaths.

Van der Venn swivelled his gun. 'Go on. Be quick. Ms Monte and I were in the middle of something.'

Nina threw an incredible stare at the man.

'It's about Gianluigi. You met him last night in a pub and apparently you were the last person he talked to.'

Van der Venn said nothing.

Alessandro tried to calm his breathing. 'Very friendly, middle-aged, short hair, grey soul patch below his lower lip. Gianluigi. Chef in my kitchen.'

The man stared at him, as if deciding whether to believe in that story or to shoot him. Alessandro lowered his hands warily and wiped his moist palms against his trousers.

'Gianluigi, huh?' van der Venn said. 'Old, small and needy. And quite fainthearted. Just like you.'

'You're pointing your gun at me. What do you expect?' Alessandro said, his voice cracking. 'So ... did you talk to Gianluigi before his death? Did you see what happened?'

The man let down his gun. 'Wasn't your friend too curious? Yes, he was! Did I tell him to go away? Yes, I did! Did I see what happened to him? No! I *made* it happen.'

Alessandro's facial muscles became so tense he thought he wouldn't be able to speak anymore. 'What ... are you telling me?'

The man's gaze pierced Alessandro, and he remembered what Sean said about not wanting to see the stranger again.

Alessandro looked at Nina. She stared at van der Venn. Her mouth was open, the lower jaw slightly stuck out, her body rigid with anxiety.

'Mr Pini, you're an intruder on *Snovia*, who may have also overheard too much. This is no longer relevant, though,' the man said in a flat voice. 'Your Q and A time has come to an end.'

The police sirens shot through the air, as if triggered by van der Venn's rising arm.

'Drop your weapon and put your hands on your head!' Raffaele Lombardi shouted through the loudspeaker from on board his patrol boat. 'I repeat! Drop your weapon and put your hands on your head! We're coming on board!'

A spotlight blinded van der Venn. He lowered the gun and covered his eyes with his other hand. Other than that, he looked unmoved.

When Raffaele climbed on the yacht, Alessandro's voice returned. 'Raffaele, arrest that man! He has just admitted to killing Gianluigi.'

Van der Venn laughed. 'Mr Pini, please do not put words in my mouth.' He turned to Raffaele and continued in a polite, innocent manner that triggered a chilling undercurrent in Alessandro's veins. 'Officer, this is a thief who trespassed on my yacht with intention to steal from me.'

'Nonsense!' Alessandro threw his hands in the air. 'There is nothing here I would want to take! Nina, tell them!'

Nina shook her head as if trying to shake off her dismay, or to tell him to shut up.

Van der Venn pointed with his gun to the wooden chest. 'This is full of gold coins.'

Alessandro let out a high-pitched sound that resembled, 'What?'

Raffaele crossed to van der Venn, holding his own pistol at waist level. 'I said drop your weapon!'

'I have a permit for it,' Van der Venn said but let down the gun. It thudded on the deck.

Raffaele motioned to Alessandro and said, 'Pick it up and give it to me.'

'Officer, do you really intend to let the intruder go unpunished?'

'Alessandro,' Raffaele said, 'let's go.'

'What about him? Arrest him!'

'This is not the time. Now, come on.'

Alessandro pointed at Nina. 'What about her?'

'Should I arrest her also?' Raffaele said, irritated.

'She must go with us. You can't leave her alone with that psycho!'

'Mr Pini, I told you that Ms Monte and I were in the middle of something, and after this awkward affair comes to an end, I intend to continue,' van der Venn said evenly.

Nina's face turned pale. She stepped away from van der Venn, but he followed her.

Raffaele raised his gun higher. 'Move back!' He turned to Nina. 'I don't know who you are, Signora, or what your business affairs are with this man, but Alessandro knows you, so if you are feeling uncomfortable here, you can go with us.'

Alessandro saw a surge of relief on Nina's face. She nodded. 'Thank you. Just one last thing,' she said and ran into the cabin.

She returned, carrying a strange briefcase. Van der Venn's casual expression darkened.

'I have to take it with me,' Nina said to Raffaele, then she glanced at van der Venn, holding the briefcase close to her chest. 'Mr van der Venn, I believe you've completed your job, and *this* will no longer stay in your possession. However, I cannot promise you that I will keep the incident I've just witnessed to myself.' She tried to speak with confidence, but her voice faltered.

Then the three of them jumped back to the patrol boat.

Alessandro noticed one more policeman. 'Raffaele, there're only *two* of you?'

'Ms Monte!' Van der Venn stood by his yacht's side, arms crossed on his chest. 'Do you really think you can take away the hunter's trophy and just disappear with it?'

There was something unnatural in it; he didn't raise his voice, and still his words were clear and resonant.

'Beppe,' Raffaele said to his man, 'take us to the shore!'

Alessandro watched van der Venn's silhouette shrinking, glad he didn't have to look into his eyes anymore. He feared them before. Now, he imagined, they were full of rage, and unbearable.

CHAPTER 21

NINA SLUMPED ON a chair fixed to the deck of the police patrol boat, holding onto the briefcase with the tablet secured inside. She pushed it to her hammering heart, as if it could make her stop shaking.

'Raffaele, why didn't you arrest him?' Alessandro shouted.

'Calm *down*, this is a dangerous man.'

'Really? I wouldn't know why!' Alessandro gesticulated with his hands, furious. 'He murdered Gianluigi and tried to shoot me!'

Nina couldn't blame him for his outburst. If someone pointed a gun at her, she might have collapsed on the spot.

'Calm *down*, Alessandro. I couldn't risk anything with you and Signora on board,' he said and looked at Nina.

Dozens of thoughts spun in her head, as if they were pinned to a wheel of fortune, making it impossible for her to concentrate on one thing.

'My name is Nina Monte. I don't understand what happened over there, but thank you for taking me with you.'

'Raffaele Lombardi, a police inspector in Malcesine,' he said. 'I will have to ask you a few questions regarding Lammert van der Venn.'

'She doesn't know anything,' Alessandro cut in. 'But how did you find me?'

They reached the shore, and Nina saw that they were farther south from the pier where Klaff had taken her from.

'Beppe, take the boat to our pier, go to the station and wait for me there,' Raffaele said to his man.

'Yes, Inspector.'

'You two,' he said, turning to Alessandro and Nina, 'are coming with me. I have a car parked nearby.'

During the short walk, Nina kept peeking over her shoulder. Then she scrambled to the rear seat of the old police Alfa Romeo.

Alessandro took a seat next to Raffaele and repeated, 'How did you find me?'

Raffaele reversed the car and hit the main street, burning the tyres. Nina placed the briefcase on her lap and fastened the seatbelt.

'Who said I was looking for you?' Raffaele said, not shifting his gaze from the road.

'So, you simply changed your mind and decided to talk to that man?'

'Wrong again, Alessandro. This is why you shouldn't have played a policeman in your spare time.'

'Someone had to!'

They drove through the outskirts of the town. Nina caught a glimpse of a bustling restaurant. It felt like an entirely different world to her.

'One hour ago, Carabiniere arrested six men who crashed someone's private party in town,' Raffaele said. 'I've established that all of them came from the yacht in question. I thought I would take a closer look. Then we heard the gunfire, and I decided to move in.' He looked at Alessandro. 'I'm glad I did.'

Raffaele glanced at Nina's reflection in the rear-view mirror. 'Signora, how do you feel?'

'Thank you, I'm better,' she lied.

Sitting in the police car hadn't cooled her nerves yet. She had that pesky feeling in her stomach that she was up for another long night.

'What were you doing on that boat, and what can you tell me about that man?'

Nina took a deep breath. 'I met him half an hour ago. I was sent here by our Ministry of Culture to help him on a job that the Ministry hired him to do.'

'Really?' Raffaele said. 'What job?'

'This is confidential, I'm afraid.'

'Does it have something to do with the suitcase you're squeezing there?'

Nina looked down at her lap, grasped the tablet's case and pressed it to her chest. She nodded but wasn't sure if he noticed the slight motion of her head.

Raffaele opened the glove compartment and pulled out a sheet of paper. 'If your Ministry is doing business with people like him, then—'

'You misunderstood. I'm not a Ministerial worker. I'm a professor at the University of Padua.'

Alessandro took the document from the inspector and switched on an overhead light. 'This is a fax from Interpol.'

Raffaele turned on the police siren for a second and overtook a car in front of them, then said, 'Read it out loud, Alessandro.'

'Lammert van der Venn: extravagant millionaire; fifty-two years old; raised—'

'There.' With his finger, Raffaele pointed to the bottom of the page.

Alessandro read, 'Suspicions of illegal extraction and traffic of priceless artefacts; bribery of influential politicians from several European and Caribbean countries; tax evasion; money laundering, and … murder.'

'You don't know what you've got yourself into, Alessandro,' Raffaele said. 'If in your presence he admitted to committing a crime, he made you a crown witness, and you are not safe.' He glanced at Nina. 'The same stands for you, Signora.'

Nina cringed in her seat. All of a sudden she had become a witness in a criminal investigation.

'He has too much to lose,' Raffaele added. 'I didn't arrest him because there is no concrete proof against him, and because the jail at the station is full of his people. But they will be out tomorrow morning.'

He reached into his jacket and produced a gun, secured in a plastic bag. 'Do you know what this is?'

Alessandro recoiled. 'Put it away! He almost shot me with that thing.'

Raffaele stuffed it back into his pocket. 'This model of Glock is reserved for military and law enforcement agencies *only*. One of van der Venn's men had the same on him.'

He changed gears. 'Alessandro, I can protect your family, but it would be better if, for now, you were out of town.'

Alessandro leaned his head to the windscreen. 'This isn't the way to the police station!'

'You're taking a night train to Milan,' Raffaele said, then glanced into the mirror. 'Both of you. I have a good friend, a policeman, there. On the back of the fax is his number.'

'So … what does all of this mean?' Alessandro said.

Nina wondered if he felt the same way as she did—like a fugitive.

Alessandro shook his head. 'I can't go anywhere. I've lost my wallet.'

'One day you will lose your head,' Raffaele said. 'You haven't lost your wallet. You left it on the table in the restaurant where we talked this morning. I have it at the station.'

'Great,' he muttered.

'I have no cash on me,' Raffaele said and adjusted his mirror. 'Signora Monte, for the time being, would you be so kind as to take care of both your expenses?'

Nina leaned forward. 'I can do that.'

'Thank you,' Raffaele said.

After a moment of silence, Raffaele glanced at her. 'Were there really gold coins in that chest?'

'Yes, there were.'

Alessandro turned back to her. 'Gold? Is this what you have in that briefcase, what made him so furious when we left?'

'No!'

'So what is it?'

The car climbed a twisty road farther from Malcesine. Nina looked down at the black pool of Lake Garda.

'Something priceless.' She squeezed the briefcase harder. 'Something that belongs to the world of science.'

Now her thoughts were like those lights below them, hardly visible, then gone, then appearing back. None of them were bright. The wind was swishing its melody through a half-open window.

Nina shut her eyes and listened.

CHAPTER 22

NINA COUNTED SEVEN people in a small, brightly lit waiting area of the Rovereto railway station. On a bench, a teenage girl with earplugs swivelled her foot to the rhythm of some music, typing fast on her smartphone.

A man in his late sixties was reading *La Gazzetta dello Sport*. Two younger men were talking loudly, holding each other's hands; their conversation made the only sound in the room. Three middle-aged men who sat in different parts of the waiting room seemed to be dozing.

Five steps away from Nina, Alessandro was examining the station's time table, glancing at his watch now and then. When he finished, he had a relieved grin on his mouth.

'Intercity to Verona leaves in twelve minutes,' he said, approaching Nina. 'From there we shouldn't have any problems catching a train to Milan.'

Nina gave him a subtle smile and crossed to a ticket machine.

She chose the destination, number of passengers, slid her Visa into the slot, and then entered her PIN. In two seconds the machine returned the card. Nina read on the screen: "Transaction cancelled." She sighed and repeated the same steps. The card was rejected again.

The frightening thought that van der Venn had something to do with it, that he already knew where they were going, crossed her mind. She wanted to take a look over her shoulder but forced herself not to. She was a member of a civilised society. She obeyed the law. She shouldn't have anything or anyone to fear, should she?

It was so easy to say, but hard to accept after what had happened on that yacht, and after she found out about those terrible things van der Venn was suspected of.

She inhaled through her nose, choosing again their destination and number of passengers. Holding the Visa in both hands, she let the machine swallow it. Then she carefully entered the first two numbers of her PIN. She hesitated. She remembered the other two digits but wasn't sure about their order. How did she enter them before? Six and nine, or nine and six. Nine and six. That's it. Transaction complete.

She glanced around. Alessandro took a seat next to the girl with earplugs. He was rocking his head. When Nina neared him she handed him his ticket. She heard the faint melody coming from the girl's earplugs.

'Thanks,' he said. 'Really.'

Nina scanned the waiting area. One of the sleeping men was now gone. No one else had moved.

'Let's go,' she said. 'It's almost over.'

'What's over?'

She ignored his puzzled expression and turned away.

They walked onto the platform when the speaker announced an upcoming train.

As soon as it stopped, they climbed on board. Nina didn't take the first free seat, or the second. She continued down the aisle. In the next carriage, although it was empty, she didn't slow down either.

'Nina!' Alessandro said behind her back. 'What's wrong with *these* seats?'

'Nothing is wrong with those seats,' she said. 'It's the train that I'm concerned about.'

'What? Explain!'

She hastened her walk, passing through another carriage, and another. Her analytical mind was running again. She turned to the exit door and jumped off the train.

'What are you doing? Nina!'

She waved at him without turning back. 'Come!'

'Nina!'

She pulled up her skirt a little bit and ran through a tunnel under the rails, then took stairs to another platform.

A train was sitting there. The speaker was announcing its departure.

Nina looked back. Alessandro had only just appeared on the platform. 'Faster! You're slower than a girl in a pencil skirt!'

She jumped on board the EuroCity express that was gaining momentum. She held the door open.

Alessandro sprinted, made a few long steps, grabbed the handrail and pulled himself inside the train that was accelerating in the opposite direction from Milan.

He leaned over and propped his hands on his knees, looking up at Nina. 'What was that?'

'Honestly? You should exercise sometime.'

He gasped for breath. 'What?'

'At your age you should look much better after a one-hundred-metre sprint.'

He straightened up and gave her the same bewildered look he had two minutes ago at the station.

Nina turned on her heel. She slid open the door to the first-class carriage for six persons. It was empty. She took a seat at the window and embraced the briefcase.

Alessandro sat down beside her. His breath returned to normal, but she felt his angry gaze on her.

'A lot has happened in my life today, Nina,' he said. 'Why do you keep adding to this mess?'

'I'm sorry,' she said in a low voice. 'For your friend and for what happened on that yacht.'

He shook his head. 'None of that was your fault.'

'Then I'm sorry for my sense of humour?'

He let out a nervous chuckle. 'There you're guilty as charged.'

Nina smiled.

'Where is this train going?'

'We can't go to Milan. He might find out.' She raised her hand, sensing his next question. 'I don't know how.'

Alessandro put his palms on his knees. 'Where then?'

'Heidelberg Castle.'

He frowned. 'As in Heidelberg, Germany?'

'Yes,' she whispered. 'I'm sorry I didn't give you a choice.'

He sighed. 'Nina, why there?'

'Everything started there. It must end there. Some people will hold a meeting in Heidelberg tomorrow.'

'What p—'

'People who hired me to join van der Venn, and who, I'm sure, have no idea what a madman he is.'

Alessandro shifted in his seat. 'Didn't you hear what Raffaele said? Van der Venn is *insanely* rich. He bribed high-profile politicians. How do you know that the people you're talking about are not among them?'

'I … I didn't think about that,' she said.

Could it be that Massimo Campana, Christoph Gerst, and Julien Traverse had conspired with van der Venn?

'And?'

She met his eyes. 'If that's the case, I can't see any other option left, Alessandro. Whom else can I trust? Having in my hands this briefcase, the answer is absolutely no one.'

'Okay, listen. This is what we do—'

Nina stood up. 'Maybe there is one person, though.'

'Who?'

'I have to make a call,' she said and walked out to the corridor, closing the door behind.

Criminals like van der Venn could bribe politicians, but they couldn't infiltrate the Catholic Church. She dug out a business card from her purse and dialled.

'*Pronto*,' someone answered slowly. 'Hello.'

'Cardinal Esposito? This is Nina Monte.'

There was a short silence on the other end, and then the cardinal said, 'Good evening, Signora Monte. What happened?'

Alarmed, Nina touched the base of her neck. 'Why do you think something must have happened?'

'I assume that you wouldn't call at ten thirty at night, otherwise. I was just finishing my evening prayers.'

Nina winced and let her head bang on the window.

'The usual track of time no longer applies to my life, Cardinal Esposito,' she said. 'I need your guidance.'

'I am all ears.'

Nina told him what had happened on the lake, and who the man in charge of the exploration was. And that she had decided to travel to Heidelberg, but she didn't really know whom to trust.

Esposito listened to her without interruption; she heard his heavy breathing in the receiver.

When her story slowed down, and she started to repeat herself, he asked, 'Signora, did you say that you retrieved the item?'

Nina looked in the direction of the carriage where she had left the briefcase, and felt uneasy. 'I have it with me.'

'In what condition is it?'

'I had no time to examine the tablet, but, for something that originated twenty-five centuries before Christ, I'd say it looks impressive.'

'Tablet, you say … hmm.'

Complete silence this time. 'Cardinal, are you there?'

'Signora Monte, is your train going directly to Heidelberg?'

'No, it terminates in Austria, in Innsbruck. Then I will have to change trains.'

'All right, Signora. I will hang up now. Please wait for a return call from me.'

'Cardinal, when do you—' she started, but he was gone. She slowly lowered her phone. '*When* will you call me back?' she said to herself.

The train clicked on the rails, picking up its speed, then slowing down again. She looked out the window. There was no human activity on the horizon. Normal people were in their beds, getting their rest before another mundane day.

Her phone vibrated in her hand. She pressed the green icon before it started to play the ringing tone.

'Signora Monte,' the cardinal said. 'The meeting has been rescheduled for your convenience. It will take place tomorrow in Austria. Please disembark in Innsbruck and find accommodation there.'

Nina sighed with relief. 'Thank you, Cardinal Esposito.'

'Please come to the Court Church, *Hofkirche*, at eleven a.m. You shouldn't have any problems finding it. It's on every brochure of the city.'

'Court Church at eleven. Thank you!'

'God be with you!'

He hung up for good, and it was only then that Nina realized that she didn't ask if Massimo Campana and the two other men would be present. But that was obvious. Who else would choose another popular tourist destination for a confidential meeting?

Nina rubbed her eyes and headed back to Alessandro.

'Everything is sorted,' she said and took hold of the briefcase. She checked it to see if he had tried to open it – not caring if he would feel offended. She decided that it was secured as before, and the weight seemed to be the same also.

'Who did you talk to?'

She stared at him for half a minute. She could tell him that much without breaking any confidential agreement. 'I've talked to Cardinal Vittorio Ermanno Esposito from Milan. He arranged everything. I'll be meeting him and others in Innsbruck tomorrow.'

Alessandro drew the corners of his mouth down.

'This is good news,' Nina said. 'We … I don't have to go all the way to Germany.'

'Yes. But, it's just that my mother made me learn the names of all our cardinals. I can't recall the name Esposito,' Alessandro said. 'She would be mad at me.'

'Anyway,' Nina continued, 'tomorrow, everything will get back to normal.'

Suddenly Alessandro's face looked even more confused and tired. 'What will get back to normal, Nina? You will return the briefcase to those people, and then what? How will they protect us from him?'

'I'm sure that once we pass the briefcase to them, he will lose interest in us. I believe that the police in Malcesine overreacted about us being crown witnesses,' she said, although her own words didn't sound that convincing even to her.

'Maybe. But the problem is,' he said, 'that *I* will not lose interest in him. He must pay for Gianluigi's death.'

'And I intend to back you up on that, but for now let's concentrate on one thing at a time.' She glanced at the briefcase.

He nodded, his eyes vacant. 'Will you finally tell me what's so precious in what you're carrying there?'

She drew a breath. 'I suppose that you deserve to know a little bit more.' It felt exhilarating to have someone with whom she could talk about it.

'I agree, Nina.'

'Van der Venn retrieved the contents of this briefcase from the bottom of Lake Garda. It was carried by the medieval galley, *Santa Lucia*. And *Santa Lucia* was sunk during the battle of Maderno in 1439. I presume that this thing had been brought to Europe from Asia, and then had been lost somewhere in the Roman Empire.'

'What thing?'

'Now, we established that *somewhere* means Lake Garda. If van der Venn found it on this sunken galley, I think that the clergymen had intended to deliver it to the pope, taking advantage of a strong military escort.'

'Why take a route through the lake if that thing was coming from Asia?'

Nina had similar doubts, and a number of theories started to crystallize in her head, but she couldn't concentrate to make much sense out of them. 'I only know that the cardinal said it was once under Church protection.'

'Okay.' Alessandro knocked on the briefcase. 'This is the moment when you tell me what's inside.'

She pulled it tighter to her chest. 'If you really have to know … inside is a stone tablet in which a text is engraved.' She turned her body to him and said, 'It might be the *oldest* religious message ever found on our planet.'

Alessandro gave her an astounded look. 'Is that all?'

She opened her mouth to protest. 'I … I've just shared a monumental discovery with you.'

'C'mon, Professor. Listen to yourself,' he said. 'You presume, you think, it might. It doesn't sound credible. Besides, after you've told me about that chest full of gold coins … Don't you think so?'

'No, I don't.'

'Please don't tell me I almost got shot because of what could be an ancient and worthless piece of rock.'

'I don't intend to discuss it further with someone who has no idea about ancient religions,' she said and sat back.

'I know my religion. That's enough for me,' Alessandro said in a calm tone. 'But you're right. I know nothing about prehistoric times, so … if you say this thing is somehow important, I believe you. Let's forget about gold coins.'

She scrutinized his face, searching for signs of sarcasm,

but Alessandro's look was honest. That sounded better; he understood her. A little bit. At least.

Nina took off her blazer and tucked her white shirt into her skirt. The carriage was cosy and warm. She felt like she was losing control over her eyelids. She opened them wider, but soon they slipped. Her body was telling her that it was time to go to bed, as every evening it did, before 11:00 p.m. She deserved a good night's sleep.

'Earlier, aboard van der Venn's yacht,' Alessandro said in a low voice, 'I overheard you saying something about a fast track to God. Did I get it right?'

'Yes.'

'And?'

Nina kicked off her shoes and curled up her legs. 'Some people are convinced that whoever understands the text will reach a state of enlightenment and … will find a way to the One God.' Her words were becoming longer and slower.

'What crazy individuals are those?' Alessandro said. 'And can you read it?'

'A … a little. Small part of it.'

'Do you know someone who can read everything?'

Her head fell on his shoulder. 'I guess…'

'What does it exactly mean, Nina? One God.'

'I presume … that whoever … finds … the text…'

CHAPTER 23

EUROCITY EXPRESS FROM Rovereto pulled into the platform in Innsbruck Central Station. It was 1:20 a.m. on Alessandro's wristwatch.

While Nina slept on his shoulder for the entire journey, he didn't close his eyes for more than he needed to blink. The face of the man who tried to kill him, and the constant ringing of gunfire in his head, was too sharp when he let his eyelids drop.

For the last three hours he only moved as much as was necessary to stretch out his legs. At least one of them could get rest. Now he really needed to stand up, though.

'Nina,' he whispered and gently moved his shoulder. 'We're here.'

She recoiled and looked around. 'What? Where are we?'

'We have arrived in Innsbruck.'

'Where is the briefcase?'

'Next to me, on the other side.'

She gave him a distrustful look, got up and grabbed it. Then she touched her forehead and plunked herself back down on the seat.

'Easy.' He put his hands on her shoulders. 'Are you okay?'

She yawned and curled her back. 'Did you sleep, too?'

'Sort of,' he lied. 'Let's go. We need to find a place to stay overnight.'

Nina put on her blazer, checked her hair in the mirror above the seats, and rubbed her eyes. 'Let's take a taxi to a hotel.'

'No,' he said. 'Come.'

He opened the door to get out of the train. A chilly wind hit his body. Outside, the temperature wasn't higher than fourteen degrees. He looked back at Nina and her business-like outfit, and especially at her knee-length skirt—that would not keep her warm.

'What are you waiting for?' she said.

Alessandro jumped onto the platform. Nina stepped down after him. He watched her body cringe.

She shuddered and glanced up at him. 'I take it back. There was no need to hurry up.'

He took off his hoodie and offered it to Nina before she managed to protest, although it didn't look that she had intended to oppose. On the platform, a few other passengers passed them by without taking notice of what they were up to.

Nina pulled the hoodie over her head, jumped two times and let it envelop her upper body; it reached almost to her knees.

Alessandro gave a tight-lipped smile, put his arm around her, then led her to the exit. 'I know a nice place not far from here. I stay there when I come to Innsbruck to ski.'

'Good to hear that you do some sports, after all.'

'One more word, Professor, and I leave you here.'

'No, you won't. You're broke.'

'True. I keep forgetting about that.'

They headed off the station.

There was little activity around Central Station. Not even a single cab. Asphalt on the roads was wet after the rain. Its black surface absorbed most of the street lighting.

A patrol car slowly moved along the road. A policeman glanced at them with a detached gaze. Alessandro crossed to the other side and sped up his pace, keeping an eye on Nina, who trudged beside him, shaking in the cold.

'It's only a ten-minute walk,' he told her.

The night was quiet and moonless. The only activity he noticed on the way was an open kebab outlet where behind the window three men of Turkish origin were eating. If he had been alone he might have dropped in for a quick snack.

The door to the Innsbruck B&B was closed, but there was always someone on duty to welcome latecomers. He rang the bell and waited. After twenty seconds, he rang twice.

'Break it down. Maybe the bell doesn't work.'

'Don't worry. If it doesn't, they will hear your chattering teeth,' he said to tease her, although he already felt the chill of the Austrian mountains himself. He tried to rub Nina's shoulders.

She pushed him away and squinted. 'You know I could hit you now if my hands weren't frozen.'

'How can you still be cold, wearing my—'

The lock clicked. Alessandro pulled the door open and allowed Nina to go first.

He smelled fresh paint. The corridor of the old building must have been refurbished recently. From the top of the stairs a tall man was coming down. His head was shaven on both sides. Blond hair was combed back from the top of his head.

'Alessandro? I wouldn't expect you for another two months. Was Malcesine struck by heat waves even you can't bear?' he said in impeccable Italian, grinning at Alessandro.

'Hello, Max,' he replied. 'I didn't recognize you.'

Max raked his hand through his hair. 'I *know*. I'm in a stage of evaluating my true self.'

Nina cleared her throat.

'We're sorry for disturbing you at this hour,' Alessandro said. 'We've just arrived, and need to stay somewhere for one night. This is Nina.'

Max sent her a welcoming smile. 'No problem. I have a double-bed room available.'

Alessandro felt Nina's finger between his ribs.

'We'll take separate rooms,' he said.

Max pulled back the corners of his mouth. 'This is the only room available. Sorry. If that won't work for you, I could recommend a great B and B. It's just around—'

'We'll take it here,' Nina said. 'Just for one night.'

Alessandro leaned over to her ear. 'Don't worry. I'm not going to take advantage of you, Professor.'

She angled her head and threw him a sideways look. Alessandro pulled his lips into a goofy smirk.

'Just for one night, madam,' Max said, glancing at her from head to toe. He raised his eyebrow and added, 'Is Italian fashion taking an incredible U-turn which I know nothing about?'

Alessandro watched Nina blushing. She pulled his hoodie farther down.

'Come,' Max said. 'Your room is on the top floor. Standard rate for one night is forty-five euros. For you, thirty-five. You can pay at checkout.'

He led them up the staircase to the third floor, until they stopped in front of a yellow door. Max produced a bunch of keys, unhooked one and unlocked the door.

'There. Make yourself at home. Breakfast is from seven thirty till nine thirty. It's included with your room. Have a good night,' he said and ran back down the staircase, two steps at a time.

Alessandro switched on the light. The interior wasn't much different compared to the other rooms he had stayed in previously. Basic furniture consisted of a bed, wardrobe, table and two chairs, and a small TV set. Two one-metre-fifty-long cast iron radiators reminded him of the minus-twenty-degree winter days he experienced in Innsbruck.

Nina was still trembling, so he crossed to her and rubbed her arms and shoulders with his hands. She stood motionless, accepting this ritual without a word, and with her hands on her chest. Then she rested her head on his chest. Alessandro embraced her, and stroked her back.

He glanced at the wall behind her. A picture showing yellow, green and red changing booths standing in a row on a sandy beach hung on the wall. How farfetched an idea it was to exhibit sea holiday elements in a mountain resort. Although, he had to admit that it wasn't as farfetched as him standing here in an intimate hug with a woman he had practically just met, in a room with one bed, in the middle of the night.

Alessandro closed his eyes. He felt Nina's body relaxing, which made him relax as well, a little bit.

And then what came was that sudden and astounding affection he couldn't explain. Alessandro wanted to keep holding her in his arms. He wanted to protect her from van der Venn and everyone who would want to hurt her.

He gave her an awkward kiss on the top of her head, smelling her hair. It was sweet and fresh with a dominant coconut note. The picture of a beach on the wall wasn't that out of place after all.

'Do you want some hot tea?' he whispered, looking at an electric kettle that stood on the table.

'Yes, please.'

He put in the water, and glanced at the double-bed covered with a woollen blanket. 'I hate going to bed on an empty stomach.'

'I'm so tired I don't even care,' Nina said with half-closed eyes.

'There is a vending machine downstairs. I'll go and grab a sandwich.'

'I'll be here.'

He made his way down the stairs. A tall vending machine stood in the corner. Behind the glass he saw chocolate bars, crisps, and one Caesar chicken salad for 3.50 euros. He tried to remember if he had any change on him.

Moment of truth. He put his hands into his pockets.

They were empty.

He punched the machine with his open palm. Echo waves travelled up the stairs.

Then he remembered that Max used to keep a tip box on the reception counter. He sprinted up a flight of stairs, and smiled. Then he inserted his hand into the jar and fished out some change.

'Sorry, Max,' he said to himself. 'This is only a small loan.'

He counted 3.50 and returned the rest into the container.

After he bought the salad, he intended to get back to the room, but he assumed that Nina would already be asleep.

Instead he sat down on the steps of the top floor. He tore open the package and stuffed his mouth with chicken, lettuce and parmesan cheese. He chewed and chewed.

Chunks of food fell out of his mouth. He put the salad down. He wasn't really hungry; he just needed an excuse to be on his own.

He hadn't even thanked Raffaele for saving his life. If not for him, van der Venn may have pulled the trigger.

His fear started to fade away only now.

When he and Nina had been waiting for a train at Rovereto station, he was terrified inside, but somehow managed to conceal it. What would Nina say if she knew? What would she say if she knew that he took a seat next to that girl with earplugs in her ears because he thought that if van der Venn followed them he wouldn't risk a shot with her nearby?

He pulled on his hair, curling the strands around his finger. He was a coward. He was a selfish coward. Gianluigi was dead, and all he could think of was his own safety.

Breathe, he told himself. Just breathe.

When he opened the room, Nina was asleep, curled up like a baby girl. He heard her steady breathing. Her blazer, shirt, and the skirt were neatly folded on a chair. A table lamp, which she had left on, cast a sallow glow on her clothes. He lifted the chair and, moving on his tiptoes, placed it next to the bed so that, after waking, she wouldn't feel uncomfortable.

She stirred in the bed and wrapped the duvet around her body like a sleeping bag.

Alessandro crossed back to the table, took a seat on the second chair, and buried his head into his hands.

Did he really have anything to be ashamed of? It was a human reaction to feel scared if someone pointed a gun at him, shot at him. He was entitled to feel terrified. Wasn't he? *Wasn't* he?

Yes. He was. He just needed time to recover. He needed rest. That's all.

He straightened his spine and let out a long sigh. Then he took a sip of the tea Nina had made for him. Strong flavours of wild berries warmed him up.

He rose to his feet, spread the bed cover on the floor, pulled out a spare duvet and a pillow from the wardrobe, then stripped to his underwear, and lay down.

He felt a little better, and lighter. That inner monologue shed some burden off his chest.

He reached out and drew at the electric cord of the table lamp.

'Good night, Professor,' he whispered, pulling the duvet up to his nose.

CHAPTER 24

NINA WOKE UP in the morning at 8:15. She quietly got dressed and freshened up in a miniature bathroom that was the size of the utility closet in her apartment in Venice. Then she stepped back into the room and drew aside the floral red curtains, letting the morning sunlight flood in.

She gaped at the white peaks of the Alps, spellbound and reluctant to move.

Had those freaky events actually taken place the previous night? Or were they a projection of her scientific brain that secretly longed for adventure? She was willing to believe in that. Easily. If not for the new and hardly familiar surroundings she found herself in.

And if not for the presence of the man sleeping on the floor.

She glanced over her shoulder. Alessandro was covered up to his waist with a white, thick duvet. A silver Christian cross on a brown cord rested on his chest. His face was turned away from her.

She was grateful to him for being so thoughtful as to put her clothes closer to the bed last night. She hadn't thought about that at all. Exhausted, she had fallen asleep instantly and hadn't even heard him coming back to the room.

Nina felt her cheeks going hot when she realized that she was gazing at his naked torso. When was the last time she saw a man naked, without counting sporadic times on a TV screen?

Without making too much noise, she took a seat in the chair and put the briefcase on her lap. She scrutinized its futuristic contours. Now she was more convinced than before that what she had done yesterday was right. Taking it away from van der Venn was acting in accordance with her intuition.

She put her hands on top of it and probed its rugged surface. There was no lock or combination lock that she could see, and the line along which the case should open was barely visible. She tried to remember how van der Venn had unlocked it.

She put her fingers on both sides of the case, then underneath it, probing for a button or a latch. Not a tiny hint. She tapped on it like on a piano keyboard.

Afraid to turn it upside down, she lifted the briefcase above her head as if there were a sign on it: that way up; handle with care. She gazed at its bottom. There was nothing that could give her an idea of how to reveal its contents.

'Buongiorno,' Alessandro said.

She glanced at him, her hands still raised above her head. 'Buongiorno.'

'I thought you were more interested in the inside of that fancy box,' he said, yawning.

'I cannot open it.' She shook the case, then held her breath. 'I'm sorry.'

'For what?'

'I wasn't talking to you.'

He frowned. 'Then to whom?'

Nina looked at him with the intention of sending him a stare of rebuke, but Alessandro's sleepy face showed no signs of mockery. Most of the time, she couldn't tell if he was genuinely confused or if he was making fun of her.

He propped his elbows on his floor bed. 'Why do you think Lammert van der Venn wants it so badly? He didn't strike me as a religious person,' he said. 'And he's got those gold coins.'

'Alessandro, the world is full of gold coins.'

His eyebrow shot up. 'Is it? Then I would be most grateful if you could point me—'

'You know what I mean!' Nina crossed to the bed, sat down and gently placed the briefcase on her lap. 'Besides, he's not the only one who wants it. There are other parties interested, other countries.'

He sat up on the floor. 'You didn't mention other countries. Those people you're talking about are not Italians?'

'Not all of them.'

Alessandro got up and put on his T-shirt and shorts. She caught a glimpse of his black Versace boxers. Not intentionally, of course.

'Why are other nationalities involved? The stone was found in Italy,' he said, folding the duvet and the bedcover. Then he threw everything into the wardrobe.

'It's because…' She had asked the same question in Heidelberg.

'What is it, Nina?'

She rubbed her eyes and said bleakly, 'It's politics, Alessandro. But it makes sense why they made such a secret out of it.'

Alessandro perched on the bed, beside her.

'Even if they were sceptical, like you are, in case the discovery *is* genuine, they can't disregard the tablet and risk it falling into the wrong hands.'

'How come? I thought you told me that it was authentic?'

Nina stood up and paced the room, holding the briefcase in front of her. 'Don't you see?'

'Should I?'

'Their interest in the tablet is not motivated by its archaeological value, which is undisputed. What they want is to run experiments on the tablet in their laboratories.'

Alessandro yawned. 'Aaand to find a way to God, right?'

'Oh, no! I don't think they're of such a strong faith, but…' She took a seat on the other side of the bed and touched her temple. 'Now I understand what Julien Traverse meant by saying that the discovery had the enormous potential.'

Alessandro followed her to the other side. 'And who's that guy?'

'Julien Traverse is one of the men I'm meeting today.'

Then Nina turned her body to him. 'Traverse was talking about human revolution, but he failed to mention that the way to do so is through reaching enlightenment. Do you know what it means, Alessandro?'

'A state of being … enlightened?'

'Yes, but do you have any idea what that means to *them*? What they *think* they can achieve with the tablet?'

He shrugged his shoulders.

She got up again, not letting her hands slip off the briefcase, and crossed to the window. 'Imagine a nation with highly intelligent people. It would produce scientists initiating rapid progress in fields like biochemistry, genetics, physics, mathematics … microbiology, or create sportsmen performing on a level not known to us. Not to mention never-before-seen military solutions to guarantee peace. We could prevent new terrorists' attacks! Nowadays no country is safe! Everyone looks for protection and peace!'

Alessandro crossed his legs on the bed.

'That nation,' Nina continued, 'would become a leader in every aspect of everyday life. In everything!'

'And all of those bad things out of one ancient religious message?' Alessandro said, rubbing at his nose.

Nina scowled at him. 'What bad things?'

'I'll tell it how I see it, Nina: unlawful manipulation of the human genome; soldiers killing more efficiently, conquering other lands to make those less capable their slaves; cheating in sport, like we haven't had enough of that at the moment—'

'But you—'

'Whoever gets their hands on the tablet would use it to dominate and exploit. The protection you talk about is fictional and for politicians' sake, so that they can get re-elected. You see, that's why I don't watch much television. Except football, obviously,' he added.

Nina snorted at his hasty theories. The fan of the brainless game didn't share her enthusiasm. So what? 'You're looking at it from the wrong perspective, Alessandro.'

'Maybe yes. Maybe no,' he said. 'At least now I know what you meant by fast track to God.'

'Not exactly. This would be the first step. Only after reaching the higher understanding of our own existence comes—'

'Finding a way to God,' Alessandro finished her sentence, without hiding his scepticism.

She nodded.

'Nina.' He shook his head. 'I'm sorry, but you are a *professor*!'

'And?'

'I wouldn't expect a scholar to come up with such a fantasy.'

She raised her hand. 'Listen—'

'No. Listen to yourself. You're saying that a piece of a rock can make us smarter, faster, and better than ever in human history. And then open a door to God?' He snapped his fingers. 'Just like that.'

'You don't know all the facts about the tablet,' she said and lowered her voice. 'I know how I sound, and I never said that all of that is verified, Alessandro, because it's not. But, what *if*?'

He said nothing this time.

'And,' she went on, 'if those people I'm meeting invested their time and money—'

'That means nothing. They're probably as rich as van der Venn, so what's a million or two to splash on weird stuff?'

Nina curled her toes. She hated how he referred to the tablet: yesterday it was "a piece of rock" for him, now it was "weird stuff", although apart from that there might have been a little logic to his thinking. A little.

Alessandro glanced at her briefcase. 'Can I try to open it, so I can see that gem with my own eyes?'

She shook her head. 'There must be a secret mechanism that I can't even see embedded in the case. Van der Venn had it custom made.'

Alessandro yawned and glanced at his watch. 'Almost nine o'clock!'

'We have lots of time until eleven,' Nina said.

'Not to catch breakfast downstairs.' He stood up and threw his hoodie onto his shoulders.

Nina watched him with irritation. 'Do you ever think beyond the mundane, Alessandro?'

'I do, but not before my third espresso.'

CHAPTER 25

THE BLACK AUDI cut the Austrian highway A13 in a gracious way at the steady speed of 120 kph. The morning mist hadn't dispersed yet, and the road was slippery. In the passenger seat, van der Venn wondered if it was a good idea to let Sander Klaff drive. He could have a heavy foot sometimes.

Van der Venn was sure that it was Klaff who had provoked the fight with locals in Malcesine last night. This morning, van der Venn managed to explain to the police that his people got involved in a quarrel by accident and, apart from that, they were law-abiding guests in Italy. In reality, he'd had to be more persuasive than that. But he got his crew out. Only that mattered.

In truth, the things by Lake Garda didn't go as he had planned. The money paid to the corrupted bureaucrat from Rome was wasted. The man was supposed to call Malcesine's police so van der Venn had a free hand with the underwater excavation. But that pesky inspector had to butt in on van der Venn's affairs with Nina Monte. This morning he paid the price for snooping.

Far away, ahead of the speeding Audi, above the last patches of fog, the white peaks of the high Alps painted the landscape. On both sides of the highway, pine trees grew densely on the steep slopes.

From the rear seat, van der Venn heard animated sighs. Waaberi wriggled, moving from one window to another. Then he poked his head between him and Klaff.

'Boss, I've never been to Austria. It looks like out of this world!'

Van der Venn looked back at him. Waaberi's head swivelled from right to left; his eyes shone with excitement.

'There! End of the road!' Waaberi yelled and pointed ahead at a black entrance to a tunnel that cut into a green hill.

Klaff snorted. 'You've been nowhere, moron! You've spent the first fourteen years of your pathetic life in a Somalian dump, and the rest at sea.'

'Shut up and drive, Sander,' van der Venn said. 'And you, Waaberi, tone it down a notch.'

The ride from Italy was tiresome for him—his lower back started to hurt before they crossed the Austrian border. The one painkiller he had swallowed hadn't brought the expected relief. In spite of that, he ordered Klaff to drive as fast as it was allowed. Their destination was two hours and thirty-eight minutes away from Malcesine.

Steep slopes gave way to gentle hills dotted by detached houses with white facades and steep roofs, and the green forest.

He thought that even if Nina Monte made her hideaway somewhere out there, that wouldn't stop him from digging through every Austrian mountain to get her.

Finding the stone tablet was the most momentous discovery he had made over the last thirty years. No one could take it away from him.

'Boss, I'm hungry,' Waaberi said from the rear seat. 'How far do we have to go yet?'

'As long as it takes!' Klaff answered back.

Van der Venn looked at a clock on the dashboard: 9:20 glared back at him. He was surprised to hear Waaberi's moaning only now. None of them had eaten today.

'Boss?'

'Klaff, take the first exit and find us a place for breakfast,' van der Venn said. 'I wouldn't mind stretching my legs.'

'Thanks, boss,' Waaberi said in a happy voice.

Klaff let out a restrained sigh. He had to be hungry too. Van der Venn had him drive straight after he got them out of jail, after what was most likely a sleepless night.

After one kilometre, Klaff reduced speed and turned the steering wheel to the right. As soon as the car rolled to a stop, Waaberi jumped out and ran to the restroom. Klaff followed him at a sluggish pace.

Van der Venn strolled around the car. They parked at a gas station with an adjacent restaurant that had a big logo of Coca-Cola above the front door. Two eighteen-wheel Mercedes-Benz lorries and six passenger cars were parked nearby. A few people ambled along the rest stop, some of them snapping pictures of the landscape with their mobiles.

Van der Venn put on his sunglasses and looked into the skies. The weather had cleared up. He took off his light leather jacket and threw it on the rear seat. Then he pulled out his phone and one more time read the message he had received the previous night.

"Heidelberg meeting cancelled. Nina Monte is on her way to Innsbruck. She has the briefcase. Come to Hofkirche at 1:00 p.m."

He got back into the Audi and typed the address into the GPS device. His destination was forty-five minutes away. He sat back and exhaled. He had time.

Shortly after, Klaff brought him a cup of black coffee. Waaberi got onto the rear seat with a plastic bag filled with food. Van der Venn smelled bread and sausages. The three of them ate in silence. Then he nodded at Klaff, and the car pulled away from the rest stop.

Thirty-five minutes later, they approached the outskirts of Innsbruck. The roads got much wider. Three-storey houses lined the streets. Some of them looked like those he saw on the way, only they were much bigger here.

Klaff reduced speed to 50 kph. The wall of the mighty Alps ahead, so close now, would have the same effect on anyone. It seemed there could be nothing else behind those impregnable summits. They had to be respected. Like the ocean. A single false move and pitiless nature was the silent witness of a man drawing his last breath.

He decided he would feel good in the mountains.

When the Audi pulled into the city centre, Klaff slowed down to a pedestrian speed.

'I've never been to Innsbruck,' Waaberi said with his mouth full of a third breakfast roll. He bit into an apple. 'It looks like out—'

'Yeah, yeah, we know, like out of this—' Klaff cut short the mockery when van der Venn's hand landed on his forearm.

Looking around the bustling streets of Innsbruck, van der Venn wondered where Waaberi picked out that expression. It was accurate for this occasion; somewhere among those people was the person who had in her hands the answer to "out of this world."

On his tracking device, receiving through the satellite from the sensor built into the desert-sand-coloured briefcase, that person blinked red.

Nina Monte was on the move.

CHAPTER 26

NINA GRIMACED AT the sight of fried food when she walked into the dining room followed by Alessandro. The smell of sausages and bacon had a remarkable ability to irritate her stomach, especially in the morning.

'Guten Morgen, sleepyheads,' Max said as he ushered them to a table. 'What would you like to drink?'

'Cappuccino, please,' Nina replied.

'Same for me.'

They took their seats in the middle of the high-ceiling room with ten or so tables, out of which only three were taken.

Two opposite walls of the restaurant were painted in purple, the other two in dark yellow. To enhance the effect, every table was covered with either purple or yellow cloth. A basket with apples, oranges and bananas were placed on each of them.

That mishmash of colours worked well with the black-and-white photos of Innsbruck hanging on the walls.

Other guests were almost finished eating. More or less everyone was sipping hot drinks over a private chat, or watching local news on a small flat-screen TV placed in the corner on a chest of drawers. Nina saw that Max stored clean cutlery and napkins there. Beside the TV was an acrylic stand for brochures and maps of the city.

Max returned with two cups of coffee and a tray with pastries, toasts, butter and jam. 'In case you Italians are sick of sugar,' he smiled and winked at Nina, 'there is more food against the wall. But Alessandro will know.'

'Thanks,' she said.

Max patted Alessandro on the shoulder in a friendly manner and walked away.

Alessandro snatched a donut covered with icing and pushed it into his mouth. His jaw moved two times and he swallowed. Nina looked around to see if anyone else saw that, but she quickly realized that no one cared.

She grabbed an appetizing-looking yeast bun and took a bite. It was freshly baked, still warm and filled with apple marmalade, exactly what she needed in the morning to fully wake up.

'That thing must be destroyed, Nina.'

She almost choked. 'What are you talking about?' She checked out the bun from all angles.

'I'm serious, Professor.' He gestured with his head to the floor, where she had put the briefcase.

Nina placed the bun on a small plate. 'First, you don't even believe that the message on the tablet can do what I said it can, and now—out of the blue—you want to destroy it. Do you know what I think, Alessandro? You say it because you don't want van der Venn to have it.'

There. She could also be dead honest.

A sweet brioche disappeared next into Alessandro's mouth.

A group of three holidaymakers passed them and left the room.

'I'm so sorry about Gianluigi, I truly am,' she added, to soften her attitude. 'But you will not avenge him by taking away things van der Venn wants.'

Alessandro leaned towards her. 'I hate that guy with all my heart, Nina. Regardless, what about this scenario? You have the briefcase now. In a couple of hours you will pass it to someone else. Imagine if it falls into the hands of people like him, the people who don't value others' lives beyond their personal interest, the kind who don't hesitate to pull the trigger. Do they really deserve to get what you carry? Even if the tablet only has value purely from an archaeological point of view?'

Nina took another bite of the bun. It didn't seem to be as special as the first time. She sipped her cappuccino as an excuse not to agree with him, to some extent, at the very least.

'Besides, you are so excited about it,' he continued. 'Why do you want to give it away so quickly?'

'It's not like that. They promised I would be able to examine it.'

'Is this what they told you?'

'Of course … it is,' she said. 'My job is to confirm the authenticity of the tablet, and … Alessandro, I realize what an unscrupulous individual van der Venn is, but I'm sure he will be excluded from this thing after what he has done. And is suspected of. He must be.'

'Nina, it's not only about me detesting van der Venn,' Alessandro said, without dropping his insistent tone of voice. 'Assuming that what you told me was for real, there's another aspect of the whole matter.'

Nina listened to him, although, now and then, she shifted her gaze to the TV screen. The voice was muted, but she watched a funny weather forecast presenter. The man was dressed in a white jacket, with a tie depicting dancing snowmen.

'Nina, are you with me?'

She turned back to Alessandro. 'Go on.'

'Let's assume it is true. Now,' he cleared his throat, 'apart from the fact that people are not ready to take the responsibility you claim the tablet would give them, because I can assure you it would be used in unethical ways…'

She glanced back at the TV. She was wrong. That man wasn't funny at all; it must have been just those snowmen. Actually, he looked familiar. She had travelled to Vienna earlier this year. Maybe she met him in passing on the street. But why would she remember him? Was he dressed the same way?

Was she getting paranoid? Recently, everywhere she had seen familiar faces. First, standing on van der Venn's yacht, now this.

She shifted back to Alessandro, who stared at her. 'Nina, the only way to be closer to God is through deep prayer, and not with a help of a hocus-pocus ancient piece of rock. It's blasphemy.'

So the cross Alessandro carried on his chest wasn't just for decoration. 'I thought you were a hotelier, not a philosopher. I can agree with you on certain matters, but the God issue isn't one of them. Know why? Because I don't believe he exists.'

Alessandro's face was a picture of pure bewilderment.

Nina added, 'Do you want to come up with yet another reason to throw out this unique part of world heritage?'

He squinted at her. 'You don't believe in God. I don't get it. After everything you told me?'

A Spanish-speaking couple finished their breakfast and headed to the exit.

'And what did I tell you, Alessandro, huh?'

He straightened up and put his palms down on the table. 'The things the tablet can do to a human. What can be—'

'That has hardly anything to do with religion.'

'But it *has*.'

'No, Alessandro. Enhancing abilities of human intelligence is all science, pure and explainable chemical reactions happening in our brains. There's nothing left here for speculation.'

He spread out his hands. 'But I thought it was based on that specific religious message! What you say now is in stark contradiction to your earlier words.'

Nina waited for the last two girls to pass them. 'Really?' When they disappeared behind the door, she said firmly, 'The tablet has an unimaginable archaeological and scientific value and must be thoroughly examined one way or another.'

'You're taking an enormous responsibility on yourself. Think about it, please.'

'I appreciate your company, Alessandro, but what will happen with the tablet now is not your concern. Anyway, I shouldn't have told you that much. I shouldn't have expected you to understand the gravity of the situation.'

'At least hold on to it for some time, and examine it yourself.'

She stood up.

His hopeless gaze followed her. 'So this is it?'

Nina took another glimpse of the TV screen. A black-and-white movie was on. Her world had long ago ceased to be black and white, but the colours of life weren't exactly pure and of a high definition either.

'I'll talk to you later, Alessandro,' she said, without looking at him.

On her way out, she snatched a map of Innsbruck from the chest of drawers. She was on her own—like she had been for most of her life.

CHAPTER 27

NINA SAT DOWN on a sunny bench on Maria-Theresien Street, close to the Innsbruck City Hall. It was 10:30 a.m. She watched scores of tourists heading towards the heart of Old Town at a leisurely pace. Many of them came to a halt every few steps to photograph Gothic and Baroque facades of houses painted in shades of pastel or red that lined the street.

She browsed through the brochure she had picked up in the hotel. Her destination, Court Church, *Hofkirche*, was built by Ferdinand I in the sixteenth century. Its main feature was an empty tomb of Emperor Maximilian I, and twenty-eight bronze statues of the so-called "Black Men." A cold chill ran down Nina's body as she pictured an empty sarcophagus guarded by lifeless figures.

According to the map on the leaflet, this Gothic church was located on Universitat Street, less than one kilometre from where she sat right now.

A female tour guide holding a folded umbrella over her head and followed by a group of fifteen or so Japanese holidaymakers, stopped not far from Nina. They gathered around an old-looking plaque fixed to a building wall on which German text was engraved.

The tour guide started to explain in Japanese who the founder of that plaque was, whom it was dedicated to, what events were commemorated by that and so on. Well, this was at least what she presumed the woman with an umbrella was talking about.

But how much could be said to future generations through words engraved in stone, and what a huge value it could have for those able to decipher and comprehend such a message?

Nina lowered her head. Only some people couldn't understand that. Like Alessandro.

She shouldn't have lashed out at him like that. Waves of regret started to build up in her chest. How could he insist on disposing of the tablet? How come he couldn't comprehend what she had in her hands?

Maybe because he didn't have a degree in history of religions, like she had. And he was a religious person, and she wasn't.

And what if he was right? What if she couldn't see it objectively despite her background as a scholar, and she just wanted everything that she had written about the tablet to be true?

Alessandro made her doubt, and she hated her indecision. She hated if someone pointed that out. Did it mean she hated Alessandro? No, of course not.

She missed him, in a strange way. She wasn't sure why. He was a reckless, happy-go-lucky guy. Not her type of man. Not at all.

In spite of that, she was becoming attracted to him, and she felt safer when he was around, even if she didn't expect van der Venn and his mob to materialize out of thin air.

She wondered what would have happened if Alessandro hadn't shown up on the yacht last night. What would van der Venn have done if she had refused to cooperate? But would she have refused to cooperate? Before the shooting, she'd had no reason to distrust him. Thanks to Alessandro, she hadn't told him much.

Then, after they had gotten on the train to Innsbruck, Alessandro hadn't had to follow her here. Was it that misplaced wallet that had made him stay with her? Who knows? She was glad he had stayed, though.

The tower clock struck quarter to eleven. She folded the map, slid it into her purse and hooked it onto her shoulder.

She stood up, and at the same moment, with the corner of her eye, she caught an identical movement to her left. In the first instant she wanted to look in that direction, but she lingered a second. When she turned her head, she saw nothing suspicious.

At the pace of a first-time visitor, she headed towards Court Church, her fingers wrapped around the handle of the sand-yellow briefcase.

As the car traffic wasn't allowed here, she walked in the middle of the street to avoid shadowed places and to keep herself in an unbroken stream of sunlight. She buttoned her blazer. It might still be summer, but not the kind she was used to in Italy.

Nina continued with the flow of the street. Ahead of her, the Alps' snow-capped peaks stood like a fortress that sheltered the city. The mountains here looked much stronger and raw compared to those surrounding Lake Garda.

She walked onto Herzog-Friedrich Street.

A window display of Swarovski crystals drew her in to the right. Hundreds of small crystals were scattered on the floor. In the middle was a crystal ball that looked like a giant diamond. On its surface, Nina tried to catch the reflection of whoever might be following her. All that she could see were multiplied silhouettes.

She had a feeling that everyone who passed her gaped at her. She glanced down at the briefcase—it was its cosmic look that drew attention.

She walked into a souvenir shop, bought a T-shirt, and asked a salesperson to put it into a canvas bag. Before she left the shop, she slid the briefcase into the bag with the logo "I love Innsbruck."

Nina glanced at the Golden Roof, a major Innsbruck's tourist attraction. Then she took a right turn into a narrow alley, Hofgasse.

No more than one hundred metres to her destination.

On both sides of the alley a number of modern shops implanted in medieval architecture lured customers. There were plenty of them around to be lured—tourists who splashed their money willingly and gaily.

Through a window of a liqueur store, Nina saw hundreds of bottles of different sizes, in every possible colour, filled with homemade alcohol. It looked like a display of an alchemist store selling potions to treat all kinds of afflictions. In a way, it was exactly that for some people.

Then there was a place with cuckoo clocks. Made by skilful craftsmen, they resembled mountain cottages with scenes of everyday life depicted on them.

Farther down the alley, Nina noticed a long queue. A smell of baked apples and walnuts came from that direction. When she came closer, she saw a café that served delicious-looking strudels. Not all of them were sweet. One could also get spinach and feta, or ham and cheese wrapped in crispy dough. She inhaled the mixture of flavours.

Then she turned and sped up towards Hofkirche.

First, they would ask her the same question as van der Venn: if what she brought to them indeed had the significance they hoped for.

She would answer that she needed to have a closer look. That would give her time to look into their eyes and see if Massimo Campana, Christoph Gerst, and Julien Traverse were righteous men.

Then she would examine the tablet. They must have known from the beginning that she was the only one who might give them the answers they were looking for.

Only, what if they weren't righteous men?

She walked through the long archway. Forty metres ahead she saw what her map said was the entrance to the church. Her watch showed three minutes to eleven.

Two minutes later, Nina found herself in a courtyard in whose central point stood an inactive fountain. Around it grew a meticulously trimmed hedge, half a metre high, shaped in four rectangles with inverted rounding at each corner.

Across the courtyard she saw the entrance to the church. A muscular man dressed in a claret jersey with a big number 70 on his back pushed on the handle. It went down, but the door didn't budge.

Stunned, Nina looked around. The man in the claret top shrugged his shoulders in a disapproving manner and moved on, leaving her alone.

Although, maybe she shouldn't be surprised. They closed the church for the time of the meeting, and perhaps there was another entrance somewhere but the cardinal had forgotten to mention that to her, she thought.

Nina flinched when the tower clock struck eleven o'clock. Each strike was clear and resonant as if a bell hung in the middle of the courtyard, above the fountain.

She decided to check the main door, just in case, and then call Massimo Campana on his mobile.

Slowly, as if the meeting had already started, and she wanted to sneak in undetected, Nina headed towards the door. She put her hand on the cold handle and pressed down.

When the handle was at its lowest point, the door opened. The man who had tried to get in before her wasn't as strong as he looked.

She walked through the short hall and moved aside a heavy curtain that blocked the way.

The high dome of the church was held by ten massive columns. In the centre of the church stood the tomb of Emperor Maximilian I surrounded by a wrought-iron grille with golden embellishments. Its walls were decorated by a black marble relief, depicting armour, medieval weapons and events from the emperor's life.

On both sides of the tomb, three-metre-high bronze statues of the emperor's ancestors stood guard. They looked like kings and queens, knights and saints.

She glanced up at the Christ statue on the cross. It hung high above, and compared to the tomb, the son of God whose sacrifice was to redeem human sins looked humble.

Nina let her peripheral vision run a scan of the church. There were no other visitors. That she had already noticed. What about those who she expected to be there? Eerie silence droned in her head. She felt her neck muscles tightening.

Something touched her shoulder from behind. She jerked, turned and took a swing with her hand holding the briefcase.

It only just missed Alessandro's head.

'It's me!' he screamed.

She glowered at him, puzzled.

'Sorry, Nina. I didn't mean to scare you.'

She poked his chest with her finger. 'That's why you followed me here all the way from the hotel?'

'What? No!' He took a step back. 'I didn't follow you. I … I overheard your conversation on the train.'

'Did you?' she said with anger. But she wasn't angry at all; she threw one arm around him. 'I'm glad you're here.'

Alessandro gave her a brief hug. 'Do you think you've been followed?'

Nina shook her head. 'It's just my imagination.'

A rasping, metallic sound came from behind the heavy curtain. They turned their heads at once.

'Someone locked the main door to the church,' Nina whispered.

CHAPTER 28

NINA LET HER breath out, seeing the man with a heart-shaped smile emerging from behind the curtain. Cardinal Esposito held a bunch of keys attached to an iron ring, but the first thing Nina noticed was his civilian clothes. A black suit and black shirt had replaced his formal cassock. He didn't even wear his clerical collar.

'Welcome, welcome, Signora Monte,' he said, approaching her.

Nina let him clasp her hand into a cordial shake. 'Good morning, Cardinal Esposito. It's hard to recognize you.'

'The matter is extremely sensitive, Signora. I didn't want to cause unnecessary trouble for the home clergy here.'

That made sense, she thought. 'This is my friend, Alessandro, from Malcesine.'

Esposito extended his hand, but Alessandro got to his knee and kissed the back of his hand.

'Ah, we have a child of the Church here.' The cardinal placed his other hand on Alessandro's head. 'God bless you, my son. Now rise.'

'God bless, Father,' Alessandro said without lifting his gaze above Esposito's chest.

The cardinal turned to Nina. 'Do you carry our treasure in this simple bag? This is not unwise, I suppose.'

Nina pulled out the briefcase. 'It's protected.'

'Very well. Open it, please.'

He was trying to stay composed, but Nina heard a note of excitement in his voice. And it was weird that he didn't ask Alessandro to leave. The men she met in Heidelberg would have kicked him out.

'I can't do it,' she said.

Esposito unbuttoned the top of his black shirt. 'Why not?'

'Van der Venn secured the briefcase. I have no idea what kind of key is needed.'

Esposito reached out and gestured her to hand it over. 'Let me see.'

Nina stood motionless, staring at his unsteady hand. His age had nothing to do with it. He was nervous, as if he wanted the meeting to be over quickly.

'Signora. Please.' His gaze bounced from right to left.

'Nina,' Alessandro said. 'What's wrong? What are you doing?'

A sheen of sweat covered Esposito's forehead. He squinted at Nina. What she saw in his expression made her hold onto the briefcase even firmer—his brown eyes were full of greed.

She took a few steps back. 'Let's wait for Massimo Campana.'

The cardinal winced. 'Signora Monte, this is really not necessary.'

'Where are they? It's time. Why are they late?' she said as calmly as she could.

The cardinal outstretched his hand and started to slowly walk towards her. His other hand patted his pocket as if he were looking for something. Then he put his hand inside it.

'I don't know. They will come, sooner or later. In the meantime, Signora, please—'

The back of his head exploded like a watermelon hurled to the concrete floor from a five-storey building. And Esposito's body slumped to the marble floor of the Court Church.

Nina drew her breath and froze, hypnotized. Then she stumbled back, but found something to lean on. She let the briefcase slide to the floor, and restarted breathing.

Alessandro gaped at the dead priest with an open mouth, paralysed. Nina's stomach retched when she saw pieces of human tissue on his T-shirt. She turned away and covered her mouth.

'You have no idea how much I'm glad to see you again, Ms Monte.'

She knew that voice all too well.

Lammert van der Venn appeared out of nowhere with a welcoming smile on his mouth. His curly hair was pulled back into a short ponytail. He was dressed in a sleek white shirt and black jeans. In his hand he held the gun Nina had seen on his yacht. To the end of the barrel was attached a silencer.

Sander Klaff and Waaberi followed him.

Without looking down, van der Venn stepped over the cardinal's body and headed towards Nina. When he came close enough, she feared he would give her a greeting kiss and then shoot her. She raised her arm to shelter her face.

'Don't be afraid, Ms Monte. I've already forgotten that unpleasant incident on the yacht.'

He spoke in a way friends welcomed each other after a long separation because one forgot to send birthday wishes.

Waaberi stood next to Alessandro and clutched on his arm. He had a gun in his other hand. Alessandro's face went pale.

Van der Venn turned back and looked at Klaff, who was going through Esposito's pockets.

'Passport, five thousand euros in cash, train ticket to Munich, one Lufthansa business-class ticket to Mexico with the departure date in two days,' Klaff said in disgust. 'And one Russian Makarov pistol from the fifties.'

A broody smile pulled back the corners of van der Venn's lips. He shook his head with disappointment. 'You can trust no one these days. Well,' he said, his gaze returning to Nina, 'what's done is done. How have you been, Ms Monte?'

Nina's half-open jaw felt numb. 'Y … you shot the cardinal.'

'No, I didn't,' van der Venn said without blinking an eye.

With a trembling hand, Nina pointed at the dead man. 'I've just seen it. You blew up his head.'

Van der Venn glanced at the body sprawled on the floor, as if noticing it for the first time. He pointed his gun at Esposito. 'Him?'

'Yes!' Nina yelled, hardly recognizing her own voice. 'You've killed a man. Just like that!'

Van der Venn raised his forearm, aiming the gun at the ceiling. Nina expected that he would fire to express his anger or whatever he had inside him. But then his arm quickly slumped.

He lowered his head, although his canny eyes never left her. 'Ms Monte, it's never *just like that*.'

'You've killed the cardinal. You cannot get away with it!' Nina shouted, instantly feeling lightheaded. She shut her eyes. Why was he arguing? She had seen everything. Was he completely out of his mind?

'Please stop this nonsense, Ms Monte,' van der Venn said, in such a polite manner that it made Nina scream inside. 'And if you could just stop calling that man "cardinal." '

'What's going on here?' Alessandro cut in. If he wanted to sound brave, his words came out weak and scared.

Van der Venn spun on his heel. 'Mr Pini, I had forgotten that you're here. It's in your best interest if it stays this way. If not,' he said, pointing at the emperor's tomb, 'isn't it a shame to keep such a beautiful thing empty?'

Nina held back another scream of protest. She could move again. She crossed to Alessandro and stood by his free side, pressing her shoulder to his. Alessandro jammed his hands into his armpits.

Van der Venn motioned to Klaff, and the man picked up the briefcase.

'Tell us what is going on here,' Nina said with effort. 'Are you going to shoot us too?'

Van der Venn didn't seem to hear her, and Nina wasn't sure if she was able to repeat such an insane question. He kept staring at Esposito's body. 'Waaberi, find Mr Fini someplace so he can rest in peace.'

Nina sheltered Alessandro with her body. 'No!' Her voice reverberated in the church and bounced back with echo ripples. 'Don't do that, *please*,' she added quietly.

Alessandro put his hand on Nina's shoulder and squeezed it lightly, as if saying goodbye.

Van der Venn gave Nina a bewildered look. 'One thing at time, Ms Monte. But, I can see you have developed feelings for Mr *Pini*,' he said, accentuating Alessandro's surname.

Waaberi pulled a black plastic bag out of his backpack—large enough to put into it a grown man. Waves of heat ran through Nina, along with breaks of cold sweat. She heard Alessandro's laboured breath.

Waaberi crouched down by the cardinal, straightened him by putting his legs together, arms along the body. He unzipped the bag, spread it next to Esposito and rolled him onto it. Then he covered him with the other half of the bag and zipped it up.

'I don't understand,' Nina muttered.

'Let me reply with a quote of a great poet and traveller, Ms Monte. "Everybody, sooner or later, sits down to a banquet of consequences," ' van der Venn said, watching Waaberi's efforts. 'In this case, Mr Luca *Fini*, who up to now fabulously played his role of a Catholic cardinal, made a mistake.'

Nina heard every word he said, but their meaning as a whole was a blurry gibberish.

'Son of a bitch!' Sander Klaff kicked the bag. His foot hit a hard part of the body, because he winced and started hopping around on the other leg.

Waaberi laughed. It was like watching a scene cut out of a gruesome horror parody. Van der Venn observed, expressionless.

Klaff put his sore foot down. Waaberi lifted the bag and headed to the back of the church, probably to the same place where they had come from. Klaff drew his weapon; it was the same gun the rest of them had.

'Although the late Mr Fini informed me about the whereabouts of you two,' van der Venn said, 'he tried to mislead me. If I had arrived here at one p.m., as he reported, he would be already on the way to Munich with my belongings.'

Nina began to understand. 'You bribed him.'

'No,' he answered, shaking his head. 'I hired out his services in exchange for money. Obviously it wasn't enough. Some people can't control their greed, Ms Monte. And please don't let pity blind your judgment. He was armed not for his own protection. Who knows what would've happened if I hadn't arrived in time.'

Nina almost heard a stream of nerve impulses connecting her brain cells. The weather forecast presenter she had seen on TV in the hotel that morning was no longer a stranger to her. Three days ago, he had called himself Christoph Gerst and had posed as a meeting host in Heidelberg Castle.

'This is all staged,' she whispered. With every next word her voice grew louder. 'That thing in Heidelberg was a deception. You faked the discovery of the tablet. But why?'

Van der Venn waved his index finger. 'No. You're only right with the first part. I did arrange your arrival in the castle to get you involved. Those three guys were acting.'

'That's why they couldn't explain to me what it was all about,' she half asked, half stated.

The self-confident smirk returned to van der Venn's face. He nodded in a casual way, as if he were a person asked if something should be done to stop global warming.

'I am the one who is in charge of this whole venture, Ms Monte. I am the one who restricted their scripts to the necessary information. Just enough to convince you to join me.'

'But why all that hustle? Why didn't you just approach me upfront?'

'You were supposed to believe that you were working for your country, and Campana had been instructed to tell you to fully cooperate with—'

'You're a crook and a murderer,' Alessandro said, stepping up. 'And you're crazier than I thought if you think we will help you.'

At the same time that van der Venn raised his gun and pulled the trigger, Nina sheltered Alessandro with her body. The bullet swished above her head. It hit something with a loud clang, ricocheted up, and smashed the stained window of the church. The rain of glass hit the floor with a jolting shatter.

Nina covered her head with her hands and cringed. When the first shock abated, she could hear Alessandro's groaning. She looked up.

He covered his left ear with his palm. Drops of blood dripped from between his fingers and onto his T-shirt. His eyes were wide open; his face sickly sallow.

'He shot off my ear, Nina,' he mumbled.

She grabbed his hand. 'Let me see.' Although, she didn't want to see it at all. She felt as broken as that window.

'It's only a little bit of your earlobe,' Nina told him.

He looked at her, thunderstruck. '*Only?*'

'Mr Pini, if I didn't make it clear enough, I need no cooperation from you at all,' van der Venn said. 'You've done enough by involving the police.'

Nina produced a handkerchief and tapped Alessandro's ear. His face was a picture of pain and hopelessness.

176

'Hold it, and you'd better not speak,' she said in a low voice.

He grasped her hand. Nina felt that it was cold and clammy.

She took a breath and faced van der Venn. 'What now? Are you going to kidnap us? Everyone will be looking for us. Foremost, the police in Malcesine.'

'Forgive me, Ms Monte, but you're wrong again,' van der Venn continued in his outgoing tone of voice. 'Malcesine's finest have their own problems. You see, there was an explosion at their station. Gas, apparently. Three persons were brought to hospital. Sadly, one didn't make it.' He paused and looked at Alessandro.

Nina squeezed his hand. 'Don't let him provoke you.'

'And they say, Mr Pini, that you are dead,' he added with a grin. 'The body is hard to identify but somehow your wallet was found intact.'

Nina was shocked at how calmly he spoke about the atrocities he committed.

'As for you, Ms Monte,' he said, his smile growing wider, 'you've sent an emotional e-mail to your supervisor, asking for three weeks off to visit your sick grandma.'

'Bastard,' she hissed.

'As you can see, the scenario that someone will be looking for you is unlikely.'

'They *will* find out sooner or later,' she said.

Van der Venn shrugged his shoulders. 'I agree. But that gives me enough time.'

Waaberi rejoined them. His forehead was prickled with drops of sweat, and he was panting. 'All good, boss.'

'Excellent. Let's move,' van der Venn ordered. 'We've lost enough time here.'

Klaff took hold of Nina's arm but she shook him off. 'Tell me where you are taking us.'

Van der Venn disconnected the silencer from his gun and started to walk towards the door. 'I've told you already. We're going to see your grandma.'

How did he know so much about her family? And how could he send a fake email from her account?

Then she remembered.

In Milan, those emails marked as read and then straight again as unread … Van der Venn had been hacking her account in that very moment. And the new e-mail domain extension of the Italian Ministry of Culture in Campana's thank-you note. It wasn't new. It was bogus.

'My grandma has nothing to do with it,' she said without conviction in her voice.

He paused and glanced at her. 'Stop this game, Ms Monte. Haven't I proved that I'm always one step ahead?'

'My grandma has nothing to do with this,' she repeated. 'If you fly us to India, you're wasting your time!'

Van der Venn pouted his mouth and stared at her. Slowly, he moved towards Nina. She felt as if with his every step she had less air to breathe.

'Your grandmother is the only person I know of who can decipher the whole text on the tablet, Ms Monte. Your job is to persuade her to do it for me.'

If not for Klaff's skeletal fingers wrapped around her arm, she would have punched van der Venn with her fists and screamed to him, *Leave my family alone!*

'So which is it, Ms Monte? If I'm wrong, you'd better tell me now.'

Tears built up in her eyes. 'Maybe.'

'Maybe, you say. Well, that will have to suffice for now.'

'And then what?' Her voice was not much more than a whisper.

Van der Venn turned his gaze up to the crucified figure of Christ, and spread out his hands. 'Then, dear Ms Monte, I'll be among those who walked into the Kingdom of Heaven, *alive.*'

CHAPTER 29

ALESSANDRO WAS CONVINCED that Lammert van der Venn was a psychopath with an advanced stage of mental illness. Although, didn't the second imply the first? If psychopathy wasn't a serious condition, then what was? Van der Venn was killing people for little or no reason. And he thought that he would go to Heaven. As if it were a space shuttle trip.

Now Alessandro was jammed in a seat on a luxury private jet, and he wore a T-shirt that said "I love Innsbruck" and was two sizes too small—the one that Nina had bought that morning. It was tight, especially under his armpits. Every few minutes he pulled its short sleeves down, but the fabric was elastic, and always came back to its previous size.

When an hour earlier Waaberi had thrown him into this seat, fastened his seat belt, then examined his injured ear in a manner a butcher examined his dead stock, he had uttered no word of protest.

At least after take-off Nina had given him some painkillers she carried in her purse. Then Alessandro cleaned himself in the jet lavatory. The lavatory that made the best bathroom in his hotel look like a public toilet at a train station.

The rest of the jet had a similar design. Wide seats were covered with delicate cream leather. The glossy mahogany table in front of Alessandro, with an oriental lamp that looked like Aladdin's lamp for his genie, could serve four people. A wool carpet with a mosaic pattern covered the floor and a long sofa with embroidered pillows stood by the wall. In the middle of the cabin was a narrow partition with a TV screen taking all its width. It all made for an impression of being in a five-star suite in Dubai.

Alessandro wiped his moist palms against his trousers, forcing his pulse to return to normal. Little by little, it did. But his head throbbed. He closed his eyes, but then the pulsing grew stronger, and he got scared. So he opened them again and was able to relax a bit.

What he couldn't fight back, though, was an inner anger that he wasn't able to take care of himself; he had let others manhandle him against his will. But what could he do? They were stronger. They had weapons. They knew how to use them. They *liked* to use them.

In that church, he had been even more scared than on the yacht when he had almost got shot, because on the lake it might have been accidental—it wasn't him van der Venn was after, but a potential burglar.

A dull sensation in his left ear was reminding him how close he came to ending up in a plastic bag like that poor man who they thought was a Catholic cardinal. What else was a falsification? What had he gotten himself into?

When they had left the Court Church three hours ago, Alessandro had hoped that someone would help them, that someone would notice their situation. How could people go about their life without noticing someone else being kidnapped?

Then he thought that it was impossible to fly away, because to do so he would have to have a passport, and go through a security screening. Lammert van der Venn couldn't have bribed everybody on their path to India.

But all his assumptions had been imaginary.

No one had taken notice of them when they were forced into a black Audi. At the airport, there was no customs, no passport control. They had gone straight to a small airfield, and were pushed on board a jet.

He and Nina were at the mercy of well-organized lunatics.

Alessandro leaned to the left. Behind the partition, Nina was talking to van der Venn about something. It must be about that tablet. He couldn't hear them clearly. Although he could hear Klaff's annoying snoring. He was sleeping in a seat in front of the TV screen; his head was bent at a weird angle, resting on his shoulder. Waaberi was gobbling food beside him. He used only his fingers.

Nina said something to van der Venn. In response, he motioned for her to get back to her seat.

'How do you feel?' Alessandro asked when she sat down next to him.

'I don't know,' she replied through the low humming of the jet engines.

He licked his dry lips. 'What do you think he's going to do with us?'

Her eyes blinked. She looked past Alessandro, behind the window, although the blind was shut. 'Nothing. He needs us.'

'No, Nina. He needs *you*,' he said bitterly. 'I think that the only reason I'm still alive is that he doesn't want to give you another argument to refuse cooperation with him.'

Her eyes welled up. She averted her gaze and sat back.

Alessandro gritted his teeth, realizing he shouldn't have asked such a question if he didn't want to hear the truth.

'I'm sorry,' he said after a moment. 'Do you know what will happen next?'

Nina raised her eyes to the jet's ceiling. 'It's all my fault.'

'What? No.' He turned his body towards her but was afraid to unbuckle. 'We've been kidnapped by a monster, without guilt of our own, without a reason.'

'You don't understand, Alessandro,' she said, speaking through a clenched jaw. She took a deep breath and slowly exhaled, her chest jerking. 'If it weren't for that essay, we wouldn't be here.'

Nina's fingernails were biting into the armrests.

'All I knew about the tablet, I included in my paper, and I called it "Fast Track to God."' She let out a hysterical snicker. 'Which is exactly where we are right now.'

She started to shiver. Alessandro thought that she might have a panic attack. He unfastened his belt, leaned to her, and took her palms into his. Before he spoke he glanced over his shoulder.

Klaff was still asleep. Waaberi was eating. Van der Venn was working on his laptop computer; he had earbuds stuck into his ears.

'Nina, whatever you did, what happens to us is not your fault.'

'You don't understand,' she repeated, shaking her head.

'Then...' Alessandro weighed his words. 'Explain it to me, and maybe we can find a way out somehow.'

She briefly closed her eyes, took a breath, and gave a weak nod.

'Where in India is he taking us? That country is like a continent on its own.'

'Jaipur, the Pink City,' she replied. 'My grandma lives there.'

Alessandro scanned Nina's face for hints of an Indian origin. Was it her olive skin tone? Could be. Her sleek, black hair? That too, perhaps. Her green eyes that, despite their sorrow, didn't lose their hardiness?

'Is your grandma Hindu?'

'My mother was born to an Italian father but his wife, my grandma, Sati, came from India. It's a long family story.'

He squeezed her hand in an encouraging manner. She became calmer. Her jaw didn't tremble; her breath was steady.

'Sati and my granddad fell in love,' she said and smiled, absentminded. 'It was against everybody. My grandma's family comes from a high caste of priests. She was bound to find a husband with a similar background. But when she met my granddad, a handsome explorer from Italy, then an exotic country for her family, she completely lost her mind for him.'

'What did they do?'

She threw him a baffled look. 'What do you think? After the family disinherited Sati, she had no choice. They left and settled in Italy. She couldn't give birth in India.'

'Of course,' Alessandro said, as if it were so obvious, and he apologised for asking.

'Ten months after my mother was born, my granddad died. He had a heart condition. He led a hectic lifestyle. Never stopped travelling.'

'What did your grandma do?'

'My granddad left her enough money, but no friends,

and his family never treated her as their own. She never remarried, so she raised my mother alone.'

Alessandro saw that Klaff had woken up and was now coming towards them. He stopped by their row and ogled them with narrowed eyes. The hair on Alessandro's neck stood up.

'Boo!' Klaff burst into childish giggles, and then he moved on to the back of the plane.

Nina seemed not to notice it. 'My mother's marriage was arranged by Sati. Somehow she had found her an Italian husband who was a Hindu believer. Can you imagine? I have no idea how she did that.' Nina frowned. 'My grandma left everything because she fell in love, but didn't let her own daughter choose. Ironic, isn't it?'

Alessandro left it without a comment.

'My mother's name is Gita. She tells everyone that it's a short form of Giuditta. But Gita is a truly Indian name, and in Sanskrit it means "divine song",' Nina said, accenting each word with a nod. 'My mother never forgave Sati. Then, after my father died, I don't know who she blamed more for her loss, my grandma or God. She rejected Hindu religion; she rejected any religion. She separated me from Grandma and *her* God.'

Nina's eyes welled up again, but she pushed the tears back, pressing her lips together.

'I was eleven when Sati moved to Jaipur for good. She lives there alone.'

'I'm sorry you lost contact with her.'

Nina set her lips into a fragile smile. 'We didn't. She writes to me regularly, every few months. I write back to her. She doesn't like phones. When she was young all the bad news came by phone.'

Nina clasped her palms together and intertwined her fingers. 'My grandma wanted me to be part of her religion. But her letters weren't intrusive, and I liked her stories. At some point I was close to convincing my mother to go and visit. She didn't agree, though.'

Nina's expression brightened in the dim lights of the cabin. 'Over time, I think Mother made her peace with Sati. When I came of age, she didn't mind me going for a visit.'

Klaff passed by them again, leaving behind the smell of soap and sweat.

'Then Sati's letters became more religiously profound. I liked that. After all, they made me who I am today, although not exactly what Sati would want me to be.'

'You teach religions but don't believe in your teachings,' Alessandro heard himself saying. He winced and squeezed his eyes shut for a second. 'I'm sorry, Nina. I was stupid.'

'I'm a scientist exploring ancient cultures and beliefs. What's wrong with that?'

The plane jerked. Then once more. Alessandro cocked his head; the rest of the passengers were doing the same as before, except for Klaff, who now sat leaning to the TV and playing a war game. On the big screen a sniper crawled in the tall grass, and then under a military truck.

Nina continued, 'Then I got a few letters in which Sati told me a story about the sacred tablet stone, something like the ten commandments that the Christian God gave to Moses. I was ecstatic. Not because I believed in that. At that time I was looking for a subject for an important semester paper. This is how my essay came to life. Then van der Venn hijacked it, and you know the rest.'

Alessandro mused for a moment. 'Religious stories aside, it doesn't explain how he found that tablet, and why he's convinced it's a real thing? And why he thinks that your grandma can read it?'

'It *is* real. I had it in my hands. It comes from two thousand five hundred years before Christ, or is even older,' Nina said. 'As for my grandma, she comes from the highly educated social elite. Her family had been making the laws, influencing everyday life in India for twelve generations, often consulting the ancient texts, a part of the Indian heritage that had never been made public, that only the selected members of Sati's family had access to.'

Alessandro sat back and inhaled through his nose. 'This man is obviously well informed and equally mad. Like, completely crazy, only ten times worse.' He turned to her and rubbed his hands together. 'Nina, we will do everything that he says. We go with him, and we meet your grandma. She will do what needs to be done. He will see that his trip to Heaven will have to be put off, and he will lose interest in us.'

At first, it was only a faint sound of someone's chuckling. Then it grew stronger, to a laugh. And before Lammert van der Venn stood in front of them, his laughter had turned into a nauseating guffaw. He threw his head back after another wave of laughter came over him.

Alessandro wished that his windpipe would split open.

Then a rifle shot echoed from the television through the jet cabin. Klaff had found his target.

CHAPTER 30

'EXCELLENT, MR PINI. An excellent plan!' van der Venn said and clapped his hands.

When his outbreak of clowning lessened, Alessandro spoke. 'How did you hear what I said?' There was no anger in his voice; being angry around this man wasn't wise.

Van der Venn pointed with his finger to the panel above their heads. 'I listened to your conversation through a custom-made intercom. But I couldn't help myself any longer. Do you mind?'

He took a seat across from them and put his hands on the table. Alessandro noticed how massive they were, as if he had worked hard for his whole life. What terrible things those bare hands might have done.

'Mr Pini, let's make it clear that I only like the first part of your plan. What was it?' Van der Venn raised his chin and pouted his lips. 'Oh yes: "we will do everything that he says." This is also the most obvious part of your plan. Would you believe I've figured it out myself?'

Alessandro held back the reflex of bursting into the same uncontrolled laughter like van der Venn had before.

'In relation to your other idea, Mr Pini, why are you so sceptical that I'm bound to fail?'

'I'm a grown man,' Alessandro said calmly. 'I don't believe in fairy tales.'

Van der Venn glanced at Nina, seemingly content with her silence. Then he sat back and turned to Alessandro. 'Really? Let's try a little game—a quiz, if you like—and let's call it simply *Alessandro's belief system*. And let's see if it can be shaken a bit.'

Let's, Alessandro thought. And what a ridiculous name that was.

'First question, Mr Pini. By the way, if you need any assistance from our lovely companion, I will venture no veto.' He clapped his hands once, but forcefully.

Alessandro winced when the sound drilled into his injured ear. It felt as if van der Venn had smacked him with an open palm.

'And please don't worry, Mr Pini. It will be easy. At the level of a first-grade student, so even you should know the answers.'

Alessandro sat straighter.

'First question. Do you believe that Jesus Christ is the son of God?'

'Of course He is,' Alessandro replied at once. 'What has that got to do with all of this?'

'Be patient, Mr Pini. Do you believe that Christ could cure an incurable disease?'

'Yes, I *do*.'

'Excellent! Then you also believe that through profound prayer, you can receive everything you ask for.'

Alessandro glanced at Nina. Their eyes met. He knew she was thinking about the same thing. More or less, Alessandro had spoken the same words to her during breakfast in the hotel that morning: "The only way to be closer to God is through deep prayer." Had van der Venn eavesdropped on them in Innsbruck? If so, how?

'Yes, correct,' Alessandro said. 'So what?'

'Excellent!' Van der Venn was about to clap his hands again, but at the last moment he changed his mind and rested them on the table top. 'Let's keep it short. Do you believe that Christ was crucified and three days later your Lord Jesus rose from the dead?'

There was no disdain in van der Venn's voice, but Alessandro didn't like what he was getting at. 'What do you think? I'm a Catholic.'

Van der Venn's expression saddened, as if Alessandro was his guest who declared that he could no longer participate in that splendid trip to India. 'Yet, Mr Pini, you ridicule my right to believe in what I think I can accomplish only because it is through a different kind of prayer.'

'Not prayer. Superstitions. I don't believe in the supernatural.'

Van der Venn opened his eyes wider and leaned over the table. Alessandro had an impression that his eyebrows went up as far as to the middle of his forehead.

'And what do you think every religion is about, Mr Pini, if not the *supernatural*?'

Alessandro gritted his teeth. It wasn't fair. Van der Venn had dragged him into a game with rules he didn't know. Besides, the gunfire coming out of Klaff's game was jarring.

'I strongly suggest you re-evaluate your thinking,' van der Venn went on. 'You reject my right to get what I want, because my prayer is a product of a different and much older religion than yours, the religion that you weren't taught at school, that your father didn't—'

'Leave my father out of it!' Alessandro's heart raced in his chest. 'And what is the purpose of this interrogation?'

Van der Venn studied his face for a moment and then said, 'To prove that you are a hypocrite and intolerant towards other religions, Mr Pini.'

Nina grabbed Alessandro's hand and squeezed it, slipping her fingers between his. 'Don't listen to him. It's not true.'

'Is it not, Mr Pini?'

Alessandro stared at van der Venn's arrogant, self-confident face. That man did not only want him dead. No. He also was trying to humiliate him and ridicule his God.

'What do you contemplate on, Mr Pini? Let me venture a guess.' Van der Venn puckered his lips. 'You think that the man sitting across from you is insane. But this is because you're afraid to accept that behind his insanity lies logic. But you will accept it, Mr Pini. Soon. You will.'

Dozens of words sprang to Alessandro's mind. He couldn't speak up, though, as if all of them wanted to come out at once and lodged in his throat.

Van der Venn rose to his feet. 'Waaberi will bring you dinner. Then I suggest you both get some rest. We have a long day ahead.'

'I need to ask you something,' Nina said.

Van der Venn looked at her as if he wanted to say "finally." He glanced over his shoulder. 'Klaff, turn it off.' Then to Nina, 'Anything, Ms Monte.'

Klaff obeyed and for the moment Alessandro heard only the beating of his own heart.

'How is it that the essay of a twenty-five-year-old student made you believe the tablet existed, let alone that it can give you what I theoretically described?' Nina said.

He was pleased with her question; another of his grins was full of confidence. He plumped back on the seat. 'It wasn't only your paper, Ms Monte. Similar information contained in a letter I intercepted—'

'You mean, stole,' Alessandro said out loud.

Van der Venn scrutinized him. 'Just when I was beginning to tolerate you, Mr Pini. Do you know that if I threw you off the plane there wouldn't be enough of you left to run a DNA test?'

Alessandro released Nina's hand and took a strong hold of the seat armrests.

'What letter?' she said.

'In my world, I leave nothing to chance, Ms Monte. I have a group of trusted people who supply me with the information I'm willing to amply pay for. Especially if it comes from the Vatican Library.'

Van der Venn put one leg over the other and rested his hands on his knee.

'The letter belongs to the pope's Eugene IV collection. It comes from the first half of the fifteenth century. Although the signature was smudged and the paper crumbled, I managed to identify the author.' His voice took on a tone of a campfire storyteller. 'I suppose the name Mauricio de Palma doesn't sound familiar to you, Ms Monte?'

Nina shook her head.

'De Palma seemed to be an important figure in fifteenth-century Europe who preferred to live in the shadow of the pope, though. I've found out about him only thanks to the letter. He travelled as far as the Indian Peninsula. He was a collector of Christian relics, mainly remains of people who were canonized by the Church. He was quite successful in his job, which made him a favourite of Eugene IV.

Although, I'd risk saying that was exclusively thanks to the findings he had made in India, and presented to the pope.'

Van der Venn squinted at Nina. 'Your eyes are shining, Ms Monte. I'm glad to see you intrigued like that.'

'What was in that letter?' Nina asked.

'He wrote that he was on his way back home and carrying an extraordinary treasure for the pope. The return journey was long and dangerous, so he asked Eugene for a blessing and prayer. He succeeded in returning to Venice without a scratch, but it was not due to the pope's prayers.'

'Why are you so sure about that?' Nina cut in.

Van der Venn smiled. 'For a very simple reason, Ms Monte. The pope never saw that letter; it was registered to arrive in the Vatican two hundred years later.'

Nina nodded her head along. Alessandro was annoyed that van der Venn had such an impact on her, that he made her listen to him with such an interest. He added another reason to loathe him.

'I believe,' van der Venn went on, 'that when de Palma brought the tablet to the pope, Eugene IV considered it a gift sent from Heaven to convert infidels in India; after all, it was written in their language. This was, of course, ridiculous because the tablet is much older than Christianity. But let's not judge the pope so harshly; after all, he hadn't at his disposal carbon dating techniques to determine the age of the tablet.'

Van der Venn shifted his gaze to Alessandro. 'Mr Pini, please don't look at me like that.'

'How do you know all of this?' Alessandro asked, to conceal his disgust towards van der Venn.

'Books, Mr Pini. I'm sure that you're familiar with the concept of reading.'

Van der Venn could read all the books in the world, but it wouldn't make him anyone other than a thief and a murderer in Alessandro's eyes.

'I think what happened later,' van der Venn said, 'was that Eugene sent Mauricio, along with the tablet, to join the crew on *Santa Lucia*, because he believed that merely the presence of the tablet would bring victory. So, in 1439, soldiers were dispatched to fight against Milan, which was at war with Eugene's native Venice. Unfortunately for de Palma and the pope, the expedition ended tragically. Battle of Maderno, wasn't it, Ms Monte?'

Nina nodded.

Van der Venn continued. 'The galley sank; the tablet was lost. Shortly afterwards, Eugene himself went out of luck. The Council of Basel suspended him, and he was declared a heretic. They even elected their own antipope.'

Alessandro couldn't help himself and broke in. 'If even the pope wasn't successful with the tablet, and he was a holy person, why do you think you will succeed?'

Van der Venn glanced at him, but when he answered he was looking straight at Nina. 'Because he didn't know what I am about to find out. Am I right, Ms Monte?'

'It doesn't explain how you connected both documents together,' Nina said.

'Mauricio wrote how the stone was beginning to possess him, how he opened his mind to things he couldn't fathom before, and how he deeply believed that it protected him. He was convinced that only the most spiritual person close to God was worthy to have it, and to control it. Naturally, he meant the pope.'

'Not exactly what I wrote in my essay.'

'There's a strong connection.'

'Is there?'

'Yes, Ms Monte. A few peculiar words caught my interest, because it would be extremely rare to find them in the language of that time.'

'What were they? Those words,' Nina asked.

Van der Venn looked at her as if she had asked about the most obvious thing in the world. Then he said, 'Fast track to God.'

CHAPTER 31

THE PLANE'S DESCENT blocked Alessandro's ears, and he woke up. The lights were dimmed and the blinds closed. He moved his jaw sideways and his ears unblocked, but still he could hardly hear the humming of the jet engines. Either van der Venn had the noise level reduced in the cabin or the gunshot in the church had impaired Alessandro's hearing.

He gently touched his injured ear. The scab he felt at the bottom of the concha under the thin layer of bandage didn't hurt; the painkiller they had given him was efficient.

Everyone else in the cabin seemed to be asleep, apart from Klaff, who was nowhere to be seen.

The inside of Alessandro's throat felt dry and cold. He reached over to the table and grabbed a half-full bottle of water. He drained it in two long gulps.

Before they fell asleep, Waaberi had brought him and Nina dinner. It wasn't just airplane food. Van der Venn had a private cook aboard, providing a two-course dinner that consisted of creamy mushroom soup and a roasted rack of lamb served on china plates. They also got a glass of red wine, made from Nerello Mascalese grapes grown in Sicily.

To Alessandro, it felt like the last meal of a person sentenced to death.

Now it occurred to him how far from home he was. His stomach cramped when he thought what his mother must be going through. They had told her that Alessandro was dead. First Gianluigi. Now her own son.

How stupid he was not to call her from Innsbruck. What kind of son was he? He'd had plenty of time in the hotel to do so, and he wasted it lamenting over himself. Now, even if he could, he probably wouldn't want to talk to her. He might be dead very soon, and for real.

He rubbed his eyes. Better not to think about it. He looked at his watch. Twenty-eight minutes past two o'clock in the morning. He opened the blinds by his seat. A glowing red sun slipped into the cabin. He grimaced and covered his eyes. Then he opened them again and peered out. The sun was low—an early morning as it seemed.

It was the fifth time in his life he had seen the sun rising. Pristine and natural, it looked, but also cruel and distant, now that his free will had been taken away.

What was the time in India anyway? Four, five hours ahead of Italy?

He squinted out the window. The plane was low, too. No more than four hundred metres. He saw vast fields of green below, scattered households, a narrow streak of asphalt not that far ahead.

Nina sat in her seat with her eyes closed. She wasn't asleep; the muscles in her face were tensed. Should he say something to her? "Welcome to India" sounded pathetic, but a simple "good morning" should do. He looked up and abandoned the idea. He didn't want van der Venn to hear a single private word he spoke to Nina.

Instead, Alessandro took her hand. He liked the delicate feel of her skin.

197

'Did you sleep?' she said.

He wanted to answer, but Klaff was already with them, ignoring the fact that they were about to land.

'Be prepared,' he said in a demanding tone of voice.

'Prepared for what?' Alessandro said.

Klaff leaned over and poked his skeletal finger into Alessandro's chest. 'Lammert almost shot you twice. Consider yourself out of luck now.'

Then he turned to Nina. 'You say one wrong word, and you'll be watching me cutting your friend into pieces. I will start with this,' he said, and pulled on Alessandro's ear.

Alessandro squealed in a thunderbolt of pain.

Klaff laughed and patted him on the shoulder. 'You see, out of luck. And don't even think there's anyone out there who cares for you. People in India have their own problems.'

Alessandro clenched his fist and watched Klaff swaggering back to his seat.

The jet touched the tarmac of Jaipur Airport in a smooth way three minutes later.

'Was he serious?' Alessandro asked Nina. 'That we can't count on anyone to help us?'

She leaned her head back. 'I think he is serious about everything.'

The machine slowed down and whined. Then the tenor of the engines turned to a purr.

After a kilometre or so, the pilot took a left turn. Ahead, Alessandro saw a huge complex of buildings and dozens of airplanes parked all over the tarmac. Main terminal, he thought.

But they weren't heading in that direction. The pilot continued straight.

Alessandro touched his ear. It was bleeding again, and hurt. But it was bearable when compared to the helplessness that filled up his chest.

CHAPTER 32

'WELCOME TO INDIA,' Klaff said with scorn to Nina and Alessandro when the pilot switched off the engines. 'And remember what I told you before.'

Waaberi unlatched the door.

Nina leaned over and slipped her credit card and money into the lower side pocket of Alessandro's combat shorts, whispering into his ear, 'Everything will be all right. Don't—'

'Up!' Klaff grabbed her arm and pulled her out of the seat. Alessandro got up willingly, checking his side pocket.

'Leave your handbag on the plane!' Klaff ordered. 'You won't need it.'

Before van der Venn disembarked the jet, he glanced over his shoulder. If he looked at her, or at Alessandro, she couldn't say. His eyes were hidden behind fully mirrored sunglasses. He had different clothes on: creamy linen slacks and a white, half-unbuttoned shirt.

On the steps, Nina felt a sultry wave of air on her face, and a pleasant touch of morning sunrays. The temperatures were in the middle twenties. It was quiet.

The jet parked near a modern hangar, a construction with a semi-circular roof painted in orange or red; in the low sun it took on a ginger tone. The front wall of the hangar was wide open. The whole construction was big enough to accommodate five or more similar aircraft like the one van der Venn owned.

An airport security car stood by the right side of the entrance. Two people in pale green uniforms were leaning on its bonnet, lost in conversation. A small truck, with the red sign of Shell on its cylindrical tank, was parked not far away. On the other side of the entrance, a driver in a baggage car waited for a signal to approach van der Venn's jet and unload the luggage.

Nina jumped on the tarmac, followed by Klaff, who carried a backpack similar to those she saw on professionals cycling to their offices in Italy. Waaberi pushed Alessandro. He stumbled but didn't fall.

'Move, you two!' Waaberi said. 'And be quiet.'

The hangar looked bigger from the inside. It was windowless but brightly lit, like a giant sterile laboratory. A private jet, longer than van der Venn's aircraft, with a Chinese flag painted on its tail was parked nearby. People dressed in overalls bustled around it.

An oval chrome clock that hung high on the wall showed thirteen minutes past six o'clock.

Van der Venn headed towards two customs officers clad in vanilla-coloured uniforms. His stride was confident as if he were meeting his employees. He carried one briefcase. *The* briefcase.

They gave him a nod in greeting and asked for passports.

Klaff crossed to them, produced a batch of documents out of the backpack and handed them over. Then he stood beside van der Venn.

Nina's pulse sped up. She exchanged looks with Alessandro. Van der Venn had never asked for her passport. Had he searched her apartment? Waaberi put his hands on Nina's and Alessandro's shoulders; it had nothing to do with a friendly gesture.

A chubby Indian officer with a thick moustache and a high forehead scanned the documents. His eyes wandered from the passports to the faces of the newcomers. He puckered his mouth, which lifted his black moustache up and covered his nostrils.

Then he passed the documents to his colleague, who was younger and taller, or just stood straighter—compared to van der Venn, they both were short. The second man mirrored the procedure of checking the passports.

'Those two,' the taller officer said, pointing at Nina and Alessandro. 'Not the same pictures on the passports.'

Nina exhaled and glanced at Alessandro. He was tense, stifling his emotion. Was it hope he masked?

Waaberi's hand weighed her arm down.

Klaff threw a red bundle of banknotes to the chubby officer. The man caught them like a tennis ball. He focused his gaze on van der Venn, weighing them in his hand, then he shoved it into the pocket of his uniform.

'But it shouldn't be a problem, Mr...' the taller officer said and read from the passport, 'van der Venn.'

Nina felt like a lottery winner on April Fools' Day. After an initial joy, disappointment came along, fast.

'We clear?' Klaff said.

The chubby officer pointed at van der Venn's briefcase and Klaff's backpack. 'We need to x-ray those.'

'Diplomatic content,' van der Venn replied blankly.

The officer's moustache went up again. 'I see no stamps.'

'I carry them separately,' was van der Venn's answer.

The officer scratched the back of his head and looked behind.

An x-ray machine stood deeper in the hangar, half obscured by a maintenance car, whose crew was working on the Chinese jet. A third officer, who was eating breakfast while sitting on the x-ray scanner conveyor belt, shrugged his shoulders.

Waaberi crossed over to him, leaving Alessandro and Nina unattended. His heavy boots thumped against the hangar's concrete floor. He grabbed the third officer's plastic plate, and—not even so much as glancing at the food—devoured its contents with his fingers.

Three seconds later he froze, unable to swallow. His eyes bulged. He pushed his neck back and his head forward, punched his chest with his fist two times, then gulped with an effort.

A long and loud burp echoed in the hangar and bounced outside through the open wall. The three officers, people working by the Chinese jet, including someone peering through the window from that jet, and even van der Venn, were all staring at Waaberi.

He enjoyed his momentary popularity. He patted his stomach and made circular moves on it with his palm. After that he put the empty plate on the conveyor belt and said, 'Scan *this*.'

The officer by the x-ray scanner made no move; he stared at Waaberi with a questioning look. The rhythmic ticking of the clock on the wall made the sole sound in that bizarre standoff.

Finally, van der Venn nodded to Klaff. Another batch flew out of his backpack.

It hit the stout officer on his chest and bounced, but he caught it on his belly. Without fluster, he put the money into his pocket. 'Thank you, Mr van der Venn. The car you ordered is waiting outside. The key is in the ignition slot. Enjoy your stay in Jaipur.'

Van der Venn headed towards the exit, and the rest followed him; first Klaff, then Nina with Alessandro, and Waaberi at the end.

'We've been—' Alessandro shouted, but that was all he was able to get out.

Waaberi's long arm clutched his throat, cutting off his cry. He pulled Alessandro to him and started to poke his fingers into his ribs and rubbed Alessandro's skull, like old pals messing around.

When they left the hangar, van der Venn said, 'Mr Pini, the next word coming out of your mouth will be your last one.'

Alessandro dropped his head and massaged his neck with one free hand.

A shiny, silver Toyota Crossover with tinted windows was parked just outside the hangar. Five similar luxury cars stood nearby. Nina needed no better proof that this airport catered to the super-rich only.

Klaff jumped behind the wheel, van der Venn next to him. Waaberi intended to manhandle Alessandro, but he was quicker, and scrambled onto the rear seat before Waaberi was able to touch him. Waaberi let out a disappointed grunt and got in, pulling Nina along.

'It's not advisable for Europeans to drive in this country,' Nina said. 'And not only because of the left-hand traffic.'

Klaff threw the backpack under van der Venn's feet and started the engine. 'Who told you I was from Europe?'

He manoeuvred the Toyota out of the carpark. Soon they had left the airport zone behind.

Nina looked out the window. Bare earth with scarce patches of green here and there made up the landscape on both sides of the asphalt. Some buildings were scattered in the distance. The hazy air offered poor visibility although the terrain around was flat.

It was her third visit to Jaipur, but her heart didn't beat faster at the thought of seeing Sati. Not in that longing way she had once felt.

Klaff took a turn, and the car pulled onto a three-lane road where they travelled faster, but not by much. Maybe 70 kph, as the road was too congested.

The traffic consisted of two worlds. First was of a continuous flow of vehicles like trucks, cars, air-conditioned minibuses, and those in which all the windows were open; overcrowded buses, motorcycles carrying two or three passengers, tuk-tuks. People rode their bicycles on the road's shoulder; others pushed two-wheeled, loaded carts.

The second world was that of a ceaseless scream of horns, and that world could never be switched off by closing the eyes. The noise penetrated the closed car doors with ease. It was like an orchestra whose members played the same instruments but in different tones, and without hearing each other.

It was an essential part of life in India.

The sun climbed higher in the cloudless sky, but Nina shivered. The air conditioner in the car was set on maximum. She moved her body closer to the door; she didn't want to ask Klaff for anything. Sunrays pleasantly warmed the skin of her forearms.

Nina thought about her blazer. She had left it on her seat in the jet to cover a note she had scribbled on a napkin: "My name is Nina Monte. I've been kidnapped. Please help!" If it was to test the loyalty of van der Venn's crew, she had no hope for their intervention. But maybe the airport staff would find it when cleaning the plane, like that Chinese jet.

CHAPTER 33

EVERYONE WAS SILENT in the car. After all, it was the middle of the night in Europe, Nina thought; they had to be tired. The exception was the whining of Waaberi's stomach. It resembled the sound given by air escaping from a punctured squeaky toy after a person sat on it.

Nina wished she could disappear. She wished to erase from her memory the last few days, relax in some beautiful place, which India had an abundance of, with a cup of sweet, milky coffee in her hand.

'Where do we go?' Van der Venn's voice broke her fantasy.

Was he talking to her? He wasn't looking at her. Besides, it was an odd question. Unless … he hadn't known everything, and his talk that he was always two steps ahead of her was just bragging. In that instant she suddenly felt superior to Lammert van der Venn.

She shifted her head to the window and pretended to be engrossed in the view.

'Ms—'

Klaff yanked the steering wheel and cursed when a truck full of crates with empty bottles overtook them from the right with a series of angry horns, turning the driver's-side mirror into shreds. The three seconds Waaberi's body was pressed on Nina's shoulder made her feel like she was being squashed by a tree trunk.

At the back of that truck Nina saw a big sign that read *Horn Please*. Klaff must have seen that too—he jammed the heel of his palm on the Toyota's horn. Nina covered her ears.

She shouted, 'I've told you it isn't advisable—'

'Ms Monte, where do we go?' van der Venn turned back and looked at her.

Klaff's nerves were jarred. He banged on the steering wheel. A dirty yellow sedan came from the right. Its driver pointed at the cables where the mirror had been a moment ago. He screamed something to Klaff and smiled broadly. Klaff reached for the backpack, but van der Venn didn't let him take it.

'For the last time, Ms Monte. Where?'

'You're an art dealer,' Nina said. 'Shouldn't you possess at least one crystal ball? It comes in handy in moments like now.' She held her breath.

Waaberi retched and burped, holding his irritated stomach.

'I think I ate too much, boss,' he muttered.

'You haven't stopped eating since yesterday, you moron!' Klaff said through clenched teeth.

Waaberi burped again. 'I think it was that thing at the airport.'

His face took on a yellow pallor.

'Can we stop, boss?' he whined.

'Can you see any place we could stop now?' Klaff talked back to him.

Waaberi's stomach let out a series of howls, and Nina suspected that some of them went out from the other end. In less than two seconds, she knew she was right. She turned her head away to the window.

Klaff slammed his palm on the dashboard. 'You disgusting pig!' Then he opened all the windows in the car.

Traffic uproar, stuffy and polluted air rushed into the car. The warm wind battered her face.

'We have a long way ahead,' she said through the noise. 'We won't be able to stop for another two hours.'

'Don't listen to her,' van der Venn said.

Waaberi's face resembled an expression of a puppy that had pissed on a new carpet and was baffled why everyone around was agitated about it.

'It must be something you took from that customs clerk at the airport,' Nina said. 'I didn't want to mention this before, but…'

Terror grew on Waaberi's yellowish face. 'What?'

Nina waved her hand. 'It's probably nothing. Forget about it.'

He nodded.

She felt sorry for him. But not very. 'Indian food can be disastrous for a stomach,' Nina added. 'Was that thing you ate hot?'

He shook his head. 'No, it was cold. It tasted weird, and very spicy. I've never eaten anything like that before.'

Nina raised her eyebrows and pouted her lips. 'Hmm…'

Waaberi belched. 'What?'

'Don't *listen* to her,' van der Venn said again, and threw Nina an impatient gaze.

'Yes, don't listen to me,' she said. 'You'll be okay, no worries.'

'Really?'

'Yes. In two days the vomiting and diarrhoea will ease out.' She turned her head to the window. 'Actually, I've become pretty hungry myself. I'd love to have a *fat* chicken masala in a *thick* and *spicy* curry sauce.'

Alessandro let out a short chuckle.

Waaberi grabbed Klaff on the shoulder. 'Stop the car, Sander!'

Klaff cringed under Waaberi's clutch. The car skidded to the right and went out of control. A series of sharp horns invaded through the open windows. Van der Venn caught the wheel and turned it straight.

Waaberi threw himself towards the door. Before he reached the handle, his stomach crashed into Alessandro's knee. He belched loudly. A brownish substance spilled out of his mouth and between Alessandro's feet, who winced and raised his legs, trying to push Waaberi away.

'You filthy pig!' Klaff screamed.

'Pull over!' van der Venn said.

Klaff whacked the horn, changed lanes, yanked on the steering wheel, and when the Toyota swung off the road, he slammed on the brakes. Waaberi opened the door, shoved Alessandro out of his way, throwing him outside like a shopping bag, and sprang out of the car. He trampled on Alessandro's chest. Then his torso jerked and he started vomiting.

Nina jumped out after them, and the sounds of the asphalt jungle assaulted all her senses.

Alessandro, still down, rolled to the side, holding onto his chest, gasping for air. She grabbed his hand, helped him to his feet and pulled him in the direction they had travelled from.

Behind her back, van der Venn yelled, 'Klaff, get them!'

They sprinted away from the car. Nina could almost feel Klaff's breath on her back.

'We have to stop someone over there!' she screamed to Alessandro, pointing through the frantic traffic to the other road that ran parallel.

She spotted a gap between the speeding cars in the first lane, gripped Alessandro's hand and pulled him onto the road. They made it to the middle, but had to move back two steps to let a speeding bus pass by. They rushed as far forwards as half of the third lane, when a lorry left a mighty, hot blast of air on their backs, which nearly pulled them down to the ground. Nina heard a dull whack, followed by the screech of brakes.

From the corner of her eye, she saw Klaff's airborne body landing on the asphalt, next to the Toyota he had been driving before. Other cars around them started to brake. Sounds of collisions spread around.

Alessandro wrapped his arm around Nina's waist and pulled her across the last lane. They came to a halt on the narrow strip of dried grass.

Traffic on the other side slowed down. Drivers poked their heads out to see what had happened. A man behind the wheel of a white-and-green cab stopped, and Nina thought it was their best chance, until one second later a lorry jammed into its tail. The cab bounced forward, then another car going on the second lane thrust into its side. More cars rammed into those in front, blocking the traffic.

Nina pulled Alessandro to the yellow three-wheeled taxi that had stopped ten metres ahead of the smashed cab.

'Take us out of here!' Nina jumped in and plumped on the seat, followed by Alessandro.

The tuk-tuk swayed under their weight. The adolescent driver looked at them, astonished. He started to speak, but Nina put her hands into Alessandro's pocket, drew a twenty-euro note and handed it over. He grinned, mounted his saddle, the engine whined and they were on their way.

Nina yielded to the temptation and raised herself on the edge of the tuk-tuk. She glanced back. Among crashed cars, screaming drivers, and horns, Lammert van der Venn, surrounded by a small crowd, stood on the roof of the silver Toyota.

Hands tried to catch him and pull him down. He drew his gun and fired twice in the air. People screamed and scampered away. Nina hid back inside of the tuk-tuk. Her heart pounded in her chest. Her legs felt wobbly. She wouldn't be able to run anymore, but she knew it wasn't over yet.

She recalled van der Venn's words when she had escaped from him in Malcesine: "Do you really think that you can take the hunter's trophy and disappear?"

Even though Nina had left the tablet behind, she knew she had already become part of van der Venn's catch. And he would never stop hunting her.

CHAPTER 34

'GO TO THE police!' Alessandro shouted to the driver in English. 'Police! Do you know police?'

'No!' Nina said, holding the railings of the tuk-tuk tightly. 'What for?'

The petite Hindu driver, no older than seventeen, kept the taxi at a steady pace. He was glancing at them over his right or left shoulder, depending on who was speaking, squinting his eyes against the wind and the sun.

Alessandro gaped at Nina, stunned. 'Did you say *what for*? I must have heard wrong.'

Travelling in an open vehicle in the uproar of the horns, whirr of the tuk-tuk and cars' engines and more powerful trucks' engines, combined with exhaust gases, was as tangible as it could get.

'First, I have to see Sati,' Nina said louder, but not angrily, just to be heard.

'Your grandma? Why?'

'Sati, Sati!' the driver repeated. His short-sleeve striped shirt fluttered in the wind.

Other vehicles drove much faster, overtaking the tuk-tuk with a blaring of their horns. The driver took no notice of them. He kept his eyes on the road.

Nina pushed the hair from her face. 'Alessandro, has the sudden taste of freedom made you the most selfish person?'

He pulled his eyebrows together in confusion.

'We have to warn Sati,' Nina explained. 'I don't think van der Venn knows where she lives, but he's a resourceful man.'

'But this is exactly why we should involve the police,' Alessandro said quickly. 'They will take care of her, and arrest that psycho.'

'And tell them what? "Officers, bad men are in pursuit of an eighty-six-year-old woman. You must save her," ' Nina said, mimicking his voice. ' "You ask us *why*, officers? What do you mean why? Because they have a holy stone, and she knows how to use it and make them walk into Heaven. *Please,* officers, this is true. We swear!" '

Nina took a deeper breath, instantly regretting it as the dry, heavy air assaulted her throat. She coughed, swallowed, and went on, 'I can picture a whole bunch of policemen in stitches while we're presenting them the story of their lives, and then throwing us into jail, to protect us from ourselves.'

'Cut it out!' Alessandro said with narrowed eyes. 'Then let's go to our embassy!'

'We are here illegally. Without passports. Don't forget about that, too. They would have to inform the Indian authorities. Who knows when they would finally believe us, if ever?'

Alessandro gritted his teeth, looked away for a moment, then said, 'At least, I want to call my mother. I thought that it wasn't a good idea when they held us, but now we're free.'

Nina moved closer to him. 'You won't like what I have to say about that, either.'

'Just say it!'

'Okay. What would you tell your mother, Alessandro?'

'That I'm alive!' He raised his voice. 'Is it that complicated?'

'But she is convinced that you're dead,' she said in a gentle voice. 'How do you think she will react, when you call and tell her that you're not lying in a mortuary in Malcesine? But you've been kidnapped and flown on a private jet to India and, incidentally, the man who killed Gianluigi is chasing you.'

He closed his eyes and lowered his head.

'I'm sorry, Alessandro, but this is not something you should do over the phone. Not yet.'

He glanced up at her. She saw surrender in his eyes. 'Then what do you propose?'

Nina spoke to the driver in fluent Hindi.

That, he didn't expect. He jerked his head back to her, pulling the steering bar to the left. One of the rear tuk-tuk wheels lost touch with the road and the vehicle swung to the right.

Nina screamed. The driver screamed. Horns howled around.

Alessandro crashed his left shoulder into the aluminium frame of the tuk-tuk. It bounced back on its three wheels.

'Are you all right?' he asked Nina, concerned.

'I think so,' she said, her heart pounding. She was glad she had emptied her bladder before the jet landed in Jaipur.

Their driver raised his hand in a *thanks* and *sorry* gesture and turned the throttle up.

'Professor, are you sure you had a competent Hindi teacher?' Alessandro said.

'Good to hear you got back some of your humour,' Nina answered, trying to slow down her racing pulse.

Alessandro wrapped his arm around her waist and pulled her closer. She was used to it already, to his familiar gesture of tenderness. She sighed and slowly rested her head on his shoulder, letting herself drift into oblivion. Just for a little while.

CHAPTER 35

HALF AN HOUR later, the tuk-tuk drove into a densely populated district. Although the air wasn't as heavy as on the highway, and the temperature rose significantly, and the noise of the metropolis was louder, Alessandro was almost unaware of the deafening horns. His eyes were aghast. He kept turning his head from side to side, unable to decide what was more interesting or bizarre.

Old motorbikes and cars, and identical three-wheeled taxis, whose drivers had their hands glued to the horns, were moving at a sluggish pace, dominating a jam-packed two-lane street.

Other people rode their bicycles, oblivious to motorists' relentless stream of klaxons hurrying them up. Small carts were attached to those bicycles, loaded far beyond their capacity with pipes, carpets, mattresses, cardboard boxes, sacks with vegetables or fruit, and screaming chickens in cages.

His eyes grew wide when he saw a passenger on a Yamaha motorcycle holding a large windowpane in front of him. Alessandro had never imagined that a place so much different from his hometown existed.

Residential, red-brick buildings were closely erected along the street one by one. Most of them had air-conditioning units mounted to the outside walls.

A sleek silhouette of a brand new black Jaguar was half-parked on the street, half on the roadside. It looked like a spaceship that had landed in the arena of the Roman Colosseum. It delayed the traffic, but that didn't bother Indian drivers who passed it by, careful not to scratch the luxury car.

Pedestrians occupied a crammed, narrow sidewalk, carrying merchandise like those on the bikes. In whatever direction Alessandro turned his gaze, someone was hurrying away as fast as the traffic allowed.

The same was happening on the opposite street, separated from the one they travelled along by a two-metre-wide strip of sidewalk. In the middle of it ran a fence-like barricade.

Their tuk-tuk pushed its way farther and farther down the road that seemed to have no end.

When they reached the junction and waited to cross the road, Alessandro felt like they were a band of ants trying to cut across a torrent.

After a few minutes, their driver negotiated his way across the road, running the red light amid a rain of horns. Alessandro drew his breath when he noticed that the traffic coming on them didn't seem to ease. His fingers were white on the tuk-tuk's handle. He rose from the seat and mouthed, *what the hell?*

Other cars and bikes followed their tuk-tuk.

'What's the point of having traffic lights?' he said through the noise.

'There's one rule on the road in India,' Nina answered. 'Drive the way you like, but you must *not* hurt anybody.'

The driver must have sensed nervousness in their voices, as he turned back briefly to say in heavily accented English, 'Ankit good driving. Don't worry, sir.'

'Very good, Ankit!' Alessandro shouted back.

Then he took a turn into an alley, sheltering what were mostly ground-floor, crumbling houses, and a local market. He slowed down to a walking speed in order not to hit pedestrians.

***

It was much quieter there. Just a steady buzz of voices coming from stalls packed with clothes, plastic beads, toys, vegetables, ready-to-go food. Among the variety, Nina's eyes were drawn to tables covered with the cone-shaped colourful powder Hindu people used to dye fabrics, clothes, paint their bodies or to throw at each other during festivities. They were so vibrant and vivid, dashing and divergent, like the whole Indian Peninsula.

'Don't you feel a bit like a tourist?' she said to Alessandro to lighten the tension.

'I would, if not for the three sadistic individuals on our tail.'

Nina pictured Klaff's body sprawled on the street. 'Two.'

'Do you think Waaberi is really down with food poisoning?'

Nina frowned. 'Didn't you see that Klaff was hit by a truck? He was just behind us.'

Alessandro opened his mouth and stared at her for a moment. 'There were many crashes. I didn't look back. I wanted to get out of there as quickly as possible.'

Then his face became grave. 'Is Klaff dead?'

'If not that, he must be seriously injured.'

'So if Waaberi is not at his best, there's only van der Venn who will be chasing us.'

Was it relief in Alessandro's voice that Nina heard? She shrugged her shoulders. 'I guess so.'

'Miss, miss,' Ankit shouted, pointing his finger ahead.

Nina recognized the small house that stood alone at the end of the lane. It looked different from the other buildings around. It was compact and solid. Its walls were painted green, and it was built from solid bricks. Its windows and doors were wide open. They always were; Sati never shunned people. An elderly man was sitting on a bench that stood below the window.

Ankit sped up, shoving disoriented people aside with his horn and his shouting.

Nina felt a twitching sensation in her throat. She counted the years that had passed since her last visit. Seven. Was she correct? A whole seven years since she had seen her grandma. How was that possible? Was she that preoccupied with her work that the letters she exchanged with Sati gave her enough satisfaction?

Immense shame overcame her. She was afraid of what Sati looked like. Had she aged a lot? What would she say, after Nina told her the reason of this visit?

'Nina?' Alessandro put his hand on her arm.

They were by the house.

'Can you wait for us a few minutes? I'll get you something extra. Okay?' she said to Ankit, but his expression made her realize that she had spoken in Italian; the only language she spoke within her thoughts.

She repeated the same in Hindi. Ankit brightened up and waved to her reassuringly. 'Okay, okay, okay.'

Nina jumped off the tuk-tuk, followed by Alessandro. They stopped by the open door. She glanced at the white-haired man on the bench. He had age spots on his face and hands. The skin on his cheekbones was sagging. His eyes were half closed; he rested his palms, one on another, on his lap.

Nina took off her shoes, motioned to Alessandro, and he did the same. She crossed the threshold, and her feet touched a soft, colourful carpet. She inhaled the familiar scent of herbs, resins, and masala blends. A pleasant swirl in her nostrils travelled up to her head and made her feel like she was at home after a long, exhausting journey.

Soft meditation music was flowing from speakers placed on the floor. Printed indigo curtains hung on the window, letting only a few sunrays find their way into a five-square-metre room. Smoke from the incense sticks, which were set on the small shrine by the wall, danced between those rays dramatically, teasing them, challenging them to catch it.

Next to the smoking incense, dried yellow petals on a string lay around a small statue of the four-arm Vishnu god. Shy flames of two candles stood guard beside it, adding more light to the room.

Nina looked around, uneasy. 'Grandma? Hello?'

'Is it okay if I come in?' Alessandro asked from beyond the threshold.

'Yes,' she whispered. Then she turned back to the altar. 'Grandma? It's me.'

She walked by the shrine and entered the bedroom. It was modestly furnished with a single bed, a small nightstand, a chair and a wardrobe. Her gaze wandered to a framed picture on the nightstand, but then she shifted her head back to the bed.

To a half-folded Indian shirt. A man's shirt. Grandma had remarried and didn't tell her about it? Nina felt a tingling in her chest, as if she were intruding into Sati's life without permission. Maybe they weren't as close as Nina had believed.

She picked up the picture from the nightstand. Her grandma was sitting on the bench, in front of this very house. Serenity emanated from her wrinkled, wise face.

Nina crossed to the adjoining kitchen, which consisted of a fridge, cooker, and a single sink. And a table with one chair. She neared her palm to the kettle standing on the two-hob gas cooker. It was warm.

Her stomach tightened when the obvious thought pushed its way into her head. She knew what was missing, and that Sati no longer lived here.

There were no flowers in the house. Those wild roses Sati loved so much that used to bloom in every room in their Italian home. After she had moved over to India, her affection for them had never ceased.

'I know you.'

A male voice startled Nina from behind. She turned around. The man from the bench spoke to her in Hindi. He was hunching, and because of that his body frame appeared more brittle. A fragile smile crossed his mouth.

'I know you,' he repeated.

Alessandro poked his head into the kitchen. 'Is everything okay?'

Nina stood motionless. 'I don't know.'

The man reached underneath his shirt and withdrew a photograph, then extended his hand. 'Young lady, Nina.'

He pronounced her name with an impeccable Italian accent, which astonished and scared her. She took the print from him. It was an old picture of her and Sati, taken on this street when she had visited her grandma in Jaipur for the first time, twenty years ago. Nina was smiling and tightly embracing her grandma; they stood cheek to cheek. It was Sati's favourite picture of Nina.

The man pointed at the photograph, then at himself. 'Sati gave it to Raghu.'

Nina crossed her arms over her stomach and raised her moist eyes to him. 'Raghu, where is Sati?' she asked in a quiet, cracking voice.

Alessandro cleared his throat. 'I'll be outside if you need me.'

Chapter 36

VAN DER VENN whacked the Toyota's steering wheel, not taking his foot from the accelerator, and slammed the horn. If only that could help him drive faster and farther from the accident. He had no intention of explaining anything to the Indian police.

Before he had left Klaff's body behind and driven off, he had looked into his eye sockets, and saw the whites only—the impact had twisted Klaff's pupils to the back of his head. His legs were contorted underneath his torso; he had looked like a dummy after a failed test of a new car's brakes. Van der Venn had emptied the man's pockets, then dragged Waaberi to the back seat of the car.

Those stupid Hindus were yelling something at them. If he hadn't reached for his gun, they would have torn him to pieces. A few of them had fiddled with their phones.

Van der Venn turned his head to Waaberi. 'How are you feeling?'

Mumbling.

'For once, why don't you cut down on your habit to eat everything you can get your hands on?'

'Sorry, boss,' Waaberi said, and then the sound of puking hit van der Venn's ears like icy water thrown on a burning electric hob.

Van der Venn glanced down at the car mat between his legs. It was clean. Although when he lowered his head, the stench of sick invaded his nostrils, and the air in the car took on a pungent, nauseating odour. He turned off the air-conditioning and pushed the controls by the steering wheel. All four windows slid down.

Dense and heavy air swarmed inside along with the roar of the road, but a headache was a small price compared to the reek of stomach discharge.

Waaberi spat, cleaned his mouth on his navy shirt, then lifted his body and threw his arms around the front seat. His head hung over the headrest. He breathed heavily, staring at the road ahead with glossy, beaten eyes.

A silver BMW 1 Series pulled up in front of them. Van der Venn slammed on the brakes and pressed the horn. The driver took out his hand, waved, and sped farther away in the inner lane. Waaberi threw up while his head was still over the seat. Van der Venn glanced at the gun lying next to him on the passenger seat. It was now coated in green-brown puke; some had landed on the dashboard.

He stretched his fingers on the wheel, shut his eyes and thrust the gas pedal to the floor.

'Boss? Boss. Boss!'

He looked up. The front of his Toyota was half a metre from the back of a twenty-ton Tata truck with the big text *Great India* on its tail. He let off of the accelerator and touched down on the brakes for a millisecond.

Being foolish wasn't his style. First think, then act. Not so easy today. He wondered what in that entire situation had ruined his composure.

He ruled out the hectic traffic on Indian roads. It was irrelevant.

Did he miss Klaff? The idiot who allowed himself to be run over by a ramshackle lorry? Klaff had worked for him for the last seven years. Van der Venn had taken him more to destabilize the activity of his competitors in the Caribbean rather than anything else. Fortunately for Klaff, he turned out to be a good assistant.

No, he did not miss him. That wasn't it.

He thought about Alessandro Pini. It was only a passing thing, like wondering what would the weather be like the next day. Not even that. The weather had more significance for him than a schmuck from an Italian dump. He was a small inconvenience, easily written off when required.

He thought about Nina Monte. He should have planned things more carefully. He had found the stone tablet that he had hunted for the last three years. In Malcesine, she had taken it from him; she had taken it too easily. Then he had tracked her down and she escaped again. Too easily. Nina Monte was the root of his distraction. Nina Monte was resilient in a way he hadn't predicted.

That Italian professor had made a fool of him. She had shaken his self-respect too many times.

He put his head out the window and inhaled through his nose. Then he tightened his grip on the wheel and looked in the rear-view mirror. Waaberi sat sprawled in the middle of the seat. His shirt was unbuttoned, his head leaned back. His face was covered in sweat.

Yes, he was right; he didn't miss Sander Klaff. And he wouldn't miss Waaberi if he crapped himself to death. Nina Monte was free because of their indiscipline.

Jaipur loomed on the horizon, but the traffic became more congested, and he had to slow down to 30 kilometres per hour.

He had to answer himself: what was Monte's next step? Because this was where he would be heading too.

He smiled. He knew where. That was his contingency plan in case the game with Ms Monte didn't work out.

Van der Venn recollected the acknowledgments section at the end of her essay "Fast Track to God", and the first person on the list. Sati Joshi of the Vijay Nagar area in Jaipur. Ms Monte's grandmother. The reason for all of his hopes.

He could get anything from Nina Monte if only he was certain she had a thorough knowledge of the tablet. He decided that she hadn't.

On the other hand, it would be futile to put a gun to Sati's head and kindly ask her to read the message on the stone tablet. Old people cared little about their own lives. Her granddaughter was the key to unveiling the mouth of an old woman.

He needed them both.

He should have acted up front with Nina Monte. His strategy to gain her trust proved to be faulty from the beginning. After what had happened on the yacht, in the church, and everything that followed, she would not collaborate, nor would she willingly ask her grandmother to cooperate.

'Boss…' Waaberi moaned.

Van der Venn looked in the rear-view mirror. Waaberi's long body was spread out across the whole length of the seat. His Adam's apple bobbed up and down.

'How are you keeping?'

'I'm … I'm thirsty,' Waaberi stammered out. 'And I will need a toilet. Soon.'

Van der Venn craned his neck to see if there were some road signs. He couldn't catch sight of anything through the string of cars ahead.

After three kilometres, they reached the suburbs of the city and he pulled over by a roadside restaurant, a secluded one-floor building with walls painted in red and a terrace on its roof protected by a white balustrade.

It wasn't a place where tourist coaches dared to stop. It could fit in roughly twenty people. Half of the plastic red tables and chairs, some of them cracked, were sitting in the sun, covered with a thin film of dust from the road. The other half were under the roof. None of the tables were taken. The menu board on the wall was in Hindi.

He got out of the car and crossed to the stall with snacks. Waaberi lumbered after him. The sales clerk was sitting on a stool in the shadow of an umbrella and kept reading an Indian tabloid.

Van der Venn picked two packs of potato chips that looked like European Lay's, which were hanging on a cord like drying laundry. Then he grabbed two bottles of water from a glass-door fridge. He turned around and threw one bottle to Waaberi, who opened it at once and poured half a litre into his throat.

When he was paying, he noticed three men from the nearby rickshaw parking peering into the Toyota. They stuck their heads inside through the open windows.

Then one by one, as if slapped, jerked their heads out, lamenting in Hindi. They shuddered, dusted their bodies with their hands as if attacked by a swarm of wasps, then looked at each other and chuckled. One of them kicked the car tyre.

Waaberi turned to them, squinted, straightened up, and headed in their direction.

'Go and clean yourself,' van der Venn said, stopping him halfway. 'There should be a loo behind the building.'

Waaberi growled at the men. It caught their attention. They stepped back from the car.

'Waaberi!'

'Yes, boss. I'm going.'

Even in his haggard condition, Waaberi had enough strength to reduce the three slim men to one shapeless blotch on the ground.

'And clean the weapon,' van der Venn added.

Waaberi strolled towards the car. The men scampered away, observing from a safe distance. He smirked, grabbed the messy gun and shuffled off, disappearing behind the building.

The men got back to their parking and gathered around one of the cycle rickshaws.

Van der Venn walked over to them, popped open the bag of chips and stretched out his hand.

'Help yourself, gentlemen,' he said.

Two of them who were in their fifties reached into the bag one after another. Chips crunched in their mouths. They didn't look impoverished in their shabby clothes, but not well-off either. One man was clad in an azure shirt. His beige slacks were cut just above his calves, showing a surgery-like scar on his shin. The other one was all dressed in white; his shirt reached down to the middle of his loose pants. A long scarf was wrapped around his head.

The third man was in his early twenties. He wore an Adidas T-shirt and designer-ripped jeans. None of those seemed to be the original products. His face was clean shaven. Acne spots dotted his forehead and temples.

Van der Venn smiled in apology. 'I'm sorry about my friend. He had a little accident.'

'No worry,' said the young one and ran his hand through his dark, unruly hair.

The rest of them watched van der Venn, squinting their eyes with either confusion or mistrust.

'Are you the only one who speaks English?'

'Yes, sir.' He took a few chips and put them into his mouth.

'Are you from Jaipur?'

He nodded, wiped his palm against his jeans, then slipped both hands into the back pockets.

'If I give you a name, can you find someone for me?'

A wide grin crossed his lips, showing pieces of chips between his teeth. 'Jaipur, six million people, sir.'

'I have an approximate location.'

The young man goggled at him. 'I don't know … ap … approxi, sir.'

Van der Venn scanned his face, wondering if he was feisty or just honest. 'I know *more or less* where the person lives, but not exactly. Can you help?'

The man translated van der Venn's words to his companions. They shook their heads thoughtfully, spoke to each other in a chaotic way, and fell silent as if coming to the same conclusions.

Van der Venn took out from his wallet a one-hundred-euro note. 'The person I need to find is a family member. She used to live in Italy. Her name is Sati Joshi. She's eighty-six years old. The last known address is somewhere in the Vijay Nagar area of Jaipur.'

The curious expressions on their faces told him that all of them understood. If not his words, then the power of money.

The young man frowned. 'Sati your family?'

He didn't think long before answering. 'Yes. My wife is her granddaughter. I came over to India to ask Sati to come with me to Italy. It's my wife's wish. She's very sick, and she wants to see Sati one more time.' He paused, swallowing his imaginary sorrow. 'Our families lost contact years ago. I must fix that horrible mistake.'

He wasn't sure if even the English-speaking man understood his soap-opera speech. Although, it wasn't that bad at all, considering the heat, hunger, jet lag, Klaff's dead body, Waaberi's puke, and the constant pain in his lower back.

The young man motioned to his rickshaw's back seat. 'Come.'

'No. We'll take my car,' van der Venn said.

The Hindu man waved his hand in a "not for all the money in the world would I get into that car" gesture. Then he explained to his friends what was going on. Their eyes bulged and they twisted their lips.

Van der Venn produced another green one-hundred-euro note, rolled it into a tube, and pointed with it at two older men. 'Interested in earning easy money, gentlemen?' He gestured at the car.

The men headed to the guy from the snacks stall, and spoke to him. He nodded, went inside, and returned with a bucket full of soapy water, a sponge, and a cloth that used to be someone's T-shirt.

The power of money.

'How's the food here?' van der Venn asked the young man.

'Good, food good,' he replied.

'Are you hungry?'

The man shrugged. 'Little hungry.'

CHAPTER 37

VAN DER VENN devoured the last spoonful of paneer cheese, potatoes and cashew nuts—all labelled malai kofta. It resembled breaded dumplings in a curry sauce and had a decent taste.

He took a gulp of iced tea from his glass. That was like drinking ten spoonsful of sugar dissolved in tap water.

The young man sitting across from him looked more curious about van der Venn's than his own aluminium plate full of chickpeas, sliced onions, chunks of tomatoes, lemon wedges and naan bread on the side.

He chewed the food, throwing glances at his two friends who were still busy scrubbing the inside of the car. When he thought that van der Venn wasn't looking at him, his gaze returned to the stranger who had arrived in a luxury car that stunk like sewage in a slum.

Van der Venn put the spoon on his plate and moved it away. 'The person I'm looking for lives—'

'I know, I know.'

Van der Venn raised his eyebrows. 'Explain.'

'Everybody know Sati,' the man said, fiddling with a piece of bread.

'Again. Explain.'

'Sati very good. She—'

He cut off when Waaberi joined their table. He wore a new pair of cotton slacks and an unbuttoned white shirt. Its sleeves reached to half of his forearms. His face had lost some of that horrified look.

'Where did you get these clothes from?' van der Venn said but instantly raised his hand. 'I don't care.'

Waaberi pulled the Hindu man's plate towards himself, broke away a piece of naan, plunged it into the chickpeas, shovelled food, smelled it, then pushed it into his mouth.

'Take it easy,' van der Venn said. 'You do that stunt in the car again, you walk the rest of this trip.'

Waaberi took another mouthful and mumbled, 'Yes, boss.'

The young man watched Waaberi in amazement.

'Go on,' van der Venn said to him.

'Sati feeds people, poor people, she poor herself.'

'You're saying that my wife's grandma is kind of a celebrity here?'

Waaberi choked on the food, retched, then ran for the toilet.

The man stared after him, open-mouthed.

'What is your name?' van der Venn asked.

'My name is Kama,' he replied.

'As in Kama Sutra?'

He blushed. 'Kama is Hindu god of love, sir.'

Van der Venn leaned back and crossed his shoulders on his chest. 'Tell me about Sati.'

Kama glanced at the plate Waaberi had taken from him. Scraps of food surrounded it. 'I don't know.'

'What don't you know?'

'I don't know "celebrity." '

'Okay. That's fair. Let's stick to the plain English.'

Kama parted his lips. 'You have car *and* plane?'

Van der Venn clicked his fingers against the table. 'Yes, I do. Tell me why everyone knows Sati?'

Kama tilted his head from side to side, then looked around, as if the answer were painted all over the place. 'She is good to people.'

'Why is it so strange?'

'She rich, but she not like rich.'

Van der Venn lowered his head and rubbed his eyebrows. 'Two minutes ago you said she was poor.'

'Yes, sir. Sati poor. No car, no plane.'

'Do you mean that she gives away all the money she gets from her pension or whoever is supporting her?'

'Yes, yes.'

Van der Venn took a gulp of the bottled water he had bought earlier. If Kama wanted to tell him that the old woman came from a wealthy family and was a charitable person who didn't leave much for herself, it made sense why people knew her address. She might also be receiving money from Nina Monte.

'How far is Sati's house?' he asked.

'Far, far.' Kama raised his index finger. 'Rickshaw. One hour, and a half.'

Which meant around twenty-five minutes by car. Nina Monte would have enough time to warn the old woman. His sense of superiority had cheated him on this occasion. He had let her gain an advantage. Here, his resources had their limits, but he would get them sooner or later.

On the other hand, it was better if she prepared the old woman for what was coming.

'Waaberi!' van der Venn roared and stood up.

Startled, Kama threw his body back, along with his chair. He outstretched his limbs to regain his balance. Van der Venn reached over and caught him by his wrist, and pulled. The chair tumbled down. Kama winced under van der Venn's grip.

He let the boy free. 'Let's go.'

The two men who had cleaned the car stood at attention next to its front. All four doors were wide open.

The front passenger seat and the dashboard were as good as new. On the back the same was true. Van der Venn saw a big wet spot on the car mat. He pulled it out and threw it away. The pungent smell still hung in there, but if he kept the windows open it should go unnoticed.

Someone poked him on the back. He turned around to see the sales clerk. Three air fresheners dangled on his finger.

'Ten. Green money,' he said, uncertain.

Van der Venn pulled out a ten-euro note and handed it over. The man smiled, scrambled into the car and hung the Magic Trees on the inside mirror.

'Get in,' van der Venn said to Kama. Then he turned to the two men. 'Excellent work, gentlemen. You've earned it.'

One of the men snatched the money, and they were gone.

Van der Venn hopped behind the wheel, pushed the horn and started the engine. Kama wriggled in the passenger seat. He glanced around the car, content.

Waaberi ran out of the toilet, pulling up his pants. He jumped into the car. 'Boss, what is he doing here?'

'Meet Kama, our guide. Kama, this is Waaberi.'

Waaberi reluctantly put out his hand over the passenger

seat. Kama more reluctantly shook it. Then he wiped it on his jeans.

The car blasted off, leaving a cloud of dust behind.

They drove for five minutes in silence. Van der Venn, seeing a looming crossroads, asked, 'Which way?'

'Wrong way,' Kama said gaily.

'What do you mean?'

'Sati way.' He pointed in the opposite direction, raised his chin and put his elbow out the window.

'Why didn't you say something before?' van der Venn said, stifling his irritation.

Kama pointed again. 'Sati way.'

Van der Venn tugged the wheel and pressed the horn. The car made a U-turn, leaping across a patch of grass. Kama managed to take a hold of his seat. Waaberi was slower; his head banged on the car roof with the muffled sound. They found themselves on the opposite strip of the road. Seconds later, a familiar retch and fluid extraction followed.

Kama turned back. Van der Venn caught a glimpse of aversion painted all over his face.

'Look at me, Kama,' he said. 'From now on you need to tell me exactly where to go. I will not ask you any questions. You will tell me *exactly* where to go. Do you understand?'

'Kama understand,' he replied and raised his hand to the windscreen. 'Sati way.'

CHAPTER 38

'INNSBRUCK, AUSTRIA, Europe.'

Alessandro sat in the tuk-tuk, trying to explain to Ankit what the mysterious wording on his T-shirt was. Ankit grabbed the fabric of his striped shirt and pulled it several times, throwing at Alessandro a series of words the meaning of which he could only guess.

'Yes, I know it's tight. No, it wasn't my choice.'

Ankit pointed at the drops of blood on the white T-shirt, grabbed on his own ear and shook it.

'I'll be okay, thanks. It was an accident. Sort of.'

Ankit said something, held up his hand and shrugged his shoulders.

'I have no idea what you're saying either.'

Ankit touched Waaberi's boot print on Alessandro's chest, then rubbed fresh dirt and oil between his fingers.

'Yes, it's fresh, Ankit. The man who did it to me had to step in a diesel-oil puddle first. If I told you everything, you would never believe me.' Nor would he understand, he thought.

Alessandro let out a sigh of relief when he saw Nina coming from the house. She carried two bottles of water. Something was not right, though. Her shoulders were slumped, and she looked pale.

'Who was that person in the house?' Alessandro asked when she scrambled onto the seat next to him.

'My grandma's friend.'

Alessandro forced a timid smile on his face. 'So … where is she?'

'She let him live here because she moved out,' Nina said in a worrying tone of voice.

'Moved out?' Alessandro stirred in his seat. 'But that's good, right? For a moment, I thought that she was … you know.'

'I thought the same, Alessandro.'

Ankit started the engine.

'She's okay, then?'

Nina nodded, and Ankit put the tuk-tuk into motion.

'So why that gloomy face? The good news is that if you didn't know about it, there's no chance van der Venn knows.' Alessandro tried to sound confident. There was nothing certain when it came to van der Venn.

Nina buried her head in her hands and started to cry. 'Sati moved out to a guesthouse … one week ago.'

Alessandro could hardly understand her through the sobbing.

'…to the holy city of Varanasi.'

He cocked his head. 'Old people in India move to guesthouses? Impressive. Then why are you crying?'

Nina looked up at him. 'This is not the kind of guesthouse you think of; it's a sort of hospice. The reason elderly choose Varanasi is to die there, so after death their ashes can be scattered into the Ganges River.' Her chin trembled. 'And I knew nothing about it. The person I love, and I thought she loved me back, told me nothing about her

239

plans. It feels like I didn't know her at all, like she didn't trust me!'

Alessandro scratched the back of his head. What was the right way to console a person after something like that? He knew. 'Hold on! You said you communicated via letters only. I'm sure Sati wrote about it, but it's a long way from Jaipur to Italy. Is it possible that a letter is still in your mailbox?'

Nina swallowed. 'I travelled a lot…'

'You see,' he said in a soothing tone. 'Probably your grandma came up with this idea only recently, and the news didn't reach you yet.'

Nina wiped her nose with the back of her hand. 'Do you really think so?'

'Of course. What else could it be?'

'Stop, right here!' Nina screamed to Ankit.

The tuk-tuk came to a halt.

Alessandro frowned at her. 'What are you doing?'

She took a few short breaths. 'I have to go there, Alessandro, to Varanasi, but you don't. We can go separate ways here if you like. I can't ask you to continue risking your life for me. I'm heading to the train station now.'

'Train station?'

'You can go to the embassy and tell them everything. If you like. It's a personal journey for me now.'

Alessandro stared at her, chewing the inside of his cheek, then he looked away. Nina waited for an answer. Ankit was glancing at him over his shoulder.

Alessandro closed his eyes. He saw the grinning face of Lammert van der Venn. He saw his gun pointing at him. He remembered that shock and helplessness when the bullet had shot off his earlobe. The pain came later.

'Personal it is, Nina. Personal it is about Gianluigi. Personal it is about my grieving mother, about what happened to those policemen in Malcesine, and about my life that will never be the same. And…'

And most of all, it was about the panic he felt in his guts at the thought that he would have to face van der Venn again.

Nina spoke first. 'I don't feel courageous either, Alessandro. I'm terrified. My stomach is still cramped. I know I would be far worse if not for you,' she said, and then held her breath. 'And you saved us from the collision on the highway.'

'Whew.' Alessandro wiped his forehead theatrically. 'I'm not entirely useless, after all.'

She gave him a peck on his cheek. 'You're not.'

'But…' He pressed his lips together. 'I'm not a hero, Nina. I think that you have already noticed that.'

'What about in Malcesine?' she said—he saw a gleam of pride in her eyes. 'You broke into van der Venn's yacht.'

Alessandro shook his head. 'That was different, like playing football on the home pitch. Only I didn't know that my opponent was a notorious offender. Here, it was you who freed us from that car. You are a resourceful person, Nina. I would have never done anything like this.'

What he felt inside was more complex. It was a mix of fear, a longing for home and his mother, and hatred for van der Venn.

Nina stared at him hopefully.

But above all, though, he felt responsible for Nina. She had shielded him from the bullet in Innsbruck. He had seen that van der Venn had aimed at his chest, but when she popped in front of Alessandro, he had raised the gun.

Alessandro smiled and wiped her cheek with the back of his hand. 'But don't you ever think that I will leave you here on your own, Professor.'

When her eyes smiled back to him, their deep green colour had returned.

He looked away and said, 'There's that weird uneasiness I feel inside. I don't know how to describe it. I'm ashamed of that, because I never thought I would be able to loathe a person that much.' He glanced at Nina. 'I want van der Venn dead.'

She pulled back the corners of her lips, giving him an understanding smile.

'So,' he said, slamming his thighs with his palms, 'I'd like you to show me that holy city that people choose as their last home in this life. And if van der Venn somehow finds his way to follow us, maybe this will be the right place for him too.'

Then he patted Ankit on his shoulder. 'Go, my friend! *Relave stesana.*'

Ankit and Nina parted their lips at once.

'There are things you don't know about me, Professor,' Alessandro said, proud of himself. 'One of them is that I can say "train station" in fourteen different languages.'

Ankit tilted his head from side to side as if in recognition of Alessandro's skills. Then he turned on the ignition and the tuk-tuk moved at the slowest speed.

Close to the end of the alley, they had to stop. In the middle of the lane, a two-wheeled cart lay upturned. Mangos, pineapples, guavas and apples—some still rolling—dotted the ground nearby the cart. A furious Hindu man dressed in a salmon shirt yelled at a taxi driver, hitting the bonnet of the car with a stick while waving away children who were picking up his fruits.

Ankit reversed, found an adjoining alley that was nearly as narrow as the width of the tuk-tuk, and after three minutes he catapulted his taxi into the unrelenting clamour of Jaipur's traffic.

Chapter 39

Van der Venn took a turn into a narrow street. It looked like a marketplace and was overcrowded with agitated Hindu people. He pulled over, seeing a collision of a taxi with a market stall or a cart. People around were screaming. The loudest was a man in a salmon shirt holding a stick with which he was bashing the yellow-and-green cab.

'Sati house.' Kama pointed to the last building at the end of the alley.

Van der Venn reloaded his gun. 'Stay inside, Waaberi. Kama, you go with me.'

Kama's body stiffened at the sight of the weapon. 'Don't worry. It's a precaution only. Come,' he said and holstered the gun.

They got out of the car and headed to the green, solitary house. Stalls with smoking food, spices, shoes, and bike parts dotted both sides of the street.

At the end of the street a group of people were talking to a man who sat on the bench by the house. They spoke in raised voices, gesticulating with their hands.

When van der Venn and the boy neared them, he asked Kama, 'What do they want?'

'They want to know why Sati left without telling them,' he replied, disoriented.

'Is she not here?'

Kama shook his head.

'How long has she been gone?'

Kama asked that question in Hindi, then translated. 'She gone one week.'

'Ask them if there was someone else looking for Sati today.'

Kama nodded and turned to them. Then he nodded to van der Venn. 'People look Sati. Different people.'

'Who?'

'Woman and man.'

'Do you know where Sati went?'

Kama shrugged his shoulders.

'Ask *them*.'

Kama exchanged a few sentences with the group. Van der Venn heard a few English words: *wife*, *granddaughter*. Then Kama looked at him. 'Varanasi.'

Varanasi. He had heard about that city. Yes, it shouldn't surprise him that the old woman was seeking her place over there. More importantly, the advantage was back on his side. He would reach Varanasi before Nina Monte. Without travel documents, the train was her only option, and trains in India were slow.

'Kama, can you find Sati in Varanasi?'

He smiled and shook his head. 'Varanasi one million people, sir.'

Van der Venn reached out and squeezed his shoulder. 'Here, according to you, live six million, and it was a pretty easy task for you, given the odds.'

Kama cringed under the firm grip.

'I'm a businessman,' he told him and let go. 'I offer you another five hundred euros if you can find Sati in Varanasi, and of course my wife would be extremely grateful. You don't want to disappoint a dying woman, do you?'

Kama lowered his eyes, then looked at the car and scratched the back of his head.

'Plus, you get to fly on my plane,' he added. 'What do you say?'

Kama raised his chin and grinned. 'Okay.'

Van der Vcnn strolled back to the car with a new plan in his head. He would wait for Nina Monte in Varanasi, maybe even along with her grandmother. Maybe, before Monte's arrival, the old woman would tell him something about the tablet. Far from perfect, but he did have his own private interpreter.

They reached the Jaipur private airfield in less than forty minutes. Van der Venn returned the car, but didn't bother to show his identification, as the same officers were on duty. He only reported a short domestic flight. They glanced at Kama without asking questions.

When Waaberi passed the same customs clerk from whom he had taken breakfast that morning, the man waved to him with his new plate invitingly. Waaberi gagged and put his hand to his mouth.

CHAPTER 40

ALESSANDRO HAD LOVED train journeys since he was eleven years old. His mother used to take him to Milan and from there to Como. Francesca Pini had been seeking there new ideas on how to run her small business from the local hoteliers who had their holiday resorts by the lake.

For Alessandro, it was the time when he discovered that Malcesine and the lake weren't the only fascinating places where people lived. There was a multi-coloured world beyond his unconquered mountains.

When he was twenty, he had spent a school break travelling with his friends across the whole length of Italy, right to the shores of the Ionian Sea. It was a period of first times for him.

The first time he had left home for more than a week. He smoked his first joint. He made love to two girls at the same time. It was the first time he stole a bottle of wine from a supermarket (he regretted it when he got sober, and came back with the money the next day.) The first time he was beaten up by football supporters of A.S. Roma (it was also the first time he was beaten at all, and the last time, but he had never forgotten about it.)

Before he turned twenty-seven, he had set foot in the biggest train stations in Europe: Roma Termini, Paris Gare du Nord, Madrid Puerta de Atocha, Berlin Hauptbahnhof, Brussels Central, London St Pancras.

Still, nothing had prepared him for what he saw at Jaipur Junction.

With growing amazement, he watched a colourful ocean of people flowing out of a pink building of Jaipur's main railway station. It felt as if he were standing in front of the only exit out of a football stadium and someone had ordered an immediate evacuation.

Nina clung to his arm. 'Better close your mouth, Alessandro. It's only the busiest station in Rajasthan. These people came to work. Every morning is like this.'

Men and women were passing them, some with welcoming smiles, some stone-faced, some ignoring them. Alessandro had never been agoraphobic, but now he thought that this condition had lain dormant in him. He shrank his shoulders and waited for the unending human wave to pass.

Nina stood on her tiptoes and said into his ear, 'Let's try to get inside.'

'Are you serious?'

She moved ahead. Alessandro followed her with his squeezed shoulders.

The main hall wasn't larger than many train stations in Italy, and not that much different. Time tables, a large waiting area, kiosks with newspapers and snacks, and people with luggage, queuing for a ticket or at the information desk.

After a quarter of an hour, they stood in front of a ticket window.

Nina looked up at him. 'Your last chance. Should I buy one or two tickets?'

He leaned to the window slot and said in English, 'Two tickets for the first train to Varanasi, please.'

From behind the glass, he heard a series of short sentences. Although it sounded like English, it was too quick, and with a melodious accent he hadn't caught on to yet.

He spread out his hands but quickly added, 'One way, two persons.'

The sales clerk typed on her computer and printed the tickets. Alessandro pulled out Nina's credit card that she had slipped into his pocket before they left van der Venn's jet. He gave her a short, questioning glance to make sure if he could use it.

After he had paid for the tickets, they stepped back and gave way to the growing number of bodies behind them.

On the platform, there was no sign of the crowd that had arrived at the station. But it was far from deserted. People sat or slept on the cool floor or sauntered along on the platform. He noticed groups of holidaymakers from Sweden and Eastern Europe; he had learned to recognize nationality at a glance when they were coming to his hotel.

Nina and Alessandro sat down on a bench sheltered by a tin roof set on steel poles. A freight train consisting of dozens of carriages stood on the opposite track. There were seven platforms at Jaipur Junction. The farther tracks were also busy, he reckoned.

He inhaled a rich smell coming from their left, where an elderly, scrawny woman with a silky woven scarf on her head sat on the platform in a squatting position, selling Indian food packed into a range of plastic containers. They looked like those ready-to-go meals from supermarkets one would shove into the microwave before eating.

Every minute, someone bought one of them. Alessandro swallowed, trying to silence his grumbling stomach. He remembered all too well what had happened to Waaberi after he tasted Indian cuisine at the airport.

'You never told me how come you speak their language so well? You mentioned you visited your grandma only a few times.'

'I picked up a lot from her before she moved back to India,' Nina said. 'Then every letter from Sati was a new lesson. She wrote only in Hindi and insisted I did the same. I had no choice but to learn. She's a great teacher.'

Alessandro's stomach let out a high-pitched growl. Distraction hadn't been as helpful as he hoped. 'Why didn't she stay to teach people in Italy?'

'I don't think she wanted to,' Nina replied.

A speaker announced the approaching train. Alessandro caught only the name "Varanasi" out of it. More travellers showed up out of nowhere and neared a yellow line painted on the platform's edge. When the train pulled into the station, Alessandro couldn't see its end.

Nina got to her feet. He followed her, leaned and said to her back, 'If you're planning to do the same trick as in Italy, dear Professor, and we're going to jump from one train to another, better tell me now.'

Nina climbed the short stairs. She pulled herself up using the handrails so her shirt wouldn't move up too far, and hopped aboard the Intercity Express. She turned right, walked a few metres and opened the door to the two-seat-car.

'I don't want to complain, but didn't we buy first-class tickets?' Alessandro said.

She flopped down on a long seat. 'This *is* first class.'

He glanced around. 'Oh.'

Above Nina's head was another berth, and, attached to the ceiling, a fan that looked like those used in city offices. A large mirror hung on the opposite wall.

The inside of the coach was clean, but it looked shabby and seemed to be older than Alessandro. It had crumbled leather on the seats, walls, sallow electrical sockets, and a window that didn't open.

Alessandro sat down and bounced a few times to check the firmness of the seat. 'How long is the journey?'

'If there are no delays, around fourteen hours.'

He froze, breaking his mini inspection. He meant to laugh, but Nina's face showed no sign of teasing.

'I suppose we couldn't catch a plane?' he stammered.

'Not without passports.'

He sat back and flapped his hands to the sides. 'I can't believe this is happening to me.'

She gave him a confused look that made him regret his comment.

'I don't *mind* being on this train with you, Nina,' he explained. 'I just can't believe that only yesterday my life was running pretty much the same ordinary way as for the last number of years. Which I quite liked.'

The train slowly pulled out of the station.

'Come with me,' she said and grabbed his hand. 'I will show you something.'

They entered a different carriage where people were squashed onto three-storey bunks. The air was hot and sticky there, although instead of glass there were horizontal metal bars in the windows. Bureau fans mounted to the ceiling were stirring the air, cooling it a little. Most of them didn't work.

'If you think life treats you unfairly, they travel like that for hours. I'm sure many are going to Varanasi,' Nina said.

'Aren't they too young to … ?' He didn't want to say "die" in a loud voice; it felt inappropriate to use that word, although the chances that one of them spoke Italian were slim.

Nina shook her head. 'They're not going there to wait for their death. It's a festive season, celebration of light.'

'Like gigantic … fireworks?' Alessandro asked and rubbed his chin.

'They celebrate the victory of light over darkness. Light represents knowledge; darkness represents ignorance, or demonic forces that disturb the harmony in the universe,' Nina told him in an academic tone of voice.

Then she perched on a bed next to a young woman in a flowery sari and said something to her. When the girl spoke in her language, Nina listened with a bright face, nodding along.

'She's on a pilgrimage from the west of India. She also goes to Varanasi,' Nina said.

The girl continued in Hindi.

'She's excited. It will be her first visit to Varanasi,' Nina explained. 'She told me that her name is Kashi, which is exactly how religious people call Varanasi. Kashi means "City of Light." '

The girl reached into her bag.

'She's inviting us for a meal,' Nina said.

Kashi pulled out three bundles wrapped in foil. She unpacked them on the bed and handed one to Alessandro. It looked like a deep-fried, flat, donut-shaped pastry.

'No, thank you,' he said as politely as he could. 'It's too

early to eat.' He pointed at his watch. 'It's only five a.m. where I come from.'

She kept her hand outstretched.

Alessandro felt awkward. Everyone in the coach was observing him. 'Professor, would you translate my words?'

'Eat,' Kashi said to him in English. 'Good.'

He accepted the pastry, looking at Nina for her approval; she nodded.

The girl handed Nina the same thing, and she took a bite. 'Mmm … Nothing like our kind of breakfast but really nice.'

'Are you sure it's safe?' Alessandro asked, holding the greasy donut between his thumb and index finger. 'What's in it?'

'Wheat, coriander, cumin and other spices,' Nina said, munching the food. 'They call it kachori. You will offend her if you refuse to eat.'

Alessandro winced. 'I am hungry. But … isn't there a restaurant carriage in here?'

Nina smiled through her clenched teeth. 'Don't be such a baby. Besides, if we were in Europe would you try someone's home cooking or mass-produced food?'

'If we were in Europe, I would still be in bed,' he said but placed the pastry into his mouth, not without a short pause half-way.

To his surprise, it tasted amazing. It was crunchy, rich and full of flavours not known to him before. He took a bigger bite, then gobbled the rest.

'I told her we weren't married,' Nina said. 'She wanted to know your name. I think she likes you.'

'Are you haggling with her for my price?'

Nina turned to the girl and said something. Kashi put her hand to her mouth and giggled.

Alessandro raised his eyebrows. 'Did you just … ?'

Nina laughed, so did the girl. People around got curious. The girl told them what was going on, and then the whole carriage was laughing. It was a pleasant laugh, nothing close to van der Venn's sneer.

A man jumped down from his bunk, grabbed Alessandro by his bicep and squeezed it. Then he said something and they laughed more.

Alessandro put his hand to his eyebrows, sheltering himself from the stares. 'It's embarrassing. Should I show my teeth as well?'

Another girl approached him with a small bundle. The bread she offered him smelled of almonds and honey.

'What is it?'

'Have a try. Gosh! Do you always have to put a label on things?' Nina said, amused. 'I'd like to be in your shoes now.'

Alessandro took a bite. '*Mmm*, sweet, and crisp.' He broke it in two and gave Nina one piece. 'Do you think it's too much to ask them if they have coffee?'

She translated his words before he explained that he was only joking. A few people reached for their flasks.

He accepted the closest offer. It wasn't coffee, but tea. Sugary, with cream. Alessandro smacked his lips.

More people were touching him, asking questions.

They wanted to know where Nina and Alessandro were from. What was that language they spoke to each other? How long were they travelling across India? What were their occupations? How rich were they, since they could afford to come to India? How many children did they have?

Everyone was ogling Nina, who spoke Hindi with ease.

She explained over and over again that they weren't even engaged. Some passengers couldn't understand how come they weren't a couple, weren't related, and yet still travelled together. Alessandro learned that friendship between a woman and a man wasn't such a natural thing in every part of the world.

When a small boy tugged on Alessandro's arm hair, he gave a squeak. People chuckled. Alessandro glanced at Nina for an explanation.

'Many of them have never been in the presence of a white man,' she said.

'So this is how the first white people must have felt coming over here,' he said, rubbing his arm. 'The explorers became an object of exploration.'

Nina stood up, brought her hands together and bowed. 'Namaste,' she said to the girl, then to the others.

Alessandro did the same, although not as expertly or gracefully as Nina, and they headed back to their seats.

CHAPTER 41

THEIR CARRIAGE IN first class looked to Alessandro like a high-tech luxury wagon now. 'Their lives are so different than ours. It's like being on a different planet.'

'It's only an illusion created by a language and cultural barrier,' Nina said. 'Every human being is the same and wants the same things.'

'Not exactly,' he said. 'Some people's goal is to earn ten million euros a year; others are happy with ten thousand. Some want to run a marathon, others' daily activity is limited to a few steps a day from their home to the garage, then elevator to the office.'

Nina parted her lips and slowly nodded. 'True, but above all, every person wants to live in peace and abundance. What is different is the meaning of those things to each of us.'

She was right. Alessandro thought about the people he had just met. Was it an inconvenience to them that they travelled crammed one on top of another, with little privacy? They looked far from being frustrated. Was it a sense of one purpose, unity, of sharing the same or similar life?

He watched the passing landscape outside the window. Vast fields of green crops covered the ground. Now and then he saw a shack, and he wondered if people were living in it.

Cows grazed on the pastures. Rural scenery dominated this part of the railway tracks.

'Why do you think your grandma chose to move out right now to wait for her … departure in Varanasi?' Alessandro said, without thinking over his question.

Nina studied his face.

'She's not running away from anything, is she? Because,' he added, 'I must say, she couldn't have picked a better time.'

'I don't know,' Nina said, her eyes sliding to the window. 'Moving to Varanasi is like being on the last spiritual journey, which brings you closer to God.'

'Like van der Venn?' Alessandro muttered.

Nina looked up. 'How can you even compare my grandma to *him*?'

Alessandro held up his hands. 'I know, Nina. Sorry. But let me explain.'

She exhaled and gave an approving nod.

'Van der Venn gave me a lecture about the holy gospels, which means that either he is a Catholic or he's interested in this religion.'

'I think the second doesn't rule out the first.'

'Me too,' Alessandro said. 'Now he is convinced that after he finds out what someone engraved in that stone thousands of years ago, long before Christ was born, he will get himself an appointment in Heaven.'

Alessandro put his fingers to his lower lip. 'That doesn't make sense. As much as I hate to admit it, he is an intelligent, although imbalanced, individual. He believes in material things, in the power of muscles and bullets.'

'I think he used to be like that,' Nina said. 'When you

have enough gold coins, houses, and money, you're searching for something more.'

In the mirror on the wall, Alessandro saw his bewildered face. Nina had to see it too.

'I read his dossier,' she said. 'And although now I know that he wrote it himself, there was a clue he put in there. Intentional or not, I think it's valid.'

She took a breath and continued. 'It said there that Lammert van der Venn is on an ultimate quest for a spiritual treasure. I think that somehow he came to believe that he can get it.'

'Can he?'

Nina took off her shoes and pulled up her feet. 'I do believe in the possibility of an expansion of human understanding and knowledge through the increase of a brain's capacity, which we all have. That could be called being closer to God by a spiritual person.'

Alessandro stood up. In spite of the running fan, it was sultry in the car; his clothes stuck to his body. 'You already told me something similar, Nina. But how come van der Venn can get smarter with the help of that tablet?'

'Through meditation on the mantras engraved in it. This is supposed to extensively stimulate human nervous and endocrine systems, which in the end unblocks seven energy vortexes, or chakras in our bodies, and takes you to the realm of the highest spirituality, knowing and understanding.'

Alessandro shook his head. 'Wait. So all he needs to do is sit down, cross his legs, chant ancient texts, and wait.'

'Don't make fun of this. Through practise of a disciplined meditation and the breath control, everyone can achieve spiritual perfection,' she said in an analytical tone of voice. 'Except for the last thing, which supposedly only the tablet can provide.'

Alessandro crossed his arms on his chest. 'Meeting with God, right?'

'God, creator of everything, the highest wisdom ... take your pick, they all mean the same thing.'

He scratched his face stubble. 'Have you ever tried to achieve those things?'

Nina tucked the hem of her shirt into her skirt. 'I used to meditate. I did what Sati taught me when I was ten. Initially, it felt good. I became more open to people and nature.' She gave a slight smile. 'Even my grades improved; absorbing new material was easier. But once, during an extended sitting, I felt like I was burning inside and ... like I was leaving my body. I got scared so much that I never meditated again. Instead I decided to learn how that had happened, and if that was only me. I guess, involuntarily, I chose my profession.'

'So?'

Nina gave a small shrug. 'So?'

'Have you found out what frightened you?'

'Yes. And imagine that the philosophy and science are not silent about it,' she said, raising her chin. 'Many famous people studied the subject. Would you be surprised hearing names like Socrates or Carl Jung? Many Christian saints, among them St. Teresa or St. John of the Cross, practiced contemplative prayer, which is a form of meditation.'

'No, it's *not*,' Alessandro said, sitting down beside her. 'That's ridiculous.'

'You really think that the meditation has nothing to do with Christianity?' Nina said, raising her eyebrows at him. 'Then let me tell you about *Lectio Divina*. *Lectio Divina*,

Latin for *Divine Reading* is a Christian tradition of reading the scripture that originates from the third century, and is practised until this day. It emphasises prayerful reading of the Bible as an internal dialogue with God, meaning that the person who is reading it can hear the "Living Word", the voice of God himself. So actually you can say that it's more listening aimed at deeper understanding delivered through the Holy Spirit who illuminates the person performing '

'Nina. Nina!' Alessandro raised his arms. 'Stop. You're turning again into that crazy professor from Malcesine when you tried to comfort me after I told you about Gianluigi. That was quite creepy, by the way. But I got it. Some people don't care much about dying, but I do. Some people believe in meditation; I don't. Even after what you said about those saints, and everything.'

'Haven't you heard what van der Venn said about the pope?'

Alessandro narrowed his eyes. 'You believed that story?'

She gave him no answer.

He straightened his arms and propped them on his knees. 'Please don't tell me all that babbling about van der Venn's plans to get into Heaven alive isn't anything else other than the wishful thinking of a madman.'

Nina stared into his eyes for half a minute. 'Does it matter? You've already made up your mind.'

He felt a pang of betrayal. 'Are you telling me everything?'

She averted her eyes.

'Nina, we're in this together, and you keep secrets from me?'

'No. No, I'm just tired, Alessandro,' she said softly, looking at him.

She moved closer and took his hand. 'And you have no idea how happy I am that you've decided to come with me.'

She was tired. That was good enough for him. That, he could understand. He was exhausted too, and her lecture made his head throb. He should have never thought that Nina was hiding something. Even if she were, it couldn't be significant.

He let her rest her head on his chest, and looked out the window.

The scenery didn't change much. The sky was clear, and light blue. The sky was the same everywhere; it was comforting. He pretended not to see what was below it and imagined he was back home in Malcesine.

Where the lofty face of Gianluigi greeted him.

CHAPTER 42

SATI WAS RESTING on the grass in the shadow of an old, branchy fig tree. It grew in the middle of a courtyard of a small guesthouse that stood high on the riverbank of the five-thousand-year-old City of Light, her new home.

She wore a shaded orange sari decorated with sequins and with shimmering border patch work, a gift from Nina for her seventy-seventh birthday. Although a little tatty on the hip and at the ends, and some of the sequins had fallen off, it was very comfortable.

Apart from a breeze gently rustling the leaves above her head, it was a soundless morning, as usual for the early hours. The walls surrounding the hospice were three metres high so that no one would be disturbed while awaiting salvation.

Sati had a twelve-square-metre room at her disposal. Furniture consisted of a bed with a hard mattress, an open wardrobe in which she put her few clothes, a shabby stool, and a table on which she had placed Nina's picture.

Because of her granddaughter's bright smile, it felt almost as pleasant as her house in Jaipur. Yesterday, Sati had arranged for a bunch of wild roses to be delivered to her room. It made her residence more likeable. But she would be happier if she had someone to talk to. The six other occupants led their own lives; some of them were surrounded by one or two members of their families.

A splendid view from her room almost made up for her solitude. The unglazed windows overlooked the river Ganges. Every morning at sunrise, Sati watched people bathing in the river. Three days ago she had joined them, and submerged her body into the purifying waters, letting Mother Ganga take her sins away. On the way back to the guesthouse, she felt light, happy and fulfilled, and ready for her departure.

On the next day, her strength had faded rapidly. Today, she had no energy to climb down the countless steps that led to the riverbank.

Soon someone would come for her, wrap her dead body in clean cloths and carry her on a bamboo frame to the river and let the eternal fire do the rest.

When she had arrived in Varanasi seven days ago, she arranged everything straightaway. She assumed she needed the room for three weeks at most. She paid four hundred and twenty rupees for her stay.

Then she bought two hundred kilos of timber. The sellers said that would be enough for a small person like her. She paid eleven hundred rupees for one hundred and eighty kilos of mango wood, and the same amount for twenty kilos of an aromatic sandalwood.

It meant that she had thirty-two thousand left. She told the hotel manager to give some money to people who would take care of the burning ritual. The rest he should keep as a payment on behalf of others who couldn't afford to stay in his hospice.

Sati trusted the manager. His name was Brijesha, and he looked older than some of the residents. He had been running the guesthouse for the last forty-eight years. He had told Sati that there weren't that many similar places left in Varanasi. Now the city cared more about tourists than those who came to die here.

He had told Sati something else. He considered himself to be an expert at assessing when a person was due to die. His accuracy ranged between four and five days. But in Sati's case, he couldn't say for sure. He said that sometimes God had his own ways of dealing with those matters.

An ailing man came out of his room. He walked, leaning his meagre figure on his daughter's shoulder. He was clad in one piece of cloth wrapped around his waist. His skin was sagging, his shoulder bones were protruding. They sat on a bench made from two wide chopping blocks and a solid plank nailed to them, not that far from Sati. The woman bowed politely. Sati smiled back.

Looking at her, Sati wondered if she had done the right thing in not informing Nina about her decision to leave for Varanasi. She had written a letter to her granddaughter, but it would be sent after she had died. It was another thing that she entrusted to the manager; she was worried that he would forget about the letter, so she was reminding him about it every day.

Sati didn't want to involve Nina. She wouldn't understand that death was a blessing for everyone who passed away in here. The City of Light was the only place to achieve the final release from the cycle of reincarnation.

Sati leaned forward and lit an incense stick. The smell of copal resin danced in front of her on the light wind. She waved with her open hand invitingly and inhaled. She would meditate as she had for the last eighty years of her life. In meditation, God would give her guidance, if that was His will for her to know. One week ago, He had shown her the City of Light and this hotel.

This morning she wanted to understand her dream.

She had seen Raghu in her house in Jaipur. He was packing his clothes. When she asked him what he was doing, he answered that another lady of the house had returned, and he couldn't stay there any longer. He would go to live with his nephew. His brother already lived in his son's house. It wasn't big, but it was enough for one more person. It was the only place he could go. Raghu and his late wife could not have children. Without children he had no one to take care of him. He hoped his nephew would take him. He thanked Sati for her house. He had to go now. *Raghu, wait*, Sati called after him, *what other lady?* He smiled and answered, *The young lady*. There was something more, but she couldn't remember, and she woke up with a worrying feeling in her stomach.

If she'd had no dream, or hadn't remembered it, she would have thought that it was hunger that she felt in her guts. She hadn't been eating regularly. She didn't want to go out for food. The streets were overcrowded with tourists. Besides, what difference would that make? Her time was close; her body would burn the same way, hungry or fed.

She closed her eyes and rested her hands on her lap, palms upward, left hand on top of the right. She took one deep breath, exhaled, then one more, and let the natural rhythm guide the flow of the air.

Vital energy descended from the crown of her head downwards through her spine and into every cell of her body. It flowed in waves of subtle tingling, which energised Sati in the same way the Holy Ganga nourishes its main riverbed while never forgetting its tributaries.

Sati recollected the second part of her dream.

She stood in the room of the green house and watched Raghu packing his belongings. She repeated, *What young lady, Raghu?* But he didn't hear her. He was gone. She sat down on the bed, laid her hands on its sheets, caressed them. The fingers of her left hand met an object. She picked it up. A picture. The beautiful, green eyes of her young granddaughter, who here couldn't be older than ten, peered out at her. Nina stood by the door of the Jaipur house. Her hands on her sides, she was hunching, mouth pouted like she would start crying. Sati noticed something on the ground, by Nina's left foot. Her heart fluttered.

In her vision, Sati rose and sprinted outside the house; only when dreaming could she still do that. No one was there. Nothing was there. Except him. But he was neither someone nor something. He had the same item in his hands that she saw in the picture with Nina. It was broken. He held a piece in each hand.

Sati flung her eyes open, breaking the meditation. She inhaled deeply and let the air slowly out of her lungs. Then she arose and hobbled to the arcade of the guesthouse. Her legs felt tired as if she truly had been running. She poured herself masala chai from the steel kettle that hung over the fire. Usually she would use a cooking stove and a gas cylinder, but the can had become empty yesterday. She hoped Brijesha would bring her a new one. Soon she would have to make more tea.

She would have visitors. Some were welcomed; some were expected.

CHAPTER 43

THE VIOLET LIGHT on the speaker mounted to the jet's armrest blinked. Lammert van der Venn pressed the button. 'I'm listening.'

'Mr van der Venn, our permission to take off has been delayed,' the pilot said.

'Explain.'

'The jet that was supposed to take off first was put on hold, and now blocks the airstrip.'

Some static noise came out from the speaker, then the pilot was back. 'Hold on, sir. I'm trying to get more information.'

Van der Venn peered out the window. The Chinese plane that was in front of them, in a take-off position, stood still.

The speaker next to him crackled to life once again. 'I've just got the report that the police found a suspicious vehicle in the carpark. Apparently, it was involved in a serious collision on the highway this morning.'

An airport security car rushed across the tarmac. The driver waved to the pilot of the other jet. The plane made a slow turn and headed back to the hangar.

'The police want to interview the passengers from that Cessna,' the pilot added. 'Hold on, sir.' Five seconds of silence. 'We've just been cleared. Prepare for immediate take-off.'

Van der Venn sat back and fastened his seatbelt.

Always have a back-up plan, his French mentor, Basile Lemaire, had taught him. When diving at a depth of one hundred metres, a man cannot allow himself to go down without an auxiliary oxygen tank, and cannot allow himself to lose orientation, even if his gear gives a false sense of safety.

The engines roared, and van der Venn's body was squeezed into the seat. Behind the window, details of the airfield scenery were slipping by faster and faster.

On land, he was careful to have a back-up plan too. Like a GPS locator built into the walls of the briefcase the tablet was housed in. Without it, he would have been late for a meeting in Innsbruck, and let a second-class actor, inferior to van der Venn in every respect, outsmart him. The sole thought made him cringe inside.

The pilot lifted the machine with ease.

Today van der Venn had to be vigilant too. When he had returned the Toyota, he had complained about the bad odour coming from the back seat of the car. The airport staff had made him fill out some documents. In case they wanted to follow up on that matter, he had jotted down on the car papers his next false destination—Hong Kong. The Chinese jet was the only one flying there at this time. And it had just been diverted.

The jet cut the carpet of white clouds and levelled out.

He looked over his shoulder. Waaberi was sprawled on the couch, close to the toilet. Kama sat in the same row as van der Venn, but by the opposite window.

'Kama,' he said, 'there's a bar in the middle of the cabin with snacks and drinks. Do whatever you want to do. But be quiet. We land in Varanasi in an hour.'

'Sir, you very, *very* rich,' Kama said with gleaming eyes. His feet were drumming against the carpet and he was fiddling with his seatbelt buckle.

Van der Venn turned his head away. 'Yes, I am.'

He didn't feel rich. He wanted much more, much more of something beyond tangible that no money could buy.

Van der Venn pulled out from his pocket a note his pilot handed over to him after the return from the city. It was Nina Monte's rescue-note. She was tough, wasn't giving up easily. He would have to be more wary when dealing with the Italian professor. Otherwise he might end up in Indian prison.

The pain in his lower back grew to an intolerable level. He popped two pills and closed his eyes. One hour of sleep should ease the pain.

CHAPTER 44

THE BIG MAN was rich. Kama had seen men like him in the cinema. They travelled in luxury cars or planes, like this one. Sexy ladies always surrounded them, and they didn't have to do anything for those ladies to like them.

It was Kama's first time on a plane, and it was already on the rich man's jet, not a regular passenger plane that everybody could use.

The big man told him to be quiet. Did it mean that he should not move, either? He didn't think so. Then the man wouldn't have told him about the bar and snacks.

He felt hungry. He had left his mother's house just after sunrise this morning, having a cup of cold chai and bread. He was in a hurry to meet five tourists from England, four women and one man. Kama had come across them yesterday evening not far from the train station, and he arranged sightseeing for the whole day today. He even promised them a discount. He had to; the competition from other rickshaw drivers was high.

But this morning the tourists texted him that one girl got sick and they had to cancel. He thought that it was unfortunate. Five tourists would have earned him and his two friends a lot of rupees.

And then the big man in his smelly car showed up and, with him, Kama's good luck.

The breakfast the man had bought him was delicious until the other man, the stinky man, dipped his fingers in Kama's food. After that he had lost his appetite.

Kama unbuckled his seatbelt. The clip let out a faint click. His body froze. He timidly glanced at the rich man, but he wasn't moving. Kama sighed in relief.

The stinky man was also asleep, breathing heavily and moaning now and again on a white couch. His forehead was all sweaty. He hadn't even taken off his military boots.

Kama had never seen a black man before. Except in the movies. Some of them were rich also. It didn't apply to that one. Rich men didn't shit themselves, and they listened to no one.

Although, when Kama had a second look, he thought that he wasn't really a black man at all. His skin was more yellowish-brown than black, and not that different from some Hindu. But his face was different, especially his full lips and flatter nose. And he had long fingers, and arms that weren't that big, but lean—every muscle was showing under his skin. Kama couldn't imagine how strong he was. But the rich man was strong like an elephant. Kama's wrist was still sore after he squeezed it in the restaurant.

He slowly rose to his feet and toddled to the middle of the cabin, ogling and stroking everything within his grasp: the white leather seats, the enormous TV screen, the glossy table, the soft, woven carpet.

The bar was where the rich man said the food and drinks were. A bottle of water and two glasses made of thick, cut glass stood on top of it. They looked expensive. He thought that he shouldn't touch them.

He crouched and opened the cabinet doors. His lips uttered a silent *wow*.

If only his friends could have seen him and these fancy bottles of wine, whiskey, and other stuff he didn't know, even from the movies. He pulled out his phone and took a picture, then another one of the cabin.

He wanted to upload them to his Facebook account, but there was no signal on the plane. No rush. He would do it later.

He set the photo of the bar as his phone wallpaper. It didn't fit too nicely as the screen of his old Asus was cracked, but with the money from the big man, he would buy a brand new Samsung Galaxy.

In the bar he also saw cookies, chocolate bars, and peanuts. Peanuts made his stomach bloat.

He rummaged in the basket for chocolate bars. He unwrapped one and took a bite, but his eyes lingered on the bottles.

These fancy bottles stared back at him. He looked around. No one saw him.

He gently picked up the whiskey. It had the digits "18" painted on top. He read that it was made in Ireland. He wondered if it was a country. Probably not. He had never heard of it, although he couldn't say he had heard about every country in the world.

He was glad that the bottle wasn't new. The big man had already drunk from it. Kama pulled out the cap and smelled from the bottleneck. Mmm … It was like vanilla ice cream. No wonder the rich man liked it.

He raised the bottle to his mouth but hesitated. This was not how rich people drank.

He took a glass from the cabinet and filled it to the half. Then he took a hefty gulp.

His insides ignited. His eyes bulged. It tasted nothing like ice cream. He covered his mouth and coughed. His tongue, his throat, his windpipe and his guts were searing.

He had never drunk an alcoholic drink, except Cobra beer, and it was only once, after a movie night, behind the shopping centre.

After the initial acrid taste, the whiskey actually left a sweet aftertaste in his mouth. So this is how it worked. Now Kama felt like a rich man himself.

He shut his eyes and emptied the glass. He coughed again, and the burning sensation returned, but not as strong as before.

He meant to pour another glass, but ... Why not try something else?

He took hold of a funny-shaped bottle. Bulky at the bottom, slimmer in the middle, and again wider a little bit, then slim and peaked. It read Henn ... Hene. He lowered his gaze to the bottom of the label. This he could read, "fine cognac."

This one hadn't been touched by anyone. So what? The man had said "do whatever you want." He opened it and poured to the brink of the glass. It was golden in colour. He slurped the excess and smacked his lips. It fired his stomach even better, though he didn't see much difference compared to the whiskey.

He pushed himself to his feet. Instantly, vertigo hit his head. He staggered and plopped onto the nearest seat. Cognac spilled on the carpet. *That pilot isn't good*, he thought, and took a gulp.

He liked the life of rich men. Soon he would be the richest among all his friends. The man promised him six big, green notes in euro money. He knew that money. Once, two French tourists had given him a generous tip, twenty euros. And he had only taken them for a two-hour ride. He showed them City Palace, Hawa Mahal—the Palace of Winds, Jantar Mantar Observatory, and then he had taken them to Jal Mahal—the Water Palace.

Those six notes the man would give him were like … forty thousand rupees. He couldn't imagine where else he could earn such a fortune.

But he felt sorry for the rich man. His wife was sick, and he wanted to find Sati, because she was his wife's grannie. Kama was doing a good thing. He just … he just didn't really like that the man carried a pistol. And he didn't like how the big man looked at him sometimes, and how he looked at other people.

He took another gulp from the fancy glass.

The rich man couldn't be a bad person. He was a troubled man. Kama saw it in his face. When someone's face was so cold, he had to be going through a bad time. Later, he would pray to Hanuman, his Monkey God, to release the big man from his worries.

The big man loved his wife so much that he came to India for her. Love was the greatest thing of all. "Kama" meant "God of love." God loved Kama. It was his destiny that he met the big man.

He sipped on his drink, thinking that he should quickly finish it. There were other beautiful bottles to taste.

Chapter 45

Van der Venn awoke from a deep sleep to see his jet touching down in Varanasi, at Lal Bahadur Shastri Airport. He hooked his hands behind his head and thrust out his chest, probing the reaction of his back. The pain abated.

He glanced to the side. Kama's seat was empty. He looked back. And winced. It wasn't what he'd had in mind when he told the boy to do whatever he wanted. Kama's body was on the floor, leaned against the seat by the bar's open door, his arms and legs apart, his head resting on his chest.

Van der Venn hoped the boy hadn't drunk himself to death, otherwise that meant one more dead man in his way, and he might even start believing in bad luck.

When the plane taxied beside the arrival hall, and the pilot cut the engines, he unbuckled his seatbelt and crossed to the boy.

He kicked the sole of his foot. 'Did you have fun?'

Kama opened his eyes and muttered something in Hindi.

In the bar, the Jameson whiskey was almost gone, and the Hennessey bottle was opened. The rest were intact. The boy must have had three or four glasses.

Van der Venn kicked his other foot. 'We've arrived in Varanasi. How about you start earning your salary?'

Waaberi sat up on the couch and waved hello with his floppy hand. He had grey-blue rings under his eyes and a vacant look on his face. Apart from that and his rumpled shirt, he seemed to be fit. If van der Venn had two ailing men dragging him down, he would be better off on his own.

Waaberi's clumsy movements froze when he saw Kama. 'Sorry, boss. Was I supposed to watch him?'

Van der Venn headed to the bathroom, opened a mirrored cabinet and took out a package containing a remedy Klaff had used to work off his hangover, and Klaff had sworn by it.

He filled the plastic cup with cold water and dissolved two tablets in it. Then he returned to the cabin and squatted down by the boy.

'Drink.'

Kama shook his head, holding out his hands. 'Nooo, Kama can't drink more, please, sir.'

Then he dropped his hands as if falling asleep again. Van der Venn waited a few seconds and slapped him on the face. The boy woke up.

'It's medicine. It will make you feel better.' He put the cup to the boy's mouth. 'Drink!'

Kama drank all of it. By the last gulp, he gagged and covered his mouth but didn't throw up.

'Go to the bathroom and put your head under the cold water,' van der Venn told him.

When they left the plane Waaberi and the boy shielded their eyes from the sun. Both looked as if they had partied for the straight twelve hours. Kama could barely stand on his own feet. Water was dripping from his hair and half of his T-shirt was wet. If not for Waaberi's grip under his pit, he would be going nowhere.

Van der Venn expected to move through the airport without interruptions, but halfway through the arrival lounge a short customs clerk with a bleak facial expression approached him and blocked their way.

He pointed at Waaberi and Kama, but addressed van der Venn. 'Sir, what happened to them?'

Van der Venn came to a stop. 'They were enjoying themselves.'

Waaberi and Kama broke their sluggish gait.

The man in uniform looked experienced in his job; his bearing was relaxed, apart from his narrowed eyes. Another officer watched them from a distance of ten metres with his hands crossed behind his back, his legs slightly apart.

The first officer glanced once more at Waaberi and Kama. 'What do you mean they were enjoying themselves?' His tone of voice took on a demanding tone.

'What I *mean* is that, cheap or expensive, an excess of liquor or food always brings the same ending,' he replied. 'I am not responsible for every greedy skunk that cannot control himself.'

The customs clerk's expression remained hard. Van der Venn felt an ankle holster with a smaller version of his Glock wrapped around his shin. He might have gone too far this time. The man might want to frisk them. Waaberi, who was unarmed, straightened his body.

The face of the first officer beamed, showing his uneven teeth. He waved at them to move on, adding something in Hindi, something funny judging by the wicked laughter coming from another clerk who was observing the scene.

When they walked into a pickup area of the airport, taxi drivers swarmed around them. Seeing Kama, they tried to convince him in Hindi to hire their car.

Van der Venn ignored their pestering and moved outside, away from the agitated group. He put on his sunglasses. The immediate area by the arrival building was for parking spaces only, with a few patches of green in between.

The sun was at its highest point in the cloudless sky. Without wind and humidity, a scorching swelter pouring from the sky made it hard to breathe.

Kama looked better but still wasn't fully conscious. He blubbered out something.

Van der Venn considered if he could afford to ditch the drunken kid; giving second chances wasn't his thing. But since that night in Malcesine, too many things had gone wrong, and that constant altering to his plan made him edgy. And he hated being anxious.

'Boss, should we ditch this little drunkard?' Waaberi stated more than asked.

Van der Venn raised Kama's chin with his index finger and looked into his cloudy eyes. 'Kama, do you know where Sati might be living? Do you understand me?'

For a short moment, Kama's eyes opened wider as if he were about to become more responsive, but soon his eyelids slipped, covering half of his pupils.

'Sati old … old…' was his only response.

Van der Venn raised his arm and ran his shirt's short sleeve across his forehead, wiping the sweat.

'Sati old … da … ta … n,' Kama continued in his veiled language.

'Boss,' Waaberi said, rubbing at his temple, 'I think he wants to say something.'

Van der Venn's nostrils fluttered. 'That's a truly ingenious remark.'

Waaberi rested his palm on his stomach. 'I'm sorry, boss. I'm not so good, yet.'

'From now on, you eat when I say so. Is that clear?' he snapped and spun on his heel. He needed a new plan.

'Yes, boss.'

'Sati old … ta … ta … ng.'

Van der Venn heard Kama's mumbling. He turned back to him.

Waaberi was leaning with his ear close to the boy's lips. 'I think he wants to say: Sati *old town*.'

'Sati old … town,' Kama uttered, as if a gag had been removed from his mouth. He spat saliva in doing so.

Waaberi wiped his cheek in disgust.

'That's a start,' van der Venn said. His investment in the boy had begun to repay itself.

The carpark, roughly fifty by fifty square metres, was packed with private cars and cabs. A balding man in his fifties who wore a beige fishing vest over an orange Indian kurta was rubbing the bonnet of a new-looking Hyundai Xcent with a microfiber cloth. A taxi sign was on the car's doors.

'Good day, sir,' he said when he saw them coming.

'The old town,' van der Venn said and took the front passenger seat. 'Find us a decent hotel.'

Waaberi helped Kama get in. Then he got into the car from the other side.

The driver started the ignition and said in English with a melodious Hindi accent, 'Right away, sir.'

He switched on the left indicator, and the car pulled out from the curb. 'I offer you a *very* decent accommodation in modern part of the city. I can see you and your companions travel on business.'

'What makes you think so?' van der Venn asked against his better judgment; small talk was a waste of time to him.

'Sir, I've been a taxi driver for *thirty-five* years,' he said and raised his index finger up. 'I know tourists when I see them and I know businessmen when I see them.'

He pointed at van der Venn's briefcase, lying on his lap. 'And you have only business case with you.'

According to that theory, a cabby wearing a fishing vest should be a trawler captain.

'My accommodation has a telephone, fax and internet, and is *surely* affordable for such businessmen like you,' he went on, prolonging the middle syllables in every word. 'And it's not that far from the old-town crowd, which is now full of backpackers.' He puckered his lips. 'Not a company for such a splendid businessman like you, sir.'

'Just take us to the old town,' van der Venn said and ran his hand through his greasy hair. At least he had remembered to change his shirt before they left the plane, although it felt like putting a clean tuxedo on a muddy overall.

The car pulled onto a two-lane road.

'This is my pleasure to take you to the *splendid* hotel in the old town,' the driver replied.

They drove through clamorous traffic, although not as intense as in Jaipur, unless van der Venn was simply getting used to it. Thirty minutes later they reached Varanasi's Old Town district.

Van der Venn checked Waaberi into a twin room with Kama, despite Waaberi's protest. Someone had to keep an eye on the boy, and he had no plans to be anyone's babysitter.

He told Waaberi to let Kama sleep, then to throw the boy under a shower, pour a litre of coffee into him and then to meet him downstairs in three hours.

Van der Venn opened the door to a room situated on the fifth floor of a five-star hotel. It was well maintained; the modern furniture lived up to his first-class-apartment expectations. He put down the briefcase next to the king-size bed, kicked off his shoes, and slumped on the sheets. He stretched, testing if his back would hurt. He lifted his legs and arms. He was fine.

At first the inside of the room felt nicely cool, but when his body adjusted to the temperature, which was not that much lower than outside, he started to sweat again. He didn't feel like getting up to check the air-conditioning control on the wall.

His eyelids felt heavy, as did his body. The different time zone and the long flight from Italy were catching up with him, and those painkillers made him drowsy.

He half-closed his eyes.

He had never been to Varanasi. But he sensed that was in the right place. They called this city holy. No better setting for him. The stone tablet had to be born in a holy place.

He tried to imagine what the people who engraved that message on the tablet looked like. What tools had they used? Who gave them the text?

Loud banging broke him from his reverie. His temples

pounded. Had he fallen asleep? If he had, he had never fully closed his eyes.

'Boss! Are you there?'

Van der Venn pulled up his torso and sat on the edge of the bed. He rubbed his dry eyes, then got to his feet.

He swung the door open. 'What time is it?'

Waaberi shrugged his shoulders. 'I don't know, boss, but I waited three hours like you told me. Then I tried to get something out of the boy and he said that it was useless to look for someone tonight.'

'Why?'

'He says that everyone is out, and not only tourists. Sati is out there to be too.'

'What?' Van der Venn touched his forehead. Was it food poisoning that impaired Waaberi's ability to speak clearly?

'This is exactly what *he* said, boss.'

Van der Venn opened the soundproof window and leaned on the sill. Sultry, heavy air engulfed him as if he had stuck his head into a dry sauna room. The sun was heading towards the horizon line.

He hadn't bothered to peer out the window after he had entered the room. The front wall of the hotel was set closely to other buildings, not giving away what view awaited on the other side. Now he realized that the hotel stood on the bank of the Ganges.

Hundreds of boats floated on the river that stretched out and squirmed from left to right and right to left like an enormous anaconda. From the boats, scores of tourists were snapping photos of the shoreline. Camera flashes sparkled on the river, as if the snake's skin were covered with luminous scales.

People, most of them Hindu, flocked to the concrete riverbank, sat on the stairs leading to the water, chanted, prayed, and meditated. Jingling bells galled van der Venn's ears.

He shut the window, returning to the vacuum silence of the room. 'How's Kama?'

Waaberi shrugged again. 'He's still drunk. How much did he have from your bar, boss?' A grimace of disapproval crossed his face. 'What a waste.'

Van der Venn knew that behind Waaberi's distaste was jealousy, because he had never allowed him to enjoy the bar on the jet.

'Have you eaten?' van der Venn asked.

'No, boss.' Waaberi looked down. 'You forbade me—'

'Go back to your room. Order something light. Tell them you want European or American cuisine. And get something for that boy. You both *must be* at your best first thing tomorrow morning.'

'Yes, boss,' Waaberi said in a meek voice, standing by the door with slumped shoulders. 'Boss, I'm sorry for—'

'I have things to do,' he said, cutting him off. 'Get out.'

When Waaberi left the room, van der Venn took a deep breath. His men weren't only getting sloppy, they were getting useless.

CHAPTER 46

VAN DER VENN took a sip of the coffee he had made in the shiny espresso machine that was standing on an elegant art deco table in the corner of his room. It tasted like dyed dishwater. One thing he had to give to the Italians when he stayed in Malcesine—they knew how to brew a good coffee.

He put more sugar into his cup and crossed to the window. The sun was setting, but that couldn't obscure what he already saw out there. And despised. Already, on the way to the hotel, he had taken an instant dislike to Varanasi. It really was old, and full of beggars, junkies and the sort.

He wished someone would bring the old woman to him, so he wouldn't have to leave the hotel room.

In any case, it was no disaster he didn't find Sati Joshi tonight. It would be pointless to chase after her if the whole town was out. The only person who knew what she looked like was half conscious from alcohol poisoning. Klaff's tablets were apparently efficient to beat the next-day hangover, although even that was yet to be seen.

Nina Monte and Pini shouldn't arrive in Varanasi until late, and that is only if they caught an early train from Jaipur. If they did, it was still too complicated to track them down on his own. The Indian trains were overcrowded. Newcomers were arriving in thousands. Besides, Monte didn't have the current address of her grandmother either. Otherwise, she wouldn't have gone to her house in Jaipur in the first place.

On top of everything, he had an advantage—Nina Monte had no idea he was in Varanasi. She wouldn't try to hide her grandmother from him.

He put the empty cup on the table, picked up the briefcase, and sat on the bed.

It was impossible for a burglar to open it. The lock responded only to his fingerprints, and the Kevlar shell protected the precious inside from any incursion attempt.

He stroked the briefcase with both hands.

Was he about to meet God?

He burst out laughing.

About to meet God. Did he really believe in that? Did Nina Monte and her pitiful friend? Did anyone? He was intrigued with Monte's essay. In reality, he was chasing after something else, after a different kind of treasure.

Tonight, more so than before, he had to remind himself why he was acting like a lunatic who bragged about entering the Kingdom of Heaven. People tended to be more scared of a crazy man; they tended to do as a crazy man told them to, and rarely asked questions. That's why.

Van der Venn kept his real plans regarding the tablet under wraps. They weren't as farfetched as meeting God.

Also, the less people knew about his project, the better the surprise. So he told no one.

Except for Klaff. But Klaff was gone. Van der Venn didn't think Waaberi could comprehend what was going on. His perception of the world was shallow, and existed only on the level of survival.

Van der Venn wanted much more. He wanted to achieve something monumental in his lifetime and beyond.

His collection of artefacts was vast. But nobody would remember him for his underwater excavation of gold coins, pearls, rubies and sapphires, no matter how rare they were, nor the ancient weapons, the statues dated five hundred years B.C. and everything else he had found on those forgotten galleys.

He wondered if other successful collectors had similar reflections. Some of them must have. He saluted those explorers who got themselves killed trying to become unforgettable.

Now he would surpass them all.

He had in his possession the stone tablet forged from the soul of the Holy City. The stone tablet, which was one of its kind. The message engraved in it represented the birth of all religions.

Without proper interpretation, the tablet wasn't worth as much as it would be with the full text decoded. And that would be something sublime not only for religious people, but for all of mankind.

The Louvre in Paris, the Acropolis in Athens, the British Museum in London, the Egyptian Museum in Cairo, the Prado in Madrid, and maybe even the Vatican would be begging him for the right to exhibit the tablet. Millions would be queuing to get an eyeful of it.

The name Lammert van der Venn was to be set in stone for eternity as the greatest explorer ever. Everyone would be speaking of him with great respect and adoration.

Even after his death, he would stay immortal—and so his dream would be fulfilled.

He placed the briefcase in the wardrobe. Then he checked the GPS signal on a small device. The red dot beeped. Its location overlapped with van der Venn's position. He slid the wardrobe shut.

He felt invigorated, as if the sole thought about his upcoming triumph had awoken in him latent layers of stamina. He might get lucky tonight.

He checked his weapon, grabbed the plastic key card, and left his room.

CHAPTER 47

BEHIND A ROUND reception desk with a stony, polished counter, van der Venn saw a man dressed in a black three-piece suit, a blue shirt and a diagonally striped tie who was speaking on the phone in Spanish. When he noticed van der Venn, he acknowledged his presence with a half-bow and a cordial smile. After a short while, he said into the receiver, "*Buenas noches*" and hung up.

'Good evening, sir,' he said, switching to English. 'Are you going out? If you wish, I can arrange for you a private guide, who will explain to you in *every* detail all particularities of the celebration. I *promise* you won't be disappointed.'

He spoke with a similar accent to the taxi driver, only more distinctive. Van der Venn felt like he was on a Bollywood movie set.

'What time is the next train from Jaipur?'

The receptionist looked at him as if he spoke in an unknown language.

Van der Venn rested his hands on the counter. 'Should I sing it out to you, so you can understand?'

The man gave a sheepish smile and clicked on a computer keyboard.

'The next train from Jaipur is due in Varanasi in one hour and thirty-four minutes, sir,' he said, speaking slowly in a voice that had taken on a robotic tone. 'Do you wish me to send someone there? Are your friends coming over? The second penthouse suite next to yours is available.'

'My friends are quite inventive. They will take care of themselves just fine,' he said tersely and turned away.

The ground around the hotel was kept clean by a man in a loose shirt with the hotel logo on his chest who was sweeping the stairs. When he saw van der Venn, he put the brush to the side, bowed his head, and said, 'Have a nice evening, sir.'

Van der Venn nodded and stepped out on the pavement. It was cooler than a few hours ago, but that sticky, unseen vapour still hung in the air.

There were no taxis, no rickshaws, or any form of transportation that normally occupied the front yard of any hotel in the world—there was no space for them here. This part of the old town had only alleys, too narrow for a vehicle. Everyone who wished to stay in this hotel had to negotiate the last one hundred metres on foot.

He headed to the right after a group of European-looking tourists.

After a minute of walking, the stream of people heading in the same direction grew tenfold, and the scenery around van der Venn changed.

The paint on the walls on both sides of a narrow alley was peeling off. On some buildings the work had finished after the raw plaster had been applied. Bundles of cables hung not far above van der Venn's head. He kept his eyes down. Being careless here meant stepping into mud or cow shit.

The entire place felt dirty to him.

He turned left through a dark passage. In the last moment, he recoiled, by a whisker avoiding a motorbike passing with speed.

He found himself in a touristy alley. Shops selling trinkets, candles, incense, and clothing were imbedded in two unbroken lines of walls. A group of stoned backpackers with long, disgusting dreads on their heads drank beer in an open bar, and smoked marijuana.

Van der Venn heard a loud, lengthy sound that resembled a ship's horn. He stopped and strained his ears, trying to locate its root. It died away, so he moved his way down the alley.

The farther he walked, the more intense the smell of burning incense was. He passed place after place with smoking sticks tucked into pots filled with ashes and dirt, spreading the same pungent smell.

He followed the stream of people of all ages. With every step, the sound of prayer bells and chanting grew stronger. When he was pushed out to an open space, all his previous observations were amplified.

Every square metre of wide concrete steps leading down to the water was taken by spectators. Other people sat on roofs of the nearby buildings, or on the boats floating on the river. All of them were watching a pagan ceremony taking place forty metres down on the bank of the Ganges.

He was surprised to see among the crowd so many well-dressed tourists who enjoyed those festivities of nonsense.

They chanted to the rhythm of bells and fire on the chain, which five zonked monks waved in all directions. Van der Venn would have to smoke something much stronger than marijuana to sit there and watch those lunatics. By their feet, he saw large seashells, and realized what had caused that ship horn sound minutes before.

Someone grabbed his hand. He glanced down and saw a crippled, raw-boned beggar. His toothless lower jaw was protruding from his oval skull. He had no legs.

Van der Venn jerked out his hand and cursed under his breath. It felt like being struck by the plague. He turned around and pushed his way back without a word of excuse; his bulky posture spoke for itself. With little effort he reached a less packed alley.

Even if somewhere among those people by the river was the old woman he was after, tonight it would be impossible to find her. Now he had seen that for himself. That was enough.

He felt dirty. All those hands that touched him. All those in front of him he had to touch so as not to walk into them.

He wasn't on the same path he had used to get there, but he couldn't wait to get out of this place. It should be easy to find his hotel. After all, it had taken him less than fifteen minutes to reach the river. He was moving along the street parallel to the Ganges.

A hot shower and a bloody steak were the only things he had on his mind.

He was about to speed up his pace when, out of the corner of his eye, he caught sight of something intriguing. He took another three steps when a thought sank in and he came to a halt, trying to switch off his perception of Varanasi, to let his brain find a link between the brief picture of what he had just seen and the information he already had stored in his head.

It was the same feeling as when he was under the water exploring sunken ships and spotted something unique. Like that tip of *Santa Lucia's* mast he had located at the bottom of Lake Garda.

Someone bumped into him from behind, but he hardly noticed that. The person murmured *sorry* and walked away.

Van der Venn turned his head. With narrowed eyes, he gazed at the top arch of a closed gateway that led to a vast household or shrine.

He moved closer to it and scrutinized the words engraved above it. The halogen bulb from the handmade saris shop across the alley cast some light on the gateway.

He had seen one of these words before. He had studied it on his yacht, and later on the jet with Nina Monte. They had managed to decipher the meaning of it. This was the word belonging to the first mantra engraved in the tablet.

It translated into "divine illumination."

His heart rate stayed unruffled. His palms didn't sweat, and his breath remained steady.

The times when he had become excited in a primitive way were long gone, though there was one reaction he had no control over—his sight became hazy.

His eyes shone impatiently, as if after a long time of seeing nothing but darkness, they were finally free to descry the universe.

Van der Venn pushed the gate with the pads of his fingers. It opened with a creak and he stepped inside.

CHAPTER 48

IT HAD TO be very late, Nina thought, lying stretched out in the compartment's lower berth. Her body felt heavy and difficult to coordinate, as if she were covered up to her neck with a half a metre layer of wet sand. Her skin felt clammy. Tufts of her hair stuck to her cheek. Was the air-conditioning running?

After another moment she realized that the train wasn't moving. She wondered for how long. The door opened and closed.

She lifted one eyelid and squinted her other eye. Alessandro sat beside her and leaned over.

'We've arrived in Varanasi,' he said. 'Nina? Are you awake? We're here.'

She pulled the hair out of her face. She must have looked terrible, as she always did in the morning if she didn't feel fully rested. But it couldn't be morning; it was semi-dark in the carriage.

'Are you sure?' she half asked, half yawned. 'Did they announce the station?'

She had fallen asleep when the day was still bright and the sun was high.

'Of course they did,' Alessandro said. 'My Hindi is getting better fast.'

She looked at him, raising her eyebrows; the only muscles she knew she could operate.

'What? It just feels like Varanasi to me,' he said with confidence.

Nina rubbed her eyes. Her head seemed to be the heaviest part of her body. She pulled herself up and leaned her back against the compartment partition. 'Does it?'

Alessandro rose to his feet and smiled, shaking his head. 'No. Everyone is getting off and I saw the sign with the city name.'

Nina looked around, alarmed. 'Where is the briefcase? I can't see the briefcase!'

He perched beside her and grabbed her arms in a calming grip. 'Van der Venn took it, in Innsbruck. You don't remember?'

She stared at him. Innsbruck? She remembered Innsbruck. But that felt like weeks ago; certainly half a world away. Jaipur and their escape, she could also remember. And Malcesine and their escape. She was on the run. What nonsense it was. She was a professor in Padua, not a refugee or a convict.

She put her hand to her forehead. 'What time is it?'

'In Varanasi? Ten twenty,' he said. 'In Malcesine? Ten minutes to six. No wonder I feel refreshed. I think I managed to catch a few hours of sound sleep.'

He did two rapid squats. Nina heard a loud crack in his joints, and she opened her eyes wider.

Alessandro gave a thin grin. 'Don't panic, it's normal. I was born with it.'

She put her feet on the floor and saw her reflection in the mirror. For one short second, she didn't recognize herself.

She wasn't used to the new clothes Alessandro had bought her at one of the stations during a twelve-minute stopover. He told her that he had found a ten-euro note crumpled deep in his shorts rear pocket, and had decided to make good use of it. As a result, Nina was wearing a long, cotton, printed skirt in a flaming scarlet colour with elephants and deer, and a jade vest-top with thin shoulder straps.

He had also bought a late lunch for them. It surprised her how fast he was adapting to the local cuisine, and how tastefully he had picked her clothes.

Above all, though, Nina loved that sensation of protectiveness she felt from him stronger and stronger.

She took the plastic bag, packed her sweaty designer clothes, and they left the compartment.

Alessandro stepped down on the platform, turned around and held out his hands. He must have forgotten that she wasn't wearing a tight pencil skirt anymore. She made one step, leaned forward and let him help her down.

On the platform, Hindu pilgrims and tourists with heavy backpacks kept emerging from the train. Everyone was in an organized hurry.

Nina recollected the evening when she had arrived in Heidelberg a few days ago, where everything had started. As she had walked among the people in the Heidelberg train station who hurried to watch the fireworks, here, as well, she wandered surrounded by those who came to see the celebration of light.

The air was muggy, but the night breeze kept it warm, in the mid-twenties. She was grateful for her new clothes, which didn't cling to her skin, letting the air circulate over her whole body.

Alessandro took her by the hand. 'How are we going to find a room for the night?'

'This is the first day of the celebration,' Nina said and pulled him to a cash machine. 'Let's not waste the chance to see it. *Then* we think about a hotel.'

She withdrew seven thousand rupees, which was more or less one hundred euros. Then she crossed to a taxi stand and leaned into an open window of a yellow Nissan.

'Are you free?' she asked in Hindi.

A driver raised his eyebrows, then he nodded.

They got into the cab, with an elegant forty-something Hindu driver who looked like a smile had never left his mouth. Nina asked him to take them to the old town.

The car moved out of the packed square, and pulled into the busy road. Honks of vehicles grew in strength, reminding Nina about the craziness of traffic in Jaipur. Here most of what made the clatter were motorbikes and tuk-tuks.

'Is it really the oldest city in the world?' Alessandro asked.

'Depends on whom you ask,' Nina said. 'One of the oldest, for sure. I've never been here, but the moment we left the train station it felt … welcoming.'

He turned his head away to the window. 'Well, I'm still working on it.'

Nina looked at the traffic in front of them. She wondered if it was always like that in the City of Lights. The buildings by the road weren't tall, only here and there she saw a modern high-rise block. The flow of the people was moving in one direction, but the sidewalks weren't that full. The ceremony by the river had to be in full swing.

After twenty minutes, their taxi pulled over.

'If you want to see celebration by the river,' the driver said to Nina, 'follow other people. Later, if you didn't book a hotel,' he glanced at her, and she shook her head, 'there are plenty of hostels at every corner, though I doubt you'll find anything free. Only the most expensive rooms will be vacant.'

Nina thanked him and paid him one hundred fifty rupees for the ride and another fifty for being friendly.

They headed towards the river. Even if no one else was going in that direction, Nina wouldn't have had difficulty in finding the way. They followed the jangle of hundreds of small bells that somehow broke through the traffic noise. Pious singing accompanied a fervid thudding of drums, calling the late-coming pilgrims, urging them to hurry up.

After a ten-minute walk, they reached an area by the river illuminated by halogens fixed to high poles. Street lamps were giving additional sources of light. Hundreds of smaller bulbs hung on long cords spread on and between the houses and above people's heads like Christmas decorations.

Here, the singing and the sound of bells was much louder, but Nina's ears quickly adapted to it. The scent of sandalwood travelled through the air. It reminded her of the first meditation lessons given by Sati many years ago.

Pilgrims and tourists were standing everywhere, observing the ongoing ceremony. Those who found a free place were sitting on long stairs leading to the water. There was not that much more room for latecomers.

At the end of the stairs, on a flat, concrete riverbank, several Hindu priests stood in a row, each on a thirty-centimetre podium, three metres apart from one another. They wore shiny, orange, traditional shirts and gold trousers. They moved in a synchronized manner as if dancing. In one hand they wielded candles set on brazen, cone-shaped chandeliers, and in the other they waved bells.

Behind the priests, the Ganga resembled an extension of the ground audience, where people watched the ceremony from an amphitheatre of boats crammed side by side.

Nina stood on her tiptoes and said into Alessandro's ear, 'From darkness lead us to light. This is what they're chanting.'

Alessandro stepped behind Nina, threw his arms around her, and pulled her close to his body. She held onto his hands, feeling the pleasant warmth of his embrace. They watched the spectacle for several more minutes, shoulder to shoulder with other onlookers.

Then the singing coming from the loudspeakers intensified. People clapped their hands rhythmically and drums continued pounding. Pilgrims floated candles set in small cups down the river.

'This is amazing,' Alessandro said, leaning to her neck. She felt his hot breath on her skin and it sent a warm shiver down her spine.

'Here is the biggest gathering, although they celebrate in other places,' she shouted back through the sounds of the bells. 'Varanasi won't sleep for the next five days.'

An elderly woman turned to them. She was dressed in a decorated orange sari, and had a red dot on her forehead; she put her finger to her mouth. For a split second, Nina thought that it was her grandma. Her heart thudded in her chest, as if someone had injected her veins with a shot of caffeine, and panic set in. If that really was Sati, Nina was at a loss for words.

The woman turned away, but that boost of awareness cost Nina lots of energy. She felt weary again.

She pulled on Alessandro's arm. 'We should find a place to sleep before everyone heads home.'

Then she led him down the stairs through the crowd and towards the riverbank, away from the ceremony. The farther they walked, the quieter it became. Less people strolled along the shore. Some sat on the ground, staring at thousands of candle lights floating on the Ganges.

Nina spotted a barefoot boy who sat on the steps. He couldn't be older than ten, and wore only shorts. He was selling the same candles, which pilgrims continued to drop down the river, each in a small saucer-like pot made of leaves and flowers placed in two straight rows.

'We're looking for a room,' Nina said in Hindi.

The boy looked up at her but didn't reply. He just kept his mouth open. Nina repeated the same. He still didn't seem to understand.

Alessandro put his palms together to the side of his temple and angled his head as if resting it on a pillow. 'Sleep,' he said in English.

The boy gathered his stuff, stood up, and sprinted up the stairs. When he was on the last step, he turned around and gestured to them with his hand to follow him.

Nina glanced at Alessandro. 'Sorry. I must be exhausted if I can't put together a simple sentence.'

'Have more faith in your talents, Professor,' Alessandro said and moved up the stairs. 'That boy is deaf.'

Nina ran after him. 'How do you know that?'

'When you were speaking, he was staring at your lips. I'm sure he couldn't see them properly in semi darkness. Besides, I know that look. My friend's niece is deaf.'

They followed the young Hindu through narrow, scarcely lit lanes. Once, they had to grope for the wall. Nina tried to keep her sense of direction, but after the fifth turn she had no idea where he was taking them. Most of all, they tried not to lose their guide, who moved swiftly, without peering behind his shoulder to check if they kept up with him.

Finally, the boy came to a stop by a ground-floor house with shabby walls and barred, dark windows. He glanced back at them and walked in.

In the semidarkness, Nina saw only half of Alessandro's head. The upper half was buried in someone's laundry that hung above them and was hooked to the opposite house.

She resisted a laugh. 'Don't expect anything similar to your hotel in Malcesine.'

The boy poked his head through the door and waved to them to come in.

'Any bed would be fine, Signora Monte,' Alessandro said. 'As long as you're not far away.'

CHAPTER 49

INSIDE A TINY room that looked like a reception area, Nina saw a skinny man dozing in an easy chair. His face was turned away from the candle, the flame almost dead, but the wrinkled hands couldn't belong to a young person. The Hindu boy touched his arm. It didn't wake the man, so the boy opened the drawer of a flimsy desk and took out a key.

He waved at Nina and Alessandro and led them farther through the room to a square-shaped courtyard. There was a door on each wall.

The boy opened the padlock and unbolted the door, right across the entrance they had come through. He went in and pressed the switch on the wall. A single bulb hanging from the ceiling flickered. The boy grabbed a stool from the room corner, put it under the bulb, climbed it, stretched on his tiptoes and poked it with his finger. The bulb shone brighter, so he jumped off and dropped the padlock key on the stool.

The inside of the room looked surprisingly tidy. The bare walls were painted in a beautiful amethyst colour. A double-size mattress—apart from the stool, the only furniture—covered with a white sheet and two pillows took most of the floor space. On the right side was a long, thick curtain behind which, Nina guessed, was a window.

Alessandro threw himself on the mattress and hooked his hands behind his head. 'Not a four-star hotel, but it will do.'

Nina took out a bundle of rupees she had withdrawn from the ATM. When the boy saw the money, he shook his head vigorously and pointed towards the exit.

'I see. The other man takes care of finances,' Nina said. 'But this,' she said, holding out a five-hundred-rupee note, 'is for *you*.' She pointed at the money and then at his chest. 'For. You.'

The boy stood motionless for a moment, gazing at her hand, then reached out for the note and scampered away.

Nina closed the door and checked what was to her left, behind another curtain. A bathroom. It was half the size of the room, and consisted of a toilet, a tiny sink, and a short shower nozzle sticking out of the mosaic-tiled wall. A small window was protected by a mosquito screen. Below it, a turquoise bath towel hung on a hook.

'What's in there?' Alessandro called out. 'A bathroom? Please don't tell me if it doesn't have a bathtub with a whirlpool massage and built-in loud speakers.'

Nina smiled and walked in. She had to leave the curtain open as there was no light in there. Without thinking if Alessandro could see her, she undressed and hung her clothes on the towel hook.

She opened the faucet and waited for a moment, then probed it with her hand. The water was cold, so she turned it in the opposite direction. As it didn't change much, she turned it back and waited until a lukewarm stream gushed out of the nozzle.

Her eyes opened wider when she stepped closer and the water touched her skin. She trembled and folded her arms over her chest. After ten seconds her skin got used to the temperature. She picked up the travel-size soap from the sink, unpacked it and washed herself.

Alessandro walked into the bathroom, looking into her eyes. His body was evenly tanned, slender and fit. Nina smiled, gave him space under the shower, and handed him the soap.

It felt natural to have him so close, despite feeling so vulnerable. She trusted him. They had been through a lot, and he had never left her when she needed him.

She found she was still a bit self-conscious after all, because she turned her back to him. But when she felt his hands subtly massaging her back and neck, she exhaled and relaxed. The water became warmer.

Alessandro pulled her closer, and she let a quiet moan escape her lips when he kissed her neck.

'I want you so much,' he whispered

Nina tilted her head and closed her eyes. Each time his lips touched her sensitive skin, the flame inside her grew stronger.

She didn't want him to stop. She wanted to relish every second, craving for the new waves of pleasure.

***

Nina turned on her side on the mattress and snuggled into Alessandro's chest.

After a while, he asked in a low voice, 'What're you thinking about?'

'How happy I am now,' she said softly, as if there were someone behind the door eavesdropping who could take her joy away.

'I'm thinking about van der Venn.'

Nina slapped his arm. 'Thanks a lot, Alessandro Pini! I tell you how good I feel and you think about criminals.'

'Oh, c'mon. Don't be like that.'

She cuddled him again.

'Could he make it to Varanasi?' Alessandro asked.

Nina adjusted her head on his arm. 'Even if he *is* here, the moment we arrived in Varanasi I felt that the city would somehow look after Sati,' she whispered. 'I understand why she came here. She must feel like home among these old temples and shrines.'

Alessandro propped his elbows on the mattress. 'What about us? Will this place look after us also?'

'Tomorrow, we will find Sati, make sure she's well and safe, and then we inform our embassy about everything. And you will call your mother.'

'Sounds like a good plan, Professor, but … there is just that one thing…' Alessandro's voice sounded alarmed. It made Nina uneasy.

Was he going to tell her that he had a girlfriend? She realized how little she knew about him. Her heartbeat quickened.

'Have you told me absolutely everything about that stone? On the train, I thought that you were keeping something from me.'

Nina let out a discreet sigh of relief, sat up, turned to him, and crossed her legs. 'I will tell you how my essay ends, but remember, it's only a theory. Okay?' She cleared her throat. 'The whole process of enlightenment leads not only to meeting with the Creator. If everything works, according to what Sati wrote to me, the person who recites all the mantras from the tablet one after another becomes himself *the* Creator.'

There it was. When she said it out loud, she didn't remember why she feared to do so earlier. It was only a story. But a story that van der Venn had made real in her mind.

'It doesn't mean, though,' she went on, 'that whoever does that would make a wise and merciful Creator. The tablet only enhances the traits of a human's character. The good person becomes better; the bad turns into … you know, a monster.'

Alessandro sat up. 'Then what?'

Nina took a long breath, then exhaled. 'There's another theory—you might have heard about it, and many people agree with it—that says that we are all connected to one source of knowledge and understanding, let's call it the highest knowledge, which we all take from, although not everyone knows how to tap into it.'

Alessandro frowned. 'I have heard something like that.'

'That highest knowledge represents nothing else but exactly the Creator—or God, if you will. So, returning to my essay, the changing of God also means the change of that highest knowledge. Subsequently for many of us, it would completely reorganize the way we see our world and how we act upon that view.'

'Nina, in plain language, please,' Alessandro said, scratching the back of his head.

'Taking van der Venn as a possible choice for God's … position, many would become like him, coldblooded, merciful and egoistic, because our brains would be linked to his mind. It's like a virus spreading to every computer powered by the same operating system.'

Alessandro burst out laughing and clapped his hands.

'Absurd. Good story, but still, absurd. Keeping in line with our rhetorical discussion, this is what I think, and if you ask anyone else they would say the same thing.'

Nina chewed the inside of her cheek. 'Tell me.'

Alessandro spread his hands. 'It's simple, Professor. If those things were possible, my God would never allow for them to happen.'

She smiled at him softly. 'Your God? Alessandro, if God exists, there is no *your* or *their* God. There is only one God people pray to. They just depict him differently. Do you think that nine hundred million Hindu people or one-point-six billion Muslims for that matter believe in a false God?'

Alessandro pondered for a moment what she had said. 'Is this why you were silent when van der Venn questioned me on the plane? Do you agree with him that I am a hypocrite?'

'No, I don't,' she said quickly. 'You're a religious person and you have the right to hold onto your deepest beliefs. There's nothing wrong with that.'

He looked away, so Nina moved closer to him. He clasped his hands around her.

'Remember what I told you earlier,' she said in a soft voice. 'All of that is just a theory. Tomorrow you can ask Sati about everything, if you want.'

She pulled herself up, holding onto his neck, and leaned her forehead against his. Then she kissed him, and Alessandro kissed her back.

CHAPTER 50

ALESSANDRO BLINKED HIS eyes open. He felt like he was suffocating. His breath was rapid, short and shallow. He could hardly move. He looked down at his body and frowned. He was wrapped like a mummy in the sheet he slept on. It was wet from his sweat, constraining his movement, and Nina wasn't there to help.

He rolled to the side, squirmed desperately and let himself free. He filled up his lungs with air like a diver who had emerged from the depths of a rough sea.

His head and heart were pounding. His body was clammy; it had to be at least thirty degrees in the room. He blinked a few times and pulled himself to a sitting position.

Daylight was coming from somewhere to his right. His eyes were too sensitive to look over there directly.

The chilling chanting from his nightmare didn't want to let go. It lingered in his head, confusing him about what was real and what wasn't. He massaged his temples with the heels of his palms.

He didn't remember ever having such a horrible experience in his dreams.

Usually, he didn't remember his dreams at all, and if he did, they were full of weird stuff like driving his scooter across his hometown lake, or playing football on San Siro for the audience of excited women who shouted his name, and when he scored a goal they rushed to the pitch to strip him naked.

Once, after a tough day, he had dreamt that his hotel went bankrupt. But after waking he could usually easily brush the distressing thoughts away.

Not today.

This dream was different. It was about ... What was the word? Annihilation. Destruction. Also. But not exactly. It was judgment day. It was so tangible.

Alessandro hid his face in his hands. Dried streaks on his cheeks stung. Had he been crying? Could people cry in their dreams? If they could laugh, why not cry?

In his nightmare, a four-arm giant had been sitting on a blazing throne on the riverbank, and the river was also aflame. It was night, and the surroundings were like those by the Ganges that he had seen yesterday. He heard similar chanting, although he couldn't see who was singing.

In front of Alessandro, a queue of people awaited their turn to near the four-arm monster. Alessandro was one of them.

The queue was moving forward with frightening efficiency. The giant used all of his four hands to scoop people, throwing them to the right or placing them somewhere to the left. Alessandro couldn't see where they went because the shore was steep, and he was too far away.

When the giant shoved people to the right, he did it with an imperious smirk. When he placed someone to the left, he put on a disappointed face. Men, women and children were taking his judgment in silence. No one protested, no one screamed, no one tried to run away.

Alessandro couldn't move in any other direction but onward at a steady pace, as if his feet were welded to mechanical boots that the giant controlled. It was getting hotter. He felt the fire from the river on his skin.

He thought that he should pray. He could only recall one prayer, one that his mother had taught him when he was a boy, and it had been imprinted in his memory ever since.

He recited it silently: "I believe in God the Father Almighty, Creator of Heaven and Earth, and in Jesus Christ … God from God, Light from Light—"

A short, slouching man who walked in front of him turned around. Alessandro gaped, seeing Klaff. He wanted to shout out in alarm, but his mouth was sealed.

Klaff's lips didn't move either, though Alessandro heard him in his own head: *There is no light anymore, you schmuck.* Alessandro ignored him and looked up. The giant seemed to have grown bigger.

Three hands, like arms of a mechanical crane, caught a woman and two men and threw them to the right. Now Alessandro saw where. If he could, he would stop right there and then run away, but his feet were leading him relentlessly towards the same destiny.

Disfigured demons feasted on the new bodies, like a horde of ravenous beasts. Then they threw the bones into the scorching flames of the river. Alessandro averted his gaze.

The fourth arm hoisted a child and put it down gently to the left, among a small group of other children, and a few women and men who were chanting. This was what Alessandro had heard from the beginning. An old woman sat in front of them. A white light hovered above her head like a halo.

Another person was sitting next to her, a little behind. Alessandro's pulse accelerated. It was Nina. She was naked, but he couldn't see any details of her figure, as a vivid violet light emanated from her body.

Alessandro decided that he wouldn't allow the giant to catch him. He would jump into the flames himself. He was getting closer and closer. He tried to count people to know when it would be his turn, but he couldn't get his head around it.

The huge arms hovered over him. Klaff was the last one in that round. He landed among the demons. They didn't touch him. He was becoming one of them and … Alessandro didn't look.

The heat was blistering; flames from the river consumed oxygen. He must have cried then, but the blaze dried his tears.

The arm reached for Alessandro. He felt its grip crushing his ribcage. He woke up—his unconscious couldn't bear it anymore.

As terrifying as his dream was, and impossible as it was to forget, only one thought now tormented Alessandro.

Why was he so sure he was to end up in the hands of demons?

He raised his head and took a few deep breaths. It was just a wicked dream caused by what he had seen over the last few days: that four-arm god in Sati's Jaipur house, the multitude of lights on the Ganges yesterday, Nina's stories about demonic forces that were trying to destroy the world, Klaff, and even a change in his diet. He had heard that indigestion could produce horrible dreams. Only, he actually liked the Indian food.

He turned his head to the light that was pouring into the room. The curtain was open and he saw the door, and slowly got to his feet.

Outside was a small terrace. Nina sat cross-legged on its edge, clad in her new skirt. She had pulled it up and was wearing it as a dress. She was murmuring something.

Alessandro put on his shorts and stepped out of the room. She turned her body to him, and a tenuous smile crossed her face.

'When I woke up at sunrise,' she said in a shaky voice, 'I felt so fresh and happy. I came out here, sat down, crossed my legs, and tried to remember how to meditate. It was easy. So I started, and suddenly I could perceive the vibrations of Varanasi, the Ganga, and the people. It was wonderful. Then…'

Tears welled up in her eyes.

Alessandro wanted to go to her, but his legs got heavy again like in his dream. 'What, Nina?'

'I felt an energy vibrating and buzzing at the base of my spine. It ran up and down my spine like subtle electric shocks. It was like I was being tuned to something. Finally, I felt warmth at the crown of my head, and bliss.'

'I thought that meditation was supposed be like that?' he said.

'Yes, but then a profound sorrow arose, because all my life I was afraid of something that was in me. So beautiful, celestial and genuine. I had denied its presence, but it was *always* in me.' Anger took the place of her tears. 'All my life is a fake! All my life I considered myself a scientific, logical person, which I'm not, which I don't want to be. I don't want to have an explanation to everything to confirm its right to existence!'

Alessandro raised his hand and said with tenderness, 'Listen, what we went through was dreadful. These are the consequences. This place is messing with my head too, believe me. But it's a new day, Nina. Let's find your grandma. She will tell you there's nothing to worry about.'

Nina averted her gaze. 'It's not only that, Alessandro.'

'What?'

'Something terrible is about to happen, or *is* already happening. I can't stop thinking that it has to do with the tablet.' She started to sob and threw her hands up. 'My grandma entrusted me with a great secret. I thought it was just a story, nothing more, and I published that stupid essay. I was ignorant! And look who took it seriously. One person. A murderer! People have died because of me, and who knows how many more will get killed!'

Alessandro lifted one foot, then another, and crossed to her. '*Nina*, you cannot forever blame yourself for a madman's actions.'

She twisted her mouth into a wry smile, and then said in a distant and cold voice that made Alessandro's hair bristle on his neck, 'So how do you explain this?'

She gestured down over the ledge.

Alessandro cocked his head past Nina. The terrace was higher than he expected. Yesterday, he had lost his sense of direction, though he had the impression they were climbing.

The view was hazy. He could barely distinguish the horizon line.

'Come closer,' she said and held out her hand.

His nightmare was gone, but with every step he took, it seemed so vivid, as if he were about to see those ghastly giant arms.

313

He took hold of Nina's hand and leaned over the short terrace wall. The warm breeze swept over his body. He glanced down, fifteen metres below, at the mighty Ganga.

Its riverbed was withered.

'How come so many boats floated on the water yesterday?' he said, astonished.

Now it was a barely visible creek flowing along the rugged, marshy ground, and…

He leaned farther.

Half-burnt human bones. Lots of them.

Tingling awe crawled along his body.

Nina said something, but he didn't catch her words.

Alongside the whole length of the riverbank, thousands of Hindus were sitting and chanting. It sounded like what he had heard in his dream.

'They came to the river to pray,' Nina said. 'That's the only way they know to bring back their holy waters of the Ganga.'

He glanced at her. 'Like yesterday? "From darkness, lead us to light," is that it?' He registered a strange hope in his tone, as of a person who did wrong and counted on others to mend the damage.

'No, Alessandro. There is no light anymore. They sing: "From death, lead us to immortality." '

His legs wobbled. He propped his hands on the terrace wall. *There is no light anymore.* Klaff had used the same words.

Then one more detail emerged from his nightmare, and he knew why he was so sure that he would be slaughtered by demons. The face of the four-arm monster cropped up in his mind—the callous face of Lammert van der Venn.

Alessandro clutched the crucifix hanging on his neck. 'May God have mercy on us all.'

CHAPTER 51

KAMA GRABBED HIS head and, with his forearms, shielded it from the sunshine and the banging. The sun was gone, but the banging got louder.

It was like drums rehearsing under his skull, without any rhythm to it, only bang, bang. BANG. Bang, bang, bang. Then a horrendous whack. And the drums stopped.

Kama heard the stinky man swearing aloud. He didn't know the words, but his tone of voice was angry.

Another voice called the name of the stinky man.

He heard the lock being opened. The door slammed against the wall. A person started to talk in a resonant, urgent voice that was full of authority. It was the rich man.

'Kama,' the stinky man said. He was closer now. 'Kama!'

Kama opened his mouth. Why was he shouting? He could hear him. He would have replied, only his mouth was too dry. He tried to swallow, but one cannot swallow without saliva.

The soft duvet he was wrapped into was wrenched away from him. He opened his eyes, squinted, and closed them. Someone clutched and shook his leg. He kicked it off.

'Get up!'

He felt a potent grip on his arm, hoisting him up and out of the bed. For the moment, he was fully awake.

'Wake up, you plastered stinker.'

He didn't know what "plastered" meant, but he was not a stinker, not a stinker at all.

Two arms joggled him in the air as if he didn't weigh anything. He tried to wriggle out of the catch, but it was too strong.

'Stop, sir, stop,' he screamed.

He felt he would be sick.

'Waaberi, put him down!' the rich man demanded.

Kama tumbled down onto the bed. His body trembled from the violent shake. Everything spun around him.

'How do you feel?' the rich man asked.

Somehow the urge to vomit died away, and Kama pushed himself up on his elbows. He wasn't sure where he was, but he remembered why his head throbbed so much with a dull pain. He had never drunk that much alcohol in his life. And he would never do it again.

Never.

He was ashamed. He didn't want to look at the man with the authoritative voice.

'Okay,' he answered, keeping his head low. 'Kama is okay.'

The man handed him a glass of bubbling water. Kama plucked it from his hand and drank it down. The liquid was tart, like a lemon, but refreshing. He was so glad that the man wasn't angry with him. Otherwise he wouldn't have brought him a drink. He had a job to do. For that job, the man would pay lots of his money.

While Kama dressed, he watched the two men standing by the window. The rich man was talking in a chaotic way and too fast for Kama to understand. Or he was speaking in a different language.

Then he turned around and asked Kama, 'Are you hungry?'

Kama put his palm on his stomach. It gurgled. He wasn't hungry. Even if he had been, he couldn't eat. He shook his head.

'Good,' the rich man said and passed him a piece of crumpled paper.

'Do you know where it is? Doesn't matter,' he added, 'as long as you can find those addresses. It shouldn't be too difficult. Sati lives somewhere over there.'

Kama glanced at the scribble. It was in Hindi. He could find those places.

But he was anxious. Something wasn't right with the rich man. He was agitated. Yesterday, when he told Kama that he wanted to find his wife's grandma, he sounded genuine and caring, and he had been easy-going. Today he was like a policeman who wanted to put a criminal into jail, or anybody else.

But maybe Kama was mistaken because his head was so heavy. He thought that he would need to support it with his hands to keep it straight. Probably it was just his head.

'Waaberi, and you,' the man spoke, 'get ready and meet me downstairs in fifteen minutes.'

Then he left. When Kama raised his eyesight, the stinky man was staring at him. Kama dropped his head and pretended to study the piece of paper.

The addresses were precise, which was all the better for Kama. He inhaled through his nose. Actually, he felt better.

CHAPTER 52

VAN DER VENN returned to his room and thrust the wardrobe open. He gently took out the briefcase, put it on the bed, and stretched his hands out over it. They were shaking. He shook them off.

He flared his nostrils and inhaled, expanding his chest, then the air whooshed out of his lungs. He hadn't gotten any sleep last night, but he didn't need any. He felt ecstatic.

With his thumbs, he unlocked the briefcase and opened its lid. He gazed at the tablet for a few minutes. There was something to this artefact he hadn't taken into account, something of much greater significance than he had believed.

He took it out and placed it on the sheet. It looked exactly the same as on the day he had pulled it out of Lake Garda. He ran his fingers along its coarse writing—its true value lived in this engraved message.

He sat down on the bed in front of the tablet, crossed his legs, and rested his hands on his knees, keeping his spine straight. He closed his eyes and imagined himself sitting on the stony floor of that dirty yard, chanting a mantra from the tablet a Hindu man who lived there had decoded for him.

The man had been sitting in a wheelchair and was so old that when van der Venn saw him he thought that he might be dead. A dozen candles had cast a faint light on his withered figure, dressed in the orange fabric of his slacks. His grey ponytail beard had reached to his chest and a brown, beaded necklace had hung low around his neck. He could have been one of those monks from the ceremony by the river if not for his age.

Van der Venn had explained to him that he was an Italian scholar, researching Hindu culture, in particular its ancient language, but soon realized that the man didn't know English. Instead, he showed him the picture of the first mantra from the tablet.

The cripple had studied it for too long for van der Venn's liking. He had finally reached over and tried to take the picture back. To his surprise the man held it hard. Also, his face seemed to grow brighter as if younger. Yesterday he thought that it must have been his imagination, but after what happened later, van der Venn believed it had something to do with the first mantra.

The man had gestured to him to sit down on the stone floor by his side. Van der Venn glanced around the empty yard and decided to give it a chance. The Hindu swiped his palm over his own face. Van der Venn closed his eyes, and it started.

At first, the cripple had hummed strange sounds, as if unsure what he was doing, as if probing the correct tone and sound.

Van der Venn had felt stupid and was about to end that farce. Only then the man began to chant in an effortless manner. What was coming out of his mouth had a recurrent pattern of the same sequence of words, over and over again, each time with more strength and resonance. It was similar to Hindi but with more distinctive tones.

Van der Venn had started to repeat after him.

After some time, he had felt the sounds of the mantra vibrating in his throat. They launched throbbing waves, causing ripples in his body, as if he stood too close to a high-power loudspeaker that, instead of music, emitted a silent, piercing pulsation.

An utter calmness had washed over van der Venn, releasing him from all his worries, no matter how small or large. He felt relaxed like after drinking whiskey, but unlike after the liquor, his mind remained sharp.

He had kept chanting. His heart beat faster. A tingling energy in his right leg travelled up the right side of his body. When it reached his skull, he experienced a brief moment of internal rain of a bright light. He concentrated on those sensations, but the harder he wanted them to keep going, the faster they had declined.

So he surrendered to them, and chanted eerie words that meant nothing to him, that were doing something extraordinary with his body. It wasn't why he had come to Varanasi. But now he wouldn't stop it for any price.

He had visualized his future. He sat on a golden throne. People came to him to pay homage to his achievements. Some questioned his omnipotence. Klaff took care of the unbelievers. Klaff was dead, but that was such an irrelevant detail in his kingdom.

Multiple cramps in his legs hadn't let him stay any longer in that sitting position, although incredibly his back felt all right. Then it was all gone.

He had wanted the cripple to read out more of the text, but he shook his head. He couldn't understand the rest. Van der Venn believed him, because when he took out a five-hundred-euro note, it made no impression on the Hindu man.

Then something bizarre had happened. The cripple got to his feet. In the candlelight, his face expressed awe and delight. He wobbled on his legs and made three steps. Then he toppled over like a wind-up robotic astronaut toy. A robot that a boy once owned in the orphanage van der Venn grew up in. How odd it was that out of the blue, a distant memory from his childhood came up.

The cripple had broken something. He was groaning and didn't move much. Van der Venn had stood up and got out of there.

Now his appetite for more of what he had last night was at its peak. Today would be a long day, or a very short one, and then more strength and understanding would fall on him. Who knew what else? If one mantra had such an impact on him, what would happen when the whole text was deciphered? Excitement prickled his skin.

He needed Nina Monte and her grandmother.

If Monte was right in her essay, a man could replace God. It had been laughable for van der Venn the first and every time he had read her thesis.

Not anymore.

If she was right, he had received an unforeseen chance to make himself eternal, literally eternal. That meant he would have all the time he needed to spend his fortune, and then become even richer, and to have the respect of everyone while being alive.

And to have their absolute submission, as their new God.

He needed to test Monte's theory on himself. He needed to find out how to get himself on the fast track to glory.

Van der Venn dried his moist palms on the sheet. He put the tablet on his lap and started to chant. As he remembered it. Breathing in a steady manner, trying to evoke the sensation that was still fresh.

After two minutes he gave up. He fisted his hand and punched the bed. With the presence of the cripple, it had happened on its own. Maybe because he hadn't expected any of it.

Last night hadn't been only about mantras.

A girl from a sari shop, opposite the place where he had left the cripple, wrote for him five addresses in the old part of Varanasi where an elderly, devout woman from a big city would seek shelter.

Van der Venn couldn't make any sense of the letters scribbled on a crappy piece of paper. That's why he brought Kama along.

He put the tablet back into the briefcase and then crossed to the window. There was no water in the Ganges. He had noticed that when he had spoken to Waaberi in his room. If that was a seasonal thing or something unusual, he couldn't have cared less.

Waaberi and Kama needed to be ready now.

He grabbed the briefcase, shut the door behind him, and ran down the stairs. He was too excited to wait for the elevator.

Waaberi and the boy were waiting for him on a two-seat sofa opposite the reception desk. Kama was pushed to the side, but he looked much better than before. Klaff's remedy proved efficient. His face had taken on a healthy colour; his eyes were bright and sharp, and full of guilt. When he saw van der Venn, he lowered his head. How convenient—the boy wouldn't challenge his instructions.

Van der Venn passed them by, stepped outside and paused on the stairs. He raised his head straight to the

323

sunrays. His facial muscles relaxed. He breathed deeply, in and out. The air was clear and fresh, without a trace of yesterday's fustiness.

A casual smile crossed his face. He didn't mind entering the world of beggars and cow faeces again. He was looking forward to it.

Waaberi cleared his throat. 'Boss, we're prepared.'

Van der Venn put on his sunglasses. 'I know you are.'

CHAPTER 53

VARANASI OLD TOWN felt like a labyrinth to Alessandro. He strolled after Nina along the alleys where mostly two-storey buildings made the landscape on both sides. They all looked similar to him with their shabby walls painted in light green, orange, or blue colours. Curtains made of a thick material swung on doorways.

The sun peered down at an uneven pathway made from flagstone. The morning was hot, but it was nicely cool in the shade of the buildings.

Bicycles and motorbikes were either parked by the walls or were passing them by with horns that sounded like it was their last call. If it was true, owners of repair shops—and he saw more than a few of them—ran a good business.

Some passages were so narrow that only three people could walk next to each other.

When they went into a touristy area, Alessandro saw a multitude of ads for yoga, meditation classes, and internet cafes. He heard modern Bollywood music. Guest houses invited newcomers on every corner. Shops tempted with traditional Indian shirts, dresses, trousers, handbags made of colourful fabrics, musical instruments, CDs, books, soaps, incense sticks, everything.

'How do you know it's the right way?' he asked Nina. 'Since we left the guesthouse, you haven't checked the drawing that deaf boy made for you.'

'I don't have to,' she said without emotion.

She took another turn. Local people were awaiting their customers on the steps of numerous small shops, which weren't as flashy like those in tourist parts. Others were in a hurry, carrying sacks on their shoulders, or on bikes.

A woman baked flatbread on a metal plate over a fire in a restaurant that looked like an antique kitchen without a front wall. Fantastic smells of spices and dishes Alessandro had never tasted were coming from there. He wondered if the bread was as good as the meal they had in their guesthouse.

They had eaten on their room's terrace merely half an hour ago. It had been a silent breakfast. Nina had avoided his gaze and his questions. She had spoken only when Alessandro had asked her what they were eating. She answered, 'Typical Indian breakfast.' And that was it. Then the boy they had met last night drew for her the way to the places where Sati might be staying. He was deaf, but he could read and sketch beautifully.

Nina came to a stop by a gateway to a mansion that was long past its prime. Glowing sunshine gave a soft orange tone to the sandy frontage colour.

Alessandro poked his head through the open doorway. The courtyard was as big as a tennis court. In the focal point grew a big tree, its dense branches giving shade for almost half of the yard. The tree was as high as the house that sat around it in an open rectangle. A row of arcades made the front wall of the ground floor; above it were a series of arched galleries. Dark bed sheets sheltered some of them from the sun.

In the square, elderly people were going about their everyday activities. A woman was hanging laundry and another person was sweeping the floor. Someone else peeled vegetables. They performed all these chores in a mechanical way. Alessandro wondered if it was normal like this in a hospice.

'Do you think this is it?' he said.

Nina gave him no answer.

He gazed at a woman in her thirties who accompanied a poor-looking old man on a wooden plank bench. She helped him to drink from a metal cup.

Alessandro looked at Nina. She was staring down at the doorstep.

'What is it?'

'The footprint,' she said softly.

He glanced down. It was so big that only one third of the military boot's pattern had been imprinted on the dusty threshold.

The same pattern had marked Alessandro's white T-shirt when Waaberi had stomped him in Jaipur, just before he had got to his knees and puked.

And if it was Waaberi's print, van der Venn was in town.

Alessandro felt his heart rate increasing at the thought of another confrontation with the man who had tried to kill him twice. He clenched his teeth. One criminal was making him small and weak.

'This is the place,' she said calmly, but she was trying to mask the nervousness in her voice.

'Are you sure?' he said in a squeaky tone. Nina was much better at hiding her emotions.

An attempt to take a deep breath filled his lungs only halfway. He bit on his lower lip. He wanted to say that it didn't mean that van der Venn had found her grandma in there. He might have left the place empty-handed. He and Nina should hurry up, ask around here, and move to another hospice, and get to Sati before him.

But he said none of that. Nina would have noticed his trembling voice. His traitorous trembling voice would scare him even more.

When Nina crossed the threshold, Alessandro felt a knot forming in his stomach. He blinked a few times, took a series of breaths and followed her.

Under the tree, a barefoot elderly man was doing laundry in a small washbasin. When Nina neared him, he put the wet cloth down on a plastic washboard and turned his head up. Alessandro tried to read from his face if they were welcomed here. He felt better, as he didn't see any warning in the man's eyes that they should leave because two evil men were awaiting them.

The man reluctantly raised his hand and pointed his finger to the left.

Nina started to walk. She moved in a conscious manner, softly putting one foot after another, as if the yard were full of dozing tigers.

She was heading to the house, straight into sheets of laundry drying on a string, its one end attached to the hook on the wall and the other to a tree branch. The people around them stopped what they had been doing and watched.

On one sheet, Alessandro noticed a picture of the four-armed god sitting on a glowing throne. He made the sign of the cross and shadowed Nina two metres behind, in the same shy fashion.

They had made it most of the way when a stronger breeze flapped the sheets up, and Alessandro caught sight of an elderly woman sitting under the arcade of the building.

Nina cocked her head, and broke into a sprint.

'Grandma!' she screamed, moving the sheets out of her way.

Alessandro lingered one second, then dashed after her.

He saw Nina on her knees, embracing her grandmother with passion, who was sitting cross-legged on a floral rug. Nina kissed her hands, touched her cheeks and shoulders and spoke chaotically to her, tugging on the short sleeves of her orange sari and stroking her white hair that was pulled into a knot at the back of her head.

Sati cuddled Nina back, with a caring smile. It added a few more wrinkles to her face, but she didn't look like an eighty-six-year-old person. She was nodding and saying reassuring words, because Nina clung to her and seemed to cool off.

'Ms Monte! Finally!' someone said with joy.

Alessandro felt prickles all over his body, and he held his breath.

Van der Venn emerged through the door that was behind Sati, carrying the stone tablet in his hand. Then he glanced at Alessandro. 'And you. Always *you*.'

Alessandro couldn't stand van der Venn's brazen look, so he glanced at Sati instead. A healing serenity and self-confidence emanated from her. She didn't take notice of the criminals who invaded her home.

Waaberi stood by van der Venn, holding a gun in one

hand. Next to him, on the floor, perched a Hindu teenage boy. Was he with them?

'Very touching, Ms Monte,' van der Venn said, 'but that's enough. Please step back from your grandmother.'

Nina didn't budge. Waaberi grabbed on her neck and pulled her away.

'Get off me, you monster!' Nina shouted. She lost her balance and narrowly missed a small, contained fire over which a metal kettle dangled on a horizontal bar. She landed on her buttocks three metres from Sati, pulling down a sheet from the cord, which stretched and broke.

Then she stood up. Tears welled up in her eyes. She looked helpless, but unhurt.

Alessandro's heart was hammering. His blood pressure had to have skyrocketed, as he felt thumping and throbbing in his ears. Sweat ran down his back.

Nina's face was contorted in despair, and Sati's soothing smile couldn't change that.

'Your grandmother refused to cooperate,' van der Venn said in a disillusioned tone of voice, 'even when I addressed her through her native language, thanks to this nice gentleman.' He gestured to the young Hindu.

Then he threw some euros to the boy's feet. 'The money you love so much.'

The boy lowered his head and crossed his hands behind his back without picking up the money. Alessandro thought that he blushed, as his face's dark skin tone became deeper.

Van der Venn tilted his head back. 'Well, I see this isn't as poor a country as it looks.'

He turned to Nina. 'Where was I? Ah, Ms Monte, since you're here…' He motioned to his man.

Waaberi caught Nina by her arm, forced her to crouch down and put the gun to the back of her head.

Paralysing waves of hot sweat crawled over Alessandro. He looked around for help. The hospice residents were staring, not eager to risk their fading lives. Only that younger woman got up from the bench, and meant to speak up, but Waaberi pointed the gun at her. She dropped back onto the seat.

Van der Venn placed the tablet on Sati's lap. 'Tell your grandmother to read it or to let your educated brain spoil her tea.' He picked up a cup from the floor, took a sip, and smacked his lips. 'Not bad at all!'

Nina pulled her legs underneath and sat on them. She buried her head in her palms, sobbing.

Alessandro stepped forward on tottering legs. 'Man, let's talk. C'mon,' he said, raising his hands. 'You can't do these things, please.'

Van der Venn seemed to be surprised by that. He squinted at Alessandro. 'These *things*, Mr Pini?' Then he gave a nod.

For a brief moment Alessandro believed that he would listen to him, that there was something human in him, and that he had managed to call it up.

Waaberi's interpretation was different. The last thing Alessandro saw was a big shade coming at him.

There was nothing human in Lammert van der Venn, Alessandro thought as a mighty thunderbolt struck him right in the middle of his forehead. It travelled down in a straight line, splitting him in half. Somewhere from above, he saw two parts of his body disjoin. And tumble to the right and left.

Then agony blinded his eyes.

CHAPTER 54

THE RICH MAN had fooled Kama. He wasn't looking for Sati to bring her to his country. And his wife was not sick. She was here. Her name was Ms Monte. The stinky man held a pistol to her head.

The rich man was not a good man. What kind of husband treated his wife with such cruelty?

Kama felt ashamed. He was like the stinky man, helping to hurt others. Kama's Monkey God, Hanuman, would be ashamed of him.

When Kama's mother had nagged him about learning English, she told him that it was good for his future. He wasn't sure if that was true.

Now the rich man ordered him to talk to the old lady. Kama didn't want to, but he saw what had happened to the other white man. He lay on the ground, motionless, a small trickle of blood oozing out of his head. Kama didn't know if he was still alive. He hoped that the harmed man's God was merciful.

When Ms Monte had noticed what happened, she wanted to run to her friend, but the stinky man had stopped her. He was fast, like a leopard. Now Ms Monte was crying. She must like the bleeding man a lot.

'Kama!' the rich man said, hurrying him up. He set a high tripod not that far from the old lady, and on top he attached a small camera that looked like a fancy mobile phone.

'I'm very sorry, granny,' Kama said, embarrassed, and bowed politely. 'He asks you to tell him what is on the stone.'

She smiled at Kama, and it made him feel a bit better that she wasn't angry with him. Then she looked at Ms Monte and raised her hand to her. The stinky man glanced at the rich man. The rich man allowed it, and Ms Monte hunkered down by her grandma.

The granny caressed the stone with her fingers. She opened her mouth and recited the beautiful verse. Kama was sure it was an ancient language from the Sanskrit.

He scratched the back of his head. He would never be able to tell the rich man what it was about, even if he studied the Sanskrit for many years, because it was complicated. The stinky man would hit him.

But none of this happened. The rich man shoved Kama aside and turned to the granny. 'Stop! Ms Monte, tell your dear grandmother to recite one mantra at a time, and then to pause for five seconds. I wouldn't want her to take my place.'

Kama understood the words the rich man said but not the meaning of them.

'You're out of your mind,' Ms Monte told him. She was very sad and her voice was weak.

Not like the loud and self-confident voice of the rich man, who grinned like a devil. 'Just do it!'

'She understands you,' Ms Monte said through her tears.

Kama watched and listened to the old lady reciting the second line. She stopped. Then the third line. She stopped. Then the fourth line. During all that time, she held Ms Monte's hand.

Kama wished to know what it was. He felt with all his body that it was not only beautiful but also divine.

When after another pause she started reciting again, something wonderful happened.

Kama heard the fifth text coming from Ms Monte's mouth, but the voice was of her grandma. How could that be possible when the grandma wasn't saying any words?

After the break, the sixth text came again from Ms Monte, still not in her voice. The granny was silent.

Kama thought there was something wrong with him until he saw how the stinky man was watching the women, with his mouth open, head put forward, hypnotized.

An invisible although palpable peacefulness was emanating from them. Kama felt it growing stronger and stronger. And he saw soft lights—violet and white—embracing granny and Ms Monte, although Kama's eyes were watering from emotions so those lights could have been an illusion.

The rich man was gaping with awe. His eyes sparkled like two emeralds. He was smiling, and looked as if he was going to start hopping around.

When the time came for the seventh text, only Ms Monte's lips were moving. No words came out. The rich man's face became grave in an instant.

'Tell me the last mantra!'

Ms Monte was mouthing the words silently.

'Tell me the last mantra!'

The rich man waved his arms furiously. He knocked down the camera but didn't worry about it.

Ms Monte continued her silent chanting as if not seeing or hearing him.

The rich man took the pistol from the stinky man and fired two times at the floor by her feet. One bullet hit the fire. A cloud of ashes floated in the air. Through his fingers that were glued to his face, Kama watched as the granny raised the tablet and rammed it on her knee.

There were more ashes, and it was hard to see. The granny had disappeared in a cloud of dust, and all that peaceful sensation disappeared with her.

The rich man yelled to the sky, 'The old (...) is more (...) than I thought.'

Kama didn't know what that meant.

The rich man looked around in panic. 'Where is she?' he yelled.

He fired near Ms Monte. She screamed. He shot again. The bullet bounced next to her.

Ms Monte covered her ears and head with her hands as hard as she could. She shivered like a person with a high fever.

'Tell me the last mantra!'

'Never!' she screamed.

The rich man's jaw started to shudder and his face turned red. His enormous chest went up and down rapidly. He raised his head and roared to the sky like Indra, the god of thunderstorms.

And then, seconds later, he started to laugh violently, so violently that his eyes were wet from tears. It didn't last long, though, and he became quieter. He put the pistol under his trousers leg.

'I think I know how to change your mind,' he said to Ms Monte in a sly voice.

Kama didn't want to find out what he meant by that. It couldn't be anything righteous. He turned around and ran three steps, but a big hand caught him from behind by his T-shirt and jerked.

Kama's legs soared up above his head like in a yoga pose, and then his body thumped flat onto the hard ground. He opened his mouth wide to curse the rich man, but the fall had wrenched the air out of his lungs.

He groaned, rolled to his side and curled up.

CHAPTER 55

NINA STUMBLED FOR a second time as she went down an old Varanasi alleyway, but Waaberi's strong grip on her right arm wouldn't let her fall, and wouldn't let her escape.

She looked at her fingers. They were blue. Her hand felt numb. His clasp was cutting off her circulation. She squirmed out, as hard as she could. Waaberi squeezed her arm firmer.

She winced. 'You're hurting me!'

He looked at her as if she had said a joke he didn't quite understand.

'Be a gentleman, my boy,' van der Venn said.

He walked two steps ahead of them. He puffed up, like the city belonged to him, although no more than five minutes ago he had been raging.

Back then, Nina had been afraid that he would shoot her, and everyone around them. When the gunfire started, she covered her eyes. She didn't know what had happened to Sati. When she had finally looked up, her grandma was gone. Nina's heart had almost stopped at the thought that she had been shot. She couldn't see her body. The dust was everywhere. Everything had happened so fast.

And Alessandro? When the butt of the gun had landed on his head, Nina heard a crack. She wanted to catch him but

Waaberi stood in her way; she could only watch Alessandro's limp body going down. There was nothing theatrical in it, like in a movie stunt. He had just collapsed on his back. His head had landed on the laundry Nina had pulled down before, which cushioned the impact from the stony floor. Would it matter, though, if his head was already smashed?

It was difficult to think straight. She felt worn out and dizzy after the mantras' recitation, as if she hadn't slept for days. Her body vibrated in weird, unpleasant waves like an earthquake's aftershock.

When she had recited the last mantras after Sati read them—although she wasn't sure if Sati had actually read them out loud, but she must have, otherwise how could Nina have known what to chant?—she experienced a similar feeling of being attuned to something as she had at dawn. Only much stronger.

It was like sitting on an active volcano. She had felt a rolling heat in her belly, and she had to keep her back straight to let the hot energy flow up her spine. But she'd had to stop after the sixth mantra. She feared it would blow open the crown of her head. It might have if van der Venn hadn't started shouting and firing.

After Waaberi had pushed Nina from the hospice, she lost her sense of direction. Now, though, it was becoming clear where they were taking her. To the Ganga. But why? What sinister plan could van der Venn have? Was he going to drown her? If yes, he didn't know about the water.

She gave up struggling. Waaberi's clutch was so stiff that she had to walk at his pace, otherwise he would dislocate her arm.

The closer they came to the river, the more people they met on the way. Shop shutters were being pulled down. Then their owners headed in the same direction. The news about the river was spreading.

For the first time since her childhood, Nina started to pray—or rather, to beg. She begged that this would be over soon, and that she would see Sati and Alessandro in good health again.

She begged God. Not the Hindu God, not the Christian God. Just God. She begged for God to exist, and to save the innocent. Was she among the innocent? She had published the words that brought suffering and death.

She apologised for that, first silently, then she muttered out loud, 'I'm sorry. So sorry.'

'You don't know what it is to be sorry.' Waaberi's deep voice came from above like a voice from Heaven. Was he speaking on behalf of God? Was it her answer?

'Wait till the boss starts with you.'

The boss? Van der Venn? Or God?

She caught the gaze of a young girl, who glanced at van der Venn and then buried her face in her mother's sari. Children could sense danger. Primal instincts were unspoiled in them.

Nina felt weakness in her knees. She realized they were taking her straight to the main ghat in Varanasi. To the place where, for centuries, hundreds of bodies had been burned down day and night and their ashes scattered into the Ganga River.

Was he going to burn her? No. No! It would be crazy. He couldn't. There was no holy river to accept the ashes. There could be no burning.

With every next step, the number of people grew. At the end of the lane, Nina saw a bigger group. It was a creepy view that caused shivers in her body. Everyone was standing with their backs turned to them, like living corpses obediently waiting for their turn to be set on fire.

The crowd got too congested to go through.

Van der Venn fired in the air. No one screamed; no one ran away. They just yielded the right-of-way to him, as if he were a Hindu priest coming to heal the river.

It was abnormal the people didn't scatter in panic. Then again, their holy river was gone. Nothing could be worse than that. Not for them.

Inky blurred spots dotted Nina's vision. She felt like fainting, petrified to move on.

'I need to sit down,' she said.

Van der Venn turned to her and said with a faked worry, 'Should I tell Waaberi to carry you, Ms Monte?'

Then he pushed his way ahead to the shoreline. He came to a halt by three corpses wrapped in colourful cloth that were laid on stacks made of timber. Another two dozen bodies lay on the ground in a row closely next to each other, making for a macabre queue.

Nina got a sour taste in her mouth but couldn't swallow.

Thin smoke was smouldering from a small heap of ashes, where the last body had been burnt. The ground around was soggy, covered with a layer of grey powder. Huge towers of wood were stacked nearby. Some of them were as high as twenty metres.

Waaberi's grip on Nina's shoulder eased off. She glanced up at him.

His facial expression was no longer that of a bold thug, but of a timid student who came to her lecture at university and who nervously sought a free seat; the farther from her, the better.

His head swivelled from right to left. He scanned the scene behind his back.

'Look at this, Ms Monte,' van der Venn said with excitement, gesturing to the dried river. 'Let me be honest with you. Before yesterday, I didn't believe in your story about the mighty tablet. But now? Isn't it a sign of upcoming changes?'

Nina jerked and freed her arm. Waaberi didn't try to get hold of her.

Van der Venn pointed his gun to the sky. 'I'm starting to think there is something there after all, and I *really* want to get acquainted with it.' He looked straight at her. 'Last chance. Tell me the seventh mantra, and I will let you go.'

'You're a criminal! No God would think twice of you, except how you disappointed him,' she said sternly, surprised that she had the strength to oppose him.

Van der Venn kicked one body off the stack. A Hindu man dressed in a white cloth who stood beside the corpse shrieked, raised his hands and lunged at him.

Van der Venn shot him in the chest. The man jerked back, stood still for a second and then fell to the ground.

Some people ran away, some moved back, making the circle wider around the three of them.

Nina curled her arms over her head. Stinging shame overcame her other emotions. She had brought a plague upon these people.

'Waaberi, bring Ms Monte closer,' van der Venn ordered.

Waaberi didn't move; he just pushed Nina forward.

Van der Venn motioned her to the empty pile of logs. 'Take a seat. You did want to sit, didn't you?'

Nina crossed her hands over her chest, so as not to let him see her battering heart. She held her breath and shook her head.

Van der Venn reached for her arm and forced her down on the stack.

'Comfortable, Ms Monte?' he said and grinned. 'This here is easy. You tell me the last mantra, or you will burn. That would be a shame. You see, without the water, there is no salvation for you.' He laughed. 'You've never believed in those things anyway, have you? I bet now you're reconsidering.'

Nina trembled. She couldn't control it. He would see her fear. There was no fire under her buttocks, but she felt as if she had sat down on a hot stove.

Van der Venn pulled out a lighter. It clicked without much noise, but she flinched when blue and red flame came to life. A muffled groan reverberated around.

'I'm constrained by time here. So how is it gonna be, Nina?' he said, looking at his watch. 'By the way, you don't mind me calling you Nina, do you?'

She was staring at the burning lighter, shaking her head.

Alessandro was right. This man was a monster, a psycho. Did he really expect her to just sit there and wait for the blaze to engulf her?

'If you don't tell me, you will die. Then, I will find that old witch and do the same to her.'

Nina's head was spinning. Then, Sati was alive; she had escaped! Some subdued joy arose in her heart.

Van der Venn held up his lighter and walked around her.

She smelled an awful odour by her ear. It took her two seconds to register that her hair was burning. She screamed and put out the fire with her hand. She wanted to get up, but he pressed on her shoulder. She cringed and wept.

He leaned to her ear. 'Awful, isn't it? Imagine how your skin would stink.'

Nina drew up her breath. She wanted to disappear. She wanted to turn back time. She wanted to get back to that meeting in Heidelberg and tell them all to get lost with their thrilling job offer.

'Tell me, or else I will knock you down,' van der Venn whispered, 'and you will wake up watching your beautiful skin melting down.'

She leaned forward and covered her ears, but could still hear his diabolic hiss. 'Why are you so stubborn? What do you protect? You are a *scientist*. You know that nothing happens if you tell me.'

Nina clenched her teeth on her tongue, tasting her own blood. She could tell him and finish the torment. Then he would let her go, and … She looked up.

Forty metres away, high on the stairs, a man stared into the riverbed. He must have come to take a holy bath. A long cloth of a brown-yellow dress was thrown around his arm and across his waist. His skin was reddish as if an infection spread over it. Nina blinked and held her breath. He resembled that flayed statue of St. Bartholomew from the Milan Cathedral—the first Apostle who had preached the gospel in India.

Was this a sign for her to be courageous? Or did it mean it was her end? But why? St. Bartholomew had been executed in Armenia. Not here.

Nina heard a murmur from the crowd. Frantically, she ran her fingers through her hair. She was okay.

Then the ring of people opened up and Sati trudged into the circle. Nina let out a quiet cry of despair. He had both of them now.

Sati came to a stop by the body of the shot man. She slowly raised her gaze at van der Venn and said with a placid voice, 'You must let her go. My granddaughter is only a tool in the hands of God who led you to this holy place so you could repent for your sinful life and ask for forgiveness. And resolve never to repeat your wrongdoing.'

Sati's arrival must have startled van der Venn. Nina felt his hand slipping off her, and she dashed into her grandma's arms. Waaberi neared them but didn't break their hug.

'Congratulations on your latest performance, granny,' van der Venn said. 'It was quite impressive! But now if you don't tell me what I want to know, it will be *all* of you repenting—'

He broke in mid-sentence, the last word uttered filled with distress.

Nina turned around to see his gun tumbling down from his outstretched hand that was still pointed at her head. In his other hand he clasped the blazing lighter, his forearm cramped at a right angle. His pelvis was pushed out comically, as if he were trying to do a stand-up bridge exercise. His face was distorted in suffering. Veins throbbed in his forehead and bulged in his stiff neck. His jaw was clenched. Only his lips were moving silently.

Behind him, in his unsteady hands at the height of van der Venn's lower back, Alessandro held a wooden log. His face was covered in half-dried blood.

Alessandro blinked at Nina and fell onto the ground.

She wanted to run to him, but the crowd, not held back by van der Venn's insanity, pushed her away.

First they closed down on Waaberi. They forced him to the ground. He covered his head but didn't resist when angry feet trampled him down.

Then dozens of hands gripped van der Venn. They were gentle with him, as if he were an emergency-ward patient. They laid him down on the same pile he had kicked the body from.

Someone forced his stiff arm down. He cried out and dropped the lighter.

When the flames touched his body, more than anything else—more than pain—Van der Venn's face showed liberation. Then his pelvis collapsed and he fainted.

The smell of scorching flesh made Nina's stomach retch, and she turned her head away.

A loud cheer from the back of the crowd made her look up, and she followed the stares of other people.

First, it was a stream, not much bigger than the one Nina had seen from her room. In seconds, it turned into a torrent. Soon the water was flowing with the whole width of the riverbed, and the Ganga was swelling up so fast and fiercely that the roar of water muffled the cheering of the Hindu people.

Nina shook off her amazement and glanced back to the shore. She cocked her head. She had to find Alessandro or they would trample him down, like they did to Waaberi.

She used her elbows to push her way. Alessandro wasn't in the spot where he had collapsed. She screamed his name, scanning the ground. He wasn't there.

She saw a naked and bruised Waaberi lift up van der Venn's body from the fire and jump into the river.

Then she noticed the Hindu boy who had been with van der Venn hauling Alessandro out of the crowd. He put him down higher on the stone stairs, crouching down to catch a breath. When his eyes met Nina's angry stare, he scurried away.

She sprinted to Alessandro and knelt by him.

He looked terrible. Blood on his face made for a horrific contrast to his pale skin. Her chin and hands trembled. She pushed back her tears.

It took her a few seconds before she gently shook Alessandro.

He lifted his eyelids slowly. His gaze was watery. She wasn't sure if he recognized her. 'Is it over now ... Professor?'

'Yes,' she said through her constricted throat. 'I think it is.'

Then his pupils rolled up and he dropped his head to the side.

CHAPTER 56

A PLEASANT BREEZE blowing from the south of Lake Garda caressed Nina's new, shorter hair. The azure surface of the water glimmered against the afternoon sunlight. The front yard of the building where she stood gave her a splendid view.

A single powerboat cut the lake with the speed and persistent whir of its engines, bouncing on the water, leaving frothy, white foam behind. A yellow ferryboat with tourists on the upper deck either basking in the sun or shooting pictures floated lazily through the water. High above the lake, paragliders seemed to hold still in the blue skies.

Nina kept staring at the deceptive innocence of Lake Garda. Was there anything else hiding at its bottom that should be left alone?

Her palms were sweating at the memory of her first encounter with Lammert van der Venn. Would she ever be able to forget him? At the moment, it was unlikely. At the moment, it felt like van der Venn was still after her.

She had left India at the expense of the Italian government, and landed at Leonardo da Vinci International Airport in Rome six hours ago. But with that, her life hadn't returned to normal. She wouldn't find her peace of mind until nothing remained unsettled.

She drew a deep breath, undid a button of the shirt she had bought on her way from the airport and let the air cool off her skin. If she could only calm her nerves.

Then she turned around, took a few tentative steps, and peered through the glass reception doors of the hotel.

A middle-aged woman was sitting behind the counter, her glasses resting on the bridge of her nose. She nervously fiddled with some papers as if she couldn't find something. She had dark circles under her swollen, bloodshot eyes. The skin around her mouth and on her cheeks was flabby and reddened. Her short hair was tousled in a failed attempt to make her look in vogue.

The woman paused and stared blankly at the top of the counter.

Nina walked in, but the woman didn't notice her. The news bulletin of Rai Radio Uno was set on a high volume.

"In several incidents, dams on the River Ganges in India were seized by an unknown terrorist group. The government's Special Forces regained control of the strategic objects after five hours of fierce fighting. Twenty-two terrorists, aiming to destabilize India, were reportedly shot dead on the spot. It hadn't been clear who was behind those well-organized attacks. Some experts blamed Pakistani militants. Another unidentified group had attempted to disrupt the Indian holy ceremony of burning deceased in Varanasi, in northern India. From unofficial sources we know that two Italian citizens were involved. A man—"

The radio went silent.

'Buongiorno,' the woman said, putting down the remote control she used to switch off the radio.

Nina offered her a friendly smile. 'Signora Francesca Pini?'

'Yes,' she answered, pulling out a crumpled tissue and then wiping her nose with it.

Nina clasped her hands in front of her.

'Signora Pini, my name is Nina Monte. I'm a professor at the University of Padua.'

The woman gathered her documents and put them in one pile in front of her. 'Pleased to meet you, Signora Monte.'

All the clever sentences Nina had practised on the way here now seemed to be silly and insensitive.

'We have available rooms if you are looking for accommodation,' Francesca Pini said when the moment of silence lingered too long.

'I'm not a tourist,' Nina said.

Yes, it was insensitive.

Francesca Pini smiled, as if trying to conceal her confusion. 'Do you wish to book our restaurant for a private party for your colleagues from the university? If you also take a few rooms, I can give you a discount—'

'No. Thank you, Signora Pini.' She looked around the reception and added, 'But I like your hotel, very much.'

Nina's stomach tightened when she noticed Alessandro's portrait hanging on the wall. A black stripe was attached to the upper corner of the frame.

'I'm afraid I don't understand, Signora?' Francesca Pini stared at Nina expectantly.

'I'm sorry, I don't need rooms or a restaurant.' Nina's voice lost its poise. 'This is not why I came here. I ... I know your son.'

Francesca Pini stood up and took off her glasses. 'Oh, you knew Alessandro?'

'That's not exactly what I...'

Why was it so hard to say? Because she felt guilty. Guilty of all the grief Alessandro's mother had had to go through; the grief that Nina could see in her downhearted face.

'Then, it must be some mistake,' she said, not looking at Nina. 'I don't have other sons, Signora Monte.' She grabbed the papers and moved them to the other side of the counter.

Nina knew that if she didn't start explaining, she would be asked to leave. She came over and extended her hand. 'Please. Call me Nina.'

The woman shook her hand and gave a slight nod.

'I met Alessandro last week. Since then, he helped me a lot. Without him—'

'Since *when* you say?' Francesca Pini frowned at her.

'Since the incident on the boat, and … at the police station?' Nina said softly.

Francesca Pini raised her chin and pressed her lips together in a straight line that made harsh furrows above her upper lip. 'Signora, do you know that my son died that day?'

Nina shook her head. 'He didn't.'

'Who are you?' she asked, raising her voice. 'And what do you want from me?'

She was close to a breakdown.

'Signora Pini, I'm afraid that you have been misinformed regarding Alessandro's whereabouts,' Nina said with as much compassion as she could muster.

'I don't know what game you play.' Alessandro's mother's voice was cracking. 'But how can you be so cruel and take advantage of my grief?'

'Mama!' Alessandro rushed in. 'Sorry, Nina. It wasn't going too well.'

Francesca Pini slumped onto the chair. She covered her open mouth with her trembling hand. Tears started to overflow her frightened eyes.

Alessandro crossed to her. 'It's me. I'm okay. I'll tell you everything.'

She extended her arms and hit him with her palms on his torso, not letting him get closer.

'Mama, it's me!'

She let out a loud whine. Tears streamed down her flushed cheeks in abundance. Her shaky hands probed a bandage wrapped around his head. Then she threw her arms around him.

Nina was shaking inside. Her throat shrank and twitched. She walked away.

As soon as she left the reception, the flood rushed down her own cheeks. She leaned on a tree, trying to catch a breath, then crouched down and curled her shoulders.

She wasn't sure why she was crying. She had returned to Italy. Alessandro's mother had gotten her son back. So why hold on to those destructive emotions of fear, doubt, helplessness, guilt, anger that were with her over the last days?

She composed herself and strolled to the lake.

It was so peaceful there, so different than the recent mayhem. People passed her by. Some gave her a smile or a nod.

Nina perched on a bench by the water and closed her eyes.

She listened to the wind playing with tree branches, to the water lapping on the shore, to motorboats in the distance, to the scraps of conversations from passers-by.

She raised her face up to the sun, feeling its warmth rejuvenating the inner layers of her skin, soothing her shattered frame of mind. It felt so pleasant and safe. She took a deep breath. A few tears of relief escaped from under her eyelids.

'Welcome back, Signora.' She heard a voice beside her. 'I hardly recognized you in your modern haircut, and in your a-little-less-modern clothes.' The voice let out a short giggle.

Through her hazy eyes, she glanced at an elderly man who was resting on the edge of the bench. It was the same person she had talked to when she arrived in Malcesine for the first time. Alessandro had told her what his name was.

'Signor … Giovani?'

'Yes, exactly,' he said, lifting his beret in a cordial greeting.

Nina readjusted her hair. She had it cut in the first salon she had seen in Varanasi before leaving India. She hadn't had a lot of time, and when she saw a picture of Rihanna on the wall, she just pointed at it. Now her hair was fashionably shaved on the side that had been burnt, and longer on the other. She wasn't sure if she liked it.

'I've seen women crying many times. I'm ashamed to admit'—Giovani made a penitent face—'often because of me. But I can see that your tears are not because of a broken heart.'

Nina wiped her eyes with the back of her hand. 'No, they're not.'

'Does it have anything to do with that yacht?'

'Excuse me?'

'The yacht that disappeared the day you and Alessandro asked me about it,' he said. More wrinkles covered his face. 'Poor boy.'

'Alessandro—' Nina started, but he raised his walking sick.

'Tragedy. Raffaele Lombardi, our police inspector, is still in hospital, but they say he will make it.'

Nina put her hand on his shoulder. 'Signor Giovani, Alessandro is fine.'

The old man slowly turned his body to her. 'Are you sure?'

Nina smiled. 'Yes, I'm most certain that Alessandro is well.'

'That's *glorious* news. I should know better than to listen to rumours.' He got to his feet with the help of the walking stick. 'I think I will go home earlier today, and have a small glass of Grappa for Raffaele's health and another one for Alessandro's miraculous return.' He touched the rim of his beret. 'Have a wonderful evening, Signora.'

Nina watched him hobbling away, thinking that she had just learned the secret of a long life.

She jumped when someone kissed her on the cheek.

'Here you are.' Alessandro took a seat next to her and exhaled. 'Still on edge? I'm the same. I guess it takes time to recover from that nightmare.'

'How's your head?'

'I'm on painkillers, so I don't feel anything,' he said. 'But I can't get up too quickly because then I feel dizzy. Look.' He stood up rapidly and swayed.

'Stop fooling around!'

Alessandro smiled and waved his hand with confidence. 'Don't worry, Professor. It's much harder than you think.' He made to knock on his head, but stopped at the last moment.

353

Nina raised her eyebrows. 'The only reason your head didn't split open is that you leaned back at the same moment the butt of the gun hit you.'

'Did I? Long live my reflexes—'

'Have you heard about Raffaele?'

His face saddened. 'Yes, Mama visited him in hospital in Milan today. I'll go tomorrow.'

'And how is she?'

He took Nina's hand and stroked it gently. 'I'm sorry for what happened. I thought it would be better when someone else informed her that I'm alive, but then I couldn't watch how she suffered.'

'I'm surprised that the police didn't better examine the body they found at the station. I think it's one of van der Venn's men,' Nina said.

'If so, he must have been very similar to me, I guess.'

Suddenly it occurred to her. Cesare—the man she had met on the train. He had worked for van der Venn. Van der Venn had sent him to keep an eye on her from the moment she left Milan, maybe earlier. It was him she had seen on the lake in that speedboat among the yacht's crew on their way to celebrate their pay of gold coins.

Alessandro was squinting at the lake. 'When I think about all of that, I cannot believe my luck. I've been almost killed three, four times? I started to tell Mama everything, but when I saw terror growing in her eyes, I decided to wait with the whole story. She is too emotional now.' He glanced at Nina and brightened. 'But I told her about you. I'm sure she already likes you.'

He rose to his feet. 'Come, I want to take you for a ride. It won't take long.'

'What is it that you plan to do, Alessandro Pini?'

He leaned theatrically and kissed her hand. 'Be patient, bella Signora.'

CHAPTER 57

ALESSANDRO SLOWED DOWN, came to a gentle stop, and turned the key in the ignition. The engine of his scooter died out.

'I cannot believe I've never been to this mountain before,' Nina said, dismounting from the rear seat.

Alessandro took off his helmet with caution, got off and pulled out a blanket from the locker under the seat.

He took her hand and they walked farther up the summit of Monte Baldo, dotted by limestone rocks, and then he led her twenty metres down the slope to a flat meadow. He unfolded the outdoor blanket on the grass and smoothed its corners.

He sat down, and Nina beside him. They enjoyed the freshness of the late summer air, and the silence that wouldn't be broken by cars' angry horns, or gunfire, or anything else but the mild whiff of wind and their own unrestrained breath.

'India is a beautiful country,' Alessandro said. 'But this?' He expanded his lungs. 'I wouldn't swap this view for the richest palaces of the whole world.'

Nina leaned her head on his shoulder.

Two thousand metres below, the waters of Lake Garda made a barely recognizable hazy patch of blue, and although they were sitting directly above Malcesine, from their vantage point they couldn't see the town.

On the opposite bank of the lake, tiny dots of darker blue and smudgy red formed a triangle of Limone, the small town above which ran the Alps' rugged walls of stone, one next to another, one after another, rising in a vertical manner until only their peaks were hardly perceptible in the last rows, where white fluffy carpets of clouds floated above them.

Alessandro plucked a blade of grass and put it into the corner of his mouth.

'I watched you on the plane back home, in those short moments when I was awake,' he said, chewing the grass. 'It looks like you're into that meditating thing, after all. I figured this would be an awesome place for that. Maybe you could teach me.'

Nina glanced at him and tilted her head. 'Really? I was under the impression that you would rather *not* go that way.'

'What way? I'm open to new things.'

She smiled. 'Since when?'

Since the day my head was nearly cracked open, he thought. *And I was half-dead, then brought back to life in a surge of weird heat, and since I opened my eyes and your grandmother was leaning over me.*

Instead he just said, 'Since now, Professor.'

'If you say so.' Nina crossed her legs. 'First, your body posture—'

'Nina, not now,' he said and spat out the grass. 'Do you think—do you think van der Venn will recover?'

She put her hands on her knees. 'He suffered extensive burns, second and third degree. Although I overheard some nurse saying that his wounds seem to heal remarkably fast.

357

Anyway, there are several agencies waiting to press charges. He will never leave prison.'

Alessandro wondered why he didn't have any satisfaction in that. Even if van der Venn was dead it wouldn't change things. It wouldn't bring Gianluigi back.

'What about Waaberi?'

'Indian police haven't found him,' she said. 'Last time I saw him, he was on his knees, taking punches from the angry crowd. They got him before and after he rescued van der Venn. Somehow he still managed to escape.'

Alessandro plucked another piece of grass and rolled it up between his fingers. Then he threw it away. 'Sorry, Nina, I didn't even ask how your grandma is.'

Nina stared ahead, then she said with a soft smile, 'She's well. She returned to Jaipur. She believes that her mission sent from God has been fulfilled.' Nina rolled her shoulders back and forth. 'And I spoke briefly on the phone with my mother. She was shocked. She was about to book a flight to India as soon as possible.'

Alessandro's pulse sped up. He tried to relax, gazing at the immensity of the mountains.

'That tablet wouldn't work that way, would it?' he said in a sheepish voice. 'You just can't walk into Heaven and become God?'

'Mantras are real and powerful. I felt their profound effect on my body when I recited them, holding Sati's hand. I'm glad she didn't let all that energy flow my way. My body wouldn't withstand it.'

'Do you remember the mantras?'

'No, except for the last one. The more he tried to force me to speak up, the more I rehearsed it in my head. Not sure why. Probably out of sheer stubbornness,' Nina said and grinned to herself.

Alessandro straightened his torso. 'So you remember the last one and Sati the previous mantras?'

'No. She cannot remember them. She was in a trance.'

'So they are lost, because the tablet is gone?'

Nina nodded. 'Sati smashed it into pieces.'

Alessandro squinted, looking for the proper words. 'What would you do if you could retrieve the mantras? Would you run tests on them? You know, in case there's more to it than just tingling and going into a hypnotic state of mind?'

Nina put her hands in her lap and twiddled her thumbs. 'All of them?'

Alessandro felt an excited flutter in his belly. He put his hand into the pocket of his shorts and touched the small flat shape of a camera memory card. 'Yes, all of them.'

'Well, I guess I would need time to get ready, mentally. But one day … It doesn't matter, anyway.'

'Why?'

'I'm sure the camera got trampled down by the river.'

'What camera?' he asked, trying to hide his growing anticipation.

'Van der Venn recorded everything. But at some point he knocked it down. Then Waaberi picked it up. Although it looked smashed even then.'

'Yes, you're probably right,' Alessandro said, fiddling with the card.

He already knew what was stored on it. He had checked it in his office in the hotel, when his mother stopped crying and had finally believed that he had returned home.

Alessandro had become aware of the strange item in his possession after waking up at the hospital. Nina had told him that it was that Hindu boy who was with van der Venn who had hoisted him out of the crowd at the ghat. So, it must have been him who had slid the card into his pocket.

One day, he thought.

He stashed the card deeper inside his pocket, moved closer to Nina, and put his arm around her.

'Signora Monte, would you be so kind as to have dinner with me? Also, my mother wants to talk with you.'

Nina's expression clouded. 'Are you sure she isn't mad at me?'

'Nina, Francesca Pini is the most grateful person in the world right now. It's impossible for her to be angry with anybody. This is another reason I need to get back soon, before she gives away all our rooms for free,' he said and winked.

Then he lay down and let Nina rest her head on his chest.

He closed his eyes. He wanted to forget about the last few days, and at the same time he wanted to remember them forever. Without them, he never would have met Nina.

But he wasn't going to ponder about that *one day* in the future when Nina, he or the world would be ready to understand the recording from Varanasi. He had different things on his mind: hotel renovation when the season came to an end, proving to his mother that he could be a responsible manager, and letting her retire like she deserved.

But Nina Monte was to play the most significant part in his life. He hoped she wanted to. He pulled her onto his body.

'I like your new hair,' he said, pushing an auburn wisp behind her ear.

'Finally! I thought you hadn't—'

She gave no resistance when his lips touched hers.

'It feels like it's been so long since you kissed me,' she whispered.

He caressed the small of her back. 'Have we actually been on a date, Professor?'

Nina threw him an intimidating look. 'If you call me "Professor" one more time, then … then…'

She kissed him back—first, only brushing his mouth, then sensually and long.

Alessandro stopped thinking what the future held for him. As far as he was concerned, there was no *one day*.

There was only *now*.

From the author

Thank you for reading my novel. If you enjoyed *Fast Track To Glory*, I would be very grateful if you could spend just a few minutes leaving a short review on the page where you bought the book. Honest reader reviews are the most powerful tools of getting attention for my books and help others decide if they'll enjoy this novel, too.

Thank you very much!

A note about the author

Tomasz Chrusciel wrote his first story at sixteen, but it would take another twenty years for his love affair with writing to become the central focus in his life.

After obtaining a master's degree in Political Science & International Relations in Poland, Chrusciel found himself in the corporate sector. The work stoked his passion for global politics, but his imagination craved greater freedom. After moving to Ireland and falling in love, he finally left his job to become a full-time fiction author. His debut novel *Illusive Intrusion* was followed by *Fast Track to Glory*. Both works have since earned Chrusciel a dedicated readership that continues to grow each day.

Wanderlust regularly draws the writer to extreme corners of the globe seeking new settings, personalities and historical events to inspire his next novel. When he isn't researching destinations or convincing his cat-loving fiancée to let him adopt a dog, he's at his computer furiously typing his latest scene, or chatting with his readers on social media.

Connect with the author online:

Website: http://www.tomaszchrusciel.com/
Facebook: https://www.facebook.com/tomaszchruscielbooks
Twitter: https://twitter.com/tomaszchru

Printed in Great Britain
by Amazon

73320295R00220